THE KING'S FAVORITE

JOHN VANCE

Black Rose Writing | Texas

ISBN: 978-1-68433-103-1
PUBLISHED BY BLACK ROSE WRITING
www.blackrosewriting.com

Printed in the United States of America
Suggested Retail Price (SRP) $18.95

The King's Favorite is printed in Gentium Basic
Cover artwork: Nell Gwynn by Sir Peter Lely

Special thanks to the staff at Black Rose Writing, to my children Hope and Jimmy for their love and support, and to my wife, Susan, for her enthusiasm and keen editorial eye.

THE KING'S FAVORITE

This novel combines fiction and history to illuminate one of the most fascinating periods in English History—the Restoration (1660-1700). Historical figures feature prominently in the fictional plot, although the depiction of these men and women reflects accurately the known facts about them (including a number of actual comments made by and about them). In a few instances, events and allusions have been adjusted on the calendar, but only by a few months at most. In addition to the fictional plot, this novel hopes to provide the reader with a full flavoring of the time and to illuminate the personalities of the most famous members of King Charles II's intimate circle, namely the king and his two famous mistresses, Barbara Villiers (Lady Castlemaine) and the actress Nell Gwynn.

(See the appendix for a full list of the historical figures appearing or mentioned in the novel.)

Chapter 1

London, Late Autumn 1670

"Get up, precious face. It's time for you to move your loveliness out of this bed. The king is through with you for the time being. He won't be returning this morning for any more of your moist cunny. Now up, up."

The forthright and charmingly vulgar Bridget Warren brought her candelabra closer to the bed in which young Elizabeth Keller lay. Now in middle-age, the broad-faced Bridget had done similar bedroom eviction for a dozen years now, since she was first asked by Charles Stuart to awaken one of his lovers while he was residing in exile at Antwerp. The young woman then lying in bed was the daughter of a Belgian official Charles entertained that evening—a man who claimed he would save his daughter's virginity from any suitor, "no matter the man or the title." Nothing the official uttered could have made his daughter more desirable to Charles. And with the assistance of the clever and dauntless Bridget Warren, the coupling was made and the father vanquished.

Charles found Bridget resourceful, industrious, and amusing enough to bring with him when the monarchy was restored in England in May of 1660, after the deaths of the hated Cromwell and his insufficient son Richard. Younger women felt comfortable and protected in Bridget's presence, no matter how vigorously the homely woman teased them about being mere fodder for the king's overused "cannon."

"I said get up now, sweet breath. Oh, I know. You don't have to tell me. The king was especially feeling his royalty tonight and pushed his scepter in too deep, eh? Still you must get up. My dear, what is this?" When she brought the candelabra closer, Bridget saw two streams of blood an inch or two below the young woman's knees. She had dealt with smears and trickles blood before in similar instances, always the natural demonstration of the woman's fertility or her virginity. Smiling, Bridget also noticed the bed clothes were gathered up, forming a mound of linen—from just above pretty Betty Keller's knees to the place just below her modest though well-shaped breasts.

Bridget lowered the candelabra to examine the sleeping girl's face. "Up now. Up. What? Betty? Betty—girl?" The woman was unable to stifle the panic in her voice. Young Betty's neck was craned upward and bent to the left. Her face—unmarked except for a five-inch streak of blood on her forehead, running horizontally from hairline to hairline—was frozen in an attitude of utter terror.

Bridget sagged and began to sit on the edge of the bed. But what she saw lying there was too dreadful to be near. She fled from the room, and after collecting her thoughts stirred from his sleep one of the king's advisers, who then awoke the king.

"Oh dearest God."

The king's words were barely audible—a private expression of sorrow not intended for the ears of anyone else in the room.

His sweet Betty lay on her back, her body pressed deeply into the bed clothes, the bed itself sunk around her body as if she had purposely placed herself into a pre-constructed mold. God blessed her with a natural beauty made even more enthralling by the innocence that marked every aspect of her face. The oval light blue eyes. The upturned lips. The high forehead devoid of any lines or furrows. But now the eyes were widened; the lips frozen, the lips curled hideously, and the forehead marked by a smear of her blood.

Charles reached out to brush the loose hair from the side of the dead beauty's face, but his fingers halted inches away from the soft light brown strands—the ones he played with only hours earlier—and the thick line of blood on her forehead. He turned his head and noticed his dear Betty's delicate feet pushed out from the bed coverings. He had not even touched them earlier in the night, but he had planned to spend many an hour at another time caressing and gently kissing them. Now all of her lovely toes were grotesquely splayed.

As Charles grabbed at the drawn back curtain of the canopy bed, he thought of how earlier in the night he had lain on her soft and responsive body, moving slowly yet ardently inside her. And then, as was his habit, he left her only moments after completing his lovemaking. She asked him to stay and stroke her hair just a few moments more, but he thought it prudent not to—not on this night. He feared another would soon come to demand entrance in his own bed, not far from where he was standing now.

"Your Majesty, you mustn't remain here any longer. I will have her body removed—along with the bed, which will be burned. I will see to it that all the linen is destroyed as well." The king nodded toward his friend and close adviser Henry Langston, Lord Brinton and recalled wistfully the several occasions when as a young man Brinton suggested removing the bedding in order to keep a husband in the dark about having been made a cuckold.

Brinton pressed his finger into Bridget Warren's arm. "Take away the bedding and see that it is burned—now."

"Sir, must I?"

"She need not be the one to do it, Henry."

"Very well, Your Majesty. You, woman, do as I ask." Another of the servants began to dismantle the tower of cloth piled around the mid-part of the Betty's body. When the woman managed to pull the bed clothes completely off, the others in the room gasped in unison—making it sound as if the entire room has aspirated. Only the king was silent.

Protruding from Betty Keller's lower abdomen was the handle of a ceremonial knife. Even with the rivulet of dark blood, which cascaded down and over the young woman's hips, pooling under her lower back and buttocks, all in the room stared at nothing but the hilt of the knife resting flush against Betty's tender flesh, the blade of the knife completely submerged in her body.

Charles noticed the pearl inlays on the handle. The knife was the last gift his father the king had given him, the last time they had seen each other, before the elder Charles's capture, trial, and public execution in January of 1649. That was over twenty-one years earlier, when his son, the present monarch, was not yet nineteen. And now the martyred father's own knife had taken the life of the young woman the son had made love to hours before. The woman many believed would soon be the younger

Charles's favorite mistress.

The king again heard Langston's grave voice behind him. "Your Majesty, in the morning I will speak to Mr. Devlin at the theatre and inform him that there has been an accident of the most terrible kind. And I will call it just that. An accident."

Charles nodded and was momentarily comforted by the knowledge that Langston would keep the matter discreet. He took a final look at the others in the room, all of whom had once more dropped their heads, although now all their eyes were all completely open.

"Let me . . ." The king did not finish his thought, but walked to the head of the bed to look one last time at the face of the lovely Elizabeth Keller— "Pretty Betty Keller" as she was known by patrons of the King's Theatre. Charles realized she would be sorely missed on the stage, as another of his love interests, his effervescently bawdy and witty Nellie Gwynn, was beginning to be.

Still, the king found it difficult to leave the room, even though Langston had swept his hand toward the door as an invitation to do so. He knew it now, and the others watching him must have realized it too. He had indeed fallen in love with the achingly beautiful Elizabeth Keller. Yet in a moment, anger swept the grief from his features. Now present in his mind was another face. The face of the woman who would be pleased most by the death of his dearest Betty.

CHAPTER 2

The man entered the chamber where she stood with arms folded before her and her back to the door. Without turning, she spoke with the serenity of one who had expected the visit.

"Thomas, you have some news for me?"

"Yes, my lady." The man was in the midst of catching his breath; his desire to share immediately this particular news allowed him no time to comport himself before informing her.

She waited a moment until his breathing slowed—revealing none of the impatience that so strongly marked her reputation. "Then tell me."

"There is news from Whitehall."

"Go on."

"Elizabeth Keller . . ." He halted as she slowly turned toward him. ". . . has been found murdered in her bed."

"In *her* bed or in the king's?"

"One might say in hers, my lady."

"Might say?" Barbara Villiers, known for the past nine years as Lady Castlemaine and as the king's most tempestuous and formidable mistress, changed nothing in her expression, which seemed to Thomas Lockwood so alluringly aloof. The sudden shifts of emotion that so often altered her bewitching features during many a public tempest were now controlled.

"Never mind, I understand. So tell me, how was she killed?"

"Stabbed. Low on her body. Right above her . . ." He thought it prudent to avoid naming the exact place.

"And you were told this?"

"Yes. From one of the women servants who has often shared information with me. She was in the bed chamber with several others—the king among them."

"And His Majesty's reaction?"

"He . . ." Lockwood lowered his head. He thought it wise not to share the report that the king seemed devastated. "I was told he examined her and then conversed with Lord Brinton—and finally left the room."

"I see."

"Can I do anything more for you, Lady Castlemaine?"

There was nothing Lockwood would not have done for her. He at times chastised himself for joining the ranks of those who would willingly do all they could to please this fascinating woman. Some had done more than he had attempted and had been rewarded with a simple word of praise and appreciation. Others had done less and had received so much more than that. And this was the group to which Lockwood wished to belong. He knew her position as Lady Castlemaine and soon—if the king went forward with his promise—as a Duchess would be no impediment to giving herself to a man of lesser standing. Much to her public discredit, she had done so before. Lockwood could only dream she would do so again.

"No, there is nothing further now, Thomas. But you have my gratitude for everything you have done for me."

"I am only too happy to serve you, my lady."

She sat at her vanity, her back to him. "And you may be called on to do so again soon. Now you may go."

"Yes, my lady."

Hearing the door close, Barbara examined her face in the mirror. She had only five days earlier at the end of November celebrated her thirtieth birthday. On the occasion, Charles chose not to see her; he had only sent her a note, followed a day later by a gift of a jewel and the promise of a "much larger gift to come, likely in the following month." She knew she was shortly to become a baroness, perhaps also a duchess. She briefly wondered if these gifts were undeniable proof of the king's continuing love for her and an implied promise to renew their intimacies in the months ahead. But she could not so abuse herself. No, these gifts and promises were painful consolations for Charles's denying her most fervent desire—that he still longed for her in his bed, regardless of all the others he had taken to it during the past several years. And regardless of the other men she had taken to hers. The previous occasion on which they had shared intimacies was because she demanded that they do so.

The witty slut Nell Gwynn was painful enough to endure—and now there were rumors of a young French aristocratic thing Charles had taken a fancy to. But there was something about that actress Betty Keller that had wounded Lady Castlemaine more than she expected. She had yet to determine why that was so.

Staring at her still enticing yet intimidating face, she smiled at the lewd description of it given by one of the court wits—that it was a face "to haunt forever any man who sticks his cock into it." Yes, that was her only hope. That Charles was at present vulnerable to his ghost.

Michael Devlin stood alone on the stage of the King's Theatre and recalled a London without the diversion of public theatrical displays. From 1642 to 1660, the theatres were closed—the Puritan regime having acted on its vow to end such "devil's play" the moment they ascended to power. And so it had been. The old King Charles fled the city at the commencement of the Civil War, and the new powers bolted up the theatres, sending both the carefully trained and the enthusiastic novices into retirement or to the continent in order to continue their craft. Devlin, now forty-seven, had been one of the exuberant youths whose last public performance on the London stage, before the closings almost thirty years earlier, had been as young Fenton in Mr. Shakespeare's *Merry Wives of Windsor*.

Exposure to the theatre traditions of Italy and France during the long exile of eighteen years honed the skills of Devlin and other experienced and younger English actors but also opened their eyes to the broader possibilities of the theatrical enterprise. The proscenium stage with its front curtain, the use of painted flat pieces brought on and off stage to suggest scenes, the redesign of the theatre seating with benches in the front instead of a standing area, and side boxes closer to the stage for those with title and means all impressed Devlin, and he was confident the London theatre would embrace these alterations once the Puritan Interregnum had run its course. But the most fascinating difference between the old English and the present continental theatres was the use of women players to perform their own roles. Having begun acting at fourteen, Devlin himself had taken young women's roles for three years before he performed the young male lover parts. Having looked at his weather-beaten features in the mirror upon arising an hour earlier, Devlin couldn't imagine how he ever passed for young Bianca Minola in a 1638 production of *The Taming of the Shrew*.

Devlin's boundless delight for the female actors perhaps explained his utter fascination with seven-year-old Elizabeth Keller, whose mother insisted he see perform while they were all in Antwerp with the exiled king—the second Charles—in 1658. The child captured his fancy immediately. Her talents were impressive to anyone who saw her run through her gamut of characters—from the incorrigible child to the stuffy old dowager. Betty Keller danced like a fairy and sang in a soft ethereal voice that captivated the ear. Precocity could hardly explain what she possessed. To Devlin she was everything to be hoped for—and even at that time, when he was in his mid-thirties, he fancied marrying lovely Betty when she came to a proper age. Yet he never let himself contemplate the unthinkable as he watched her as a child. He simply loved her and wanted her with him always.

Her theatrical training was his charge, given to him by Charles while they were in exile. Betty was nine upon the exiles' arrival in England in May of 1660, and during the next several months, Devlin assured her that soon the English theatre audience would behold a female actor on the public stage for the very first time since Mr. Burbage constructed the first London public theatre in 1576. And in December of 1660 it happened as he had promised: the graceful Margaret Hughes portrayed the ill-fated Desdemona in Mr. Shakespeare's *Othello*.

In the following years, Devlin continued to train the increasingly beautiful Elizabeth Keller, still determined they would eventually wed, but for the first time, soon after she had turned thirteen, he felt the sting of jealousy as one of the experienced male actors in the company placed his hand inside her dress to feel her "budding womanhood" and kissed her fully on the mouth. The moment was merely a playful one for the actor and a reflection of how easily inhibitions evaporated in the theatrical environment—but Betty demonstrated pleasure at what the player had done and, Devlin believed, looked longingly at the man as he turned and crossed the stage.

Devlin saw to it that the actor never appeared with the company again. Devlin didn't speak to Betty about the incident, but from that moment on he became tormented by thoughts of her sharing intimacies with anyone. Therefore, for the past two years Devlin had undergone the worst of suffering—made even more intense when he learned of the king's interest in the grown-up little girl he patted on the head twelve years earlier.

Devlin heard light footsteps coming from the rear of the stage area. He recognized them as he had the footsteps of everyone in his theatrical company. "Yes, William?"

The lad closed his eyes before he spoke. "I have news, Mr. Devlin."

"You look as though you are about to act tragedy, my boy. What is it?"

"It's Betty, sir."

The expansive home of Lord and Lady Durell held two different worlds on its east and west sides and a common meeting ground in the center. On the eve of their marriage, Durell agreed to all demands his wife made regarding the colors and furnishings of the rooms over which she would hold dominion, but he insisted that his own preferences be honored as well. He had no firm opinions on color provided that it "suited the male sex," but he was determined to sit—and have all of his male guests sit—on furniture reminiscent, as his wife Charlotte put it, "of the bowels of an inn on the road to Shrewsbury." Charlotte suggested they christen their home Dove-Raven House to suggest the mutually exclusive worlds the couple inhabited under the same roof.

Charlotte, one of the few females in England having this French name, kept all of her secrets on her side of the house—away from the ears and eyes of her husband and many others of his acquaintance who, like Lord Durell, found the king's personal behavior a threat to the nation. So far she had resisted the temptation to pay the servant she most trusted to inform her not only of what was being said on her husband's side of the manor but also what was being planned there. Her greatest fear was that her husband would allow some of his more notorious and politically dangerous acquaintances to pull him into a conspiracy—one that would cost him his life and her a way of life she had come to cherish. Finding herself the wife of a man banished or executed for treason was too frightening a prospect to imagine.

Although she understood the concessions her husband was forced to make to propriety, Charlotte didn't wish to end, even temporarily, the open visits paid to the "Dove" wing of the house by some of the more notorious women about whom London and most of England spoke incessantly. Among her guests were women who had lain with the king and even delivered some of his bastard children. Whereas Charlotte tended to believe her husband was unaware of her social business, she periodically had the nagging suspicion that he suspected—and that he would soon demand she betray these women by sharing what they said about the king's intimate behavior or the monarch's unguarded assessments of France, Holland, and of a host of powerful men—friend and foe alike. Lord Durell would then expect to receive this information, all in order to feed the discontent of his growing coterie, which even included a professed and obnoxious Puritan. How her husband and his friends could abide such a man, after all the misery inflicted on England by Cromwell and his like, was beyond her understanding. But now was not the time for such contemplations, for she was at present strolling on the grounds with her most trusted friend, whom she had not seen for many years.

"Oh, Abby, I'm so happy you arrived from Virginia earlier than expected. How long I have wished for you to be here with me at Dove-Raven House." Charlotte had the woman's hand firmly in her own.

"Charlotte, I always knew you would rule over such a place as this—or at least one half of it, as you have just explained. Your side, I see, has the best garden and most intriguing grounds, am I not right?"

"Of course."

Finally having Abigail Fayette in her sanctuary filled Charlotte with considerable though long-delayed pleasure and expelled all thoughts about her husband's political mischief.

"Where are we going, Charlotte?"

"You will so love this, dearest Abby. Wait until you see."

The women traversed some seventy feet of ground before they stood before an archway centered on a long hedge of some seven feet in height.

As soon as they stepped through the portal, Abigail brought her hands to her face and nearly shouted.

"Charlotte. You did it. You did what you always said you would do."

"Did you think that I wouldn't?"

The women stood at the entrance to a tall and lush labyrinth of tall hedges, immaculately kept by the gardeners. Their memories merged as each recalled the maze-like structure in France they traversed when they were ten year-old girls. At the time, their families were in exile, owing to the Puritan Interregnum. They had both grown weary of hearing their fathers speak of England's new Lord Protector Cromwell and making wagers on how long such an "abominable experiment" would last before the country would demand a return of the monarchy. Charlotte's father, an ousted member of the House of Lords at the time, thought Cromwell would suffer the same fate as King Charles and lose his head within a year. Abby's father believed England would endure "six or seven years of such folly" before all would be restored. Indeed it took a full seven years before the younger Charles would make his triumphant return to England in May of 1660.

"This is so much taller than the one in France, Charlotte. I fear that if we go in, we may never return. In a year's time they will find only skeletons in these dresses, I have no doubt."

"I know all the escapes. Just follow me."

As they moved through the entrancing maze, the women talked further of Charlotte's marriage to Lord Durell.

"And how is it that you seem to have so much say over your husband, Charlotte?"

"That is the advantage of marrying a man loosely within a generation of one's own."

"I see. So the influence is sustained in the bedchamber. And in which part of the house does that bed lie?"

"On his side." She paused, losing her smile. "I have periodically made the long pilgrimage there merely to maintain my ascendancy."

"So you have never engaged each other here in this labyrinth?" Abigail poked her finger into her friend's arm.

Charlotte's smile returned. "My husband has no interest in communing with his wife in nature. That was done only once. On an ill-advised walk in Devonshire soon after we wed. It has not been done since—at least not with Lord Durell."

"There is that same twinkle in your eye, Charlotte. Your body may be twenty-seven, but your eyes still remain ten. Oh, how I have missed seeing you these past years. In any event, I am not at all surprised by what you have told me. Ever since you were a girl you always knew how to get your way and make those suffer who refused to give it to you. Your father gave you too much free rein and you rode often and always for great distance."

"Oh, Abby. Don't use the words 'rode' or 'ride' when discussing me or any of your sister women—even in metaphor. Ever since the monarchy returned ten years ago 'to ride' has most often been used in its less than delicate meaning."

"I recall how angry your father was when he heard you speak so saucily, Charlotte."

"If you think my mouth is foul, I cannot wait until you meet Nellie Gwynn."

"Now, is she the actress? And the . . .?

"Lover of the king's—yes. With a foul mouth you will come to adore."

As the women made their way toward the center of the labyrinth, Abby marveled at how exuberant her childhood friend became with each step forward. "You love your little puzzle of hedges, don't you?"

"Yes. I feel safe here. Away from all that annoys me. All that frightens me." Charlotte took both Abigail's hands in hers. "I have so much I wish to confide in you."

"You know I will listen. Tell me what it is—all that it is."

"You may regret your generosity in this matter, Abby. Come we are almost at the center of the maze."

"They say it is a puzzle, sir. A damned infuriating puzzle. Why she was killed and by whom they do not know."

"But you are sure that it was the young one, Elizabeth Keller, who was murdered, Thomas?" Lockwood provided news to others besides Lady

Castlemaine. Besides, Lord Durell paid him most generously.

"Yes, Lord Durell. Betty Keller, the actress."

"Well. What do we make of that?"

"I cannot say, my lord."

"Thank you, Thomas. Your reports always seem dramatic as well as useful. Take this for your pains." After he handed Lockwood several coins and gestured for him to leave, Durell signaled his servant to bring wine for his two guests, who also heard Lockwood's news. The first was Sir Roger Earle, presently a conspicuous figure in Charles's court, although rumor was rife that the king wished to dismiss him from all responsibilities but only the influence of Earle's cousin Henry Langston, Lord Brinton prevented the dismissal. Earle was especially adept at establishing networks of informants not only in the English court but also in Dublin and Edinburgh.

"Lord Durell, I am sure your sources will soon know what assumptions may be formed about her death. Unfortunately, I cannot expect that any of them will judge it properly as God's will. Or as a deserved penalty exacted on the king." The servant came forward with two glasses of wine. Earle took his, but the other man refused.

"No, none for me, Lord Durell."

"Of course. My apologies, Richard. May I then offer you—"

"Nothing. Thank you—no." Richard Hansall remained standing, while Durell and Earle sat—his rustic deep brown and white clothing moreover marking the contrast between him and the other more colorfully attired men in the room.

Hansall was one of the rarest of political creatures: an unapologetic Puritan with influence on high-placed royalists. It wasn't that men like Durell and Earle approved of either Hansall's religious views or his stifling manner. Rather, he provided them with information regarding the plans the Dutch had for yet another war with England, among other matters.

It was evident to Durell that the previous Dutch wars did not settle the conflict between the two countries. There was still too much at stake economically. "I tell you the damned Dutch cannot be allowed to affect world trade the way they have, even though our king seems less than keen on engaging them since the last war—what is it—now some three years ago."

"True, my lord," Earle observed. "None of us complained of the king's nerve after he inflicted the worst naval defeat in the history on the Dutch Republic. But he could not—*would* not—sustain his success, and the Dutch redeemed themselves, which as everyone knows forced Charles to sue for terms."

Durell took the glass of wine poured for Hansall. "Yes, Roger. The miserable Dutch even sailed their ships to the mouth of the Thames."

Delighted by the anger and humiliation expressed in the room, Hansall's face altered into what, for him, might be termed a smile. "I remember well the news that the flagship *The Royal Charles* had been captured without firing a shot and dragged unceremoniously back to the western Netherlands as a trophy."

"And it remains there still," Durell added. "A humiliating and bitter reminder of Charles's ineptitude as a warrior. No, my friends, he couldn't rouse himself often enough out from between the legs of his whorish women to be such a monarch as that."

Hansall expressed his view that the events of 1665, 1666, and 1667—the horrendous plague, the devastating London fire, and the defeat by the Dutch—were evidence of divine retribution on Charles and by extension his nation. "And I am not the only one who believes so. Yet for some reason known only to God, Charles still receives much affection from the common people—and of course from his many soul-less and filthy courtiers and mistresses." Hansall had come to accept that God expected the enlightened to continue and then finish the punishment of the flawed monarch. And Hansall felt no one more enlightened than himself.

Durell lifted his second glass of Bourgogne wine and sniffed its rich bouquet. "I agree with all you have said, Richard, and I tell you, gentlemen, I feel strongly this girl's death may be another sign from the Almighty that Charles is unfit to continue as this country's monarch. It is our fortune that His Majesty has nothing but bastard children—none of whom can come to the throne, with the possible exception of the beloved Duke of Monmouth—the first of his bastard brood. But Charles's brother James will become king, and he can be reasoned with."

Earle nodded with arrogant assurance. "Now all that's left is for the king to die."

With his arms folded before him, Hansall looked down on the two men sitting and imbibing their wine. "It has begun. It only lacks a little assistance from those who wish to insist that God's will be done. The warnings from above have not been heeded. We are God's fist as well as his tongue. It is now up to us to bring that fist down and serve the wishes of the Almighty."

CHAPTER 3

In spite of the King's wishes, news of Elizabeth Keller's murder swept quickly through the court—with courtiers, ladies, servants, and guards all offering their opinions on who took the life of the beautiful young actress. Even those strolling through St. James's Park pushed aside other familiar topics of discussion to offer their assessments of the slaying. Who wanted Betty Keller dead? The most common candidate was one of His Majesty's mistresses, and the one most commonly pointed to was Barbara Villiers, Lady Castlemaine. But she wasn't the only one spoken of. The brash Nellie Gwynn was also one of the accused, but some believed it was Nellie's rival Moll Davis who couldn't bear to be reminded that yet another beauty had replaced her in the king's affections. Many cast aspersions on Moll's spending habits and character, echoing in one way or another the view of the naval administrator Mr. Pepys's late wife, who called Moll "the most impertinent slut in the world." And a few even held that Betty was killed through the machinations of the stunning young French beauty Louise de Kérouaille, who was both the maid-of-honor to Charles's favorite sister Henrietta, *Duchesse d'Orleans* and the woman the king was at present seeking to bed. With Henrietta's unexpected and recent death in France, Charles provided for Louise by making her a lady-in-waiting to his wife, Queen Catherine. Many feared Louise would convince the king to give terms too friendly to France in the treaty now being debated. But the general populace was unaware that the treaty had already been agreed to.

Voices were in addition heard whispering the names of men at court, members of the military, and of course the Puritans still embittered over their failed attempt to bury the monarchy forever and convert England into a lasting commonwealth. And there were those—Anglican and Puritan alike—who deeply resented the fact that whereas Charles had a brood of bastard children from his recent and former mistresses, he had failed to produce a legitimate air with his Portuguese wife Catherine of Braganza.

Still others wondered if Elizabeth Keller was betraying king and country to the Dutch or the French by enticing from Charles important information relating to England's military or about the sins and weaknesses of both the king and his ministers. She may have therefore been killed on orders of someone as powerful as Lord Brinton or even Charles himself. These possibilities were all in the air by the early afternoon after Betty's body was discovered, and more careful and penetrating minds were concerned there would be ramifications from the murder far more significant than the fact that Charles would now have one less lovely young woman in his bed.

There was much less speculation at the King's Playhouse in Drury Lane. Instead, there was a numbing sadness in those who kept their tears from escaping and a full emotional outpouring from those who could not. Those at the theatre—from the male and female players to those who did the most menial tasks—were deeply affected by the loss of one of their own. Unlike so many, whose fellow actors secretly wished them ill or openly confronted them over roles and lovers stolen, Elizabeth Keller had no overt enemies. Nell Gwynn adored her and the masterful actor Thomas Betterton of the rival Duke's Company made clear his desire to have Betty on his stage. "She brightens everyone who watches her—actor and audience alike," he recently said. Betty enthusiastically supported those women who performed roles she wished to attempt and never held it against any of the male actors who spoke lewdly in her presence or attempted to touch her intimately. She always very politely told them she preferred they not overstep their bounds.

Audiences simply adored her in breeches parts when she played a young male or was dressed as one to fool an unwanted suitor or oppressive father or aunt. Betty's legs were often remarked on as were her small and delicate feet. That her breasts did not fill a dress as fully as most of the other female players was never a matter spoken off disparagingly. Whenever a male patron voiced something lewd when she was on stage, the offender would meet with either a threat of or an act of violence from one of the male players after a performance concluded—and once while the play was going on. Untoward male critics suffered retribution ranging from broken noses and cracked teeth to permanent burn scars from the application of torch flame or scalding pokers. Her fellow actors were proud to have protected her honor, even when she begged them not to.

But now she was dead, and only one member of her company was considered as her possible murderer—Michael Devlin, her mentor and most ardent suitor. Devlin's affections for Elizabeth Keller generally troubled most in the company, because all but he could see her love for him resembled at best that of a daughter for her father. Some had of course taken momentary pleasure in discussing his folly in believing Betty could love him passionately and share his bed. Jokes were made behind his back about his "dead cinder" and "withered scepter," but there was never any true malice in such moments. Devlin had the company's respect as an actor and a teacher of the art. But now in the immediate wake of Betty Keller's brutal death, Devlin's reputation and general popularity counted little when it came to speculating on the murder. His farce had turned to tragedy, many of the King's Theatre players believed, although their intelligence informed them that Devlin could be only one possible suspect.

I do hope you can come to see us at Dove-Raven House. I do want you to meet my childhood friend, newly returned from America. I have no doubt you will like her and enjoy her tales of wilderness life in Virginia. Let me know as soon as possible if we may look forward to your visit.

Barbara Villiers refolded the note from Lady Durell. Perhaps she should pay a visit as soon as possible. She didn't want to receive word the king wished to see her so soon after his latest slut's death. Nothing could be more appalling than to have him ask for her shoulder to cry on.

"Thomas."

Lockwood stepped through the door. "Yes, Lady Castlemaine?"

"Take this to Lady Durell immediately." Lockwood disguised his reaction to having just returned from Dove-Raven House as Barbara dipped her goose feather pen in the ink and expressed her desire to come around four in the afternoon, after Charlotte and her friend had concluded their dinner. "Hint to Lady Durell I should like some of that new sparkling French wine she served me the last time I visited. From the *Champenois* wine makers, I think it was. Lady Durell believes the English will never like it, but I wonder." Barbara handed Lockwood the note and gave him as a gratuity a trace of a smile, the kind which Lockwood recalled very often during the day and night. He only hoped he kept his passion for his lady hidden enough so that she wouldn't dismiss or have him thrown in irons.

As soon as Lockwood took the letter and left, Barbara opened a beautiful embroidered casket constructed almost twenty years earlier and presented to Charles, then in exile during the English Civil War. The embossed casket displayed a vivid collection of colors, needlework, and imagery. Barbara had received it from Charles not long after they met in Holland, when Charles was in exile at The Hague in the Netherlands.

Barbara carefully removed and studied the jewels inside the casket, which were there when Charles presented her with the gift early in 1660. It didn't matter to Charles that she had been married less than a year to Roger Palmer, whose father let it be known she would make his son one of the most wretched men in the world. By the time she received Charles's gift, Barbara knew her father-in-law's prediction would prove accurate. Charles had been away from his native country for nine years, some two and half years after his father the king was publicly executed. Barbara had only recently turned eight when the first King Charles lost his head, and for the next ten years she, like so many other Royalist girls and women, shaped an image of the rightful new and exiled king as a brave and handsome young man who needed the support of his friends while he waited for God to put an end to vile Puritan and parliamentary rule. By the time she was sent to The Hague with letters and money—the assumption being that a young woman would arouse fewer suspicions by the government—Barbara was nineteen, a beautiful, voluptuous, and daring woman, hardly one to escape notice. When depressed, Barbara would often recall her first meeting with Charles and his reaction when she informed him that after the execution of the king, her family would gather once a year in the dark cellar of their home and drink to the younger Charles's health. When Charles asked if the occasion for the Villiers family gathering was Easter, Barbara told him no—that it was on May 29th. Charles lowered his eyes in sincere appreciation and muttered, "On my birthday, then." When he raised his eyes, he took in Barbara's expressive and full-lidded violet eyes, lush brown hair, alabaster skin, and sensuous mouth. She knew at once he was fully smitten by her, and she began at that moment formulating a way to have him sexually. That Charles was ten years older did not make him that much wiser or cleverer than she, and when he brought her hand to his mouth, she understood all she had to do was be in his presence and Charles would see to it that she would take up residence in is bed. Charles's first words after kissing her hand were "I am tall and you are tall. We should fit together wonderfully."

It wasn't long before Barbara learned about Charles's dalliance with Lucy Walter, whom Charles bedded over a decade earlier. As was her habit, Barbara sought everything she could learn about anyone she viewed as a rival or a threat—asking incessant questions to those in the royal retinue and to Charles himself. Barbara was comforted by the fact that Lucy possessed little wit but disconcerted by the opinion that Lucy had good looks. Charles was only eighteen when he and Lucy became lovers, which allowed Barbara to dismiss, though not casually, the woman's place in his heart. Barbara took delight in hearing that the royalist John Evelyn traveled with Lucy by coach and thought she was a beautiful but "insipid creature." Barbara soon became aware that when Charles left The Hague and sailed to Scotland in 1650, he left Lucy behind and that to thank him for his affections and attentions, Lucy had an affair and a child with another man. After Charles's failed attempt to defeat the parliamentarian troops at the Battle of Worcester in 1651, he escaped back to the continent and announced to Lucy their relationship was over. Barbara was more entertained than saddened to learn that Lucy drifted in and out of several scandals and was briefly imprisoned by Cromwell's government when she returned to England in 1656. But Barbara felt a stab of concern when Charles himself told her that Lucy came back to the Low Countries after she was released from prison and attempted to use the one weapon she had left to return to Charles's arms. But her attempt failed and Lucy ended up in Paris where she died of Venus's disease. Charles said Lucy was approaching thirty at the time of her death—and Barbara, then only nineteen, assumed Lucy's physical charms had withered in any event.

Pausing in her recollections, Barbara stared at her face in the mirror and touched the lines that now creased the side of each of her lovely eyes. She had with powder covered the visible creases that remained around her mouth whenever she smiled or frowned, but they were there and would only become more pronounced. Now she was about Lucy's age when the woman met her end in Paris. But Lucy had borne Charles his first child—a son James, now twenty-one and titled the Duke of Monmouth. Beloved of his father, the young man still was barred from ascending to throne since he was illegitimate. Yet he had a following, and Barbara feared without any legitimate heirs resulting from Charles's eight year marriage to Catherine of Braganza, Monmouth would eventually reign as king. As it was, Charles's brother James would rule if Charles died without legitimate issue, but James's conversion to Roman Catholicism was well known and it wouldn't take much for many to desire the Protestant Duke of Monmouth succeed his father.

Hearing voices, Barbara looked out her window and smiled. Four of the children she had with Charles—all in consecutive years from 1662 to 1665—were running, laughing, and playing hoops or in the case of the two youngest, George and Charlotte, making an attempt to mimic the skills of their older siblings. Barbara could take consolation in the fact that she delivered three more sons to the king than did Lucy Walter but still felt the indignity of knowing Charles also had a son age thirteen and as well as a daughter age twelve by Catherine Pegge, the handsome young woman who immediately preceded Barbara as Charles's favorite bedfellow. But most galling of all was Charles's most recent offspring—an infant also named Charles—from a manipulating whore, the highly popular actress Nell Gwynn. Actress—Barbara loathed the word regardless of how often she went to the theatre to be with or near the king. And to know he had his eyes on the female players—likely measuring each for their fitness as a lover—was always painful. He claimed never to have touched the lively Elizabeth Knepp, but he said little about his relations with Moll Davis—and absolutely nothing about the now slain "pretty angel" Betty Keller. But Barbara found out about her and Charles easily enough. And how many other of the female players did the king bed? "May he suffer long for this sin against me." Barbara slammed the lid shut on the casket Charles had given her a decade earlier.

CHAPTER 4

Bridget Warren pointed to the bed in which Betty Keller had been murdered. "The king has ordered this removed and burned. Take it away—now." Four men set about dismantling the bed, taking less than three minutes to break it apart and carry the pieces away. Bridget wondered if the king would simply replace this bed with another and resume his amorous play with yet another actress or married lady he would easily seduce. Charles was tall and striking with a distinct thin moustache, but more attractive were his curious manner and his confident demeanor. And why should he not have these qualities since he was the king? But it was more than his position and place. For all his other sterling and stubborn qualities, he was a man made and eager to please women—a man who let them know how much he appreciated who they were and what they willingly gave him.

Bridget leaned down to pick up two pillows the men had failed to take away. "Bridget Warren?" The voice startled her. She turned and found herself alone with Lord Brinton.

"Yes, my lord?"

"I see the bed has been removed."

"The king wished it done, my lord."

"Yes, I know." Bridget could tell Brinton expected her to say something more.

"Can I be of service, my lord?"

Brinton smiled. "Oh, come now, Bridget. It isn't becoming of you to be coy. You surely realize I know everything you claim to know about the girl's death."

She was worldly-wise and sensed the implication of Brinton's phrasing. "But I know nothing more than what I told the king—which you heard. I tried to wake the poor dear and discovered the blood—and that she was dead."

"But you said nothing to us about who you suspected committed the act."

Bridget stammered, "I . . . I have no godly idea who might have done such a thing, my lord."

He stepped toward her until he was less than a foot away, so that she was forced to look up at him. His long periwig did nothing to mitigate his expression of disappointment and anger. "Don't lie to me, Bridget. I can turn His Majesty against you very easily. Your banishment from court would only be the least of the consequences."

"My lord, I swear to you I don't know who did this. I saw or heard nothing. You must believe me."

"I believe you are in the process of concluding who might have done it but that you need more time to consider the evidence you possess so you can name with confidence the one who committed the murder—or the one who ordered Elizabeth Keller's death. I will therefore allow you to ponder your evidence and then inform me of what I—and the king—want to know. I will send word and we will talk again this afternoon—in this very place. Don't fail to meet me. If you do, you will immediately lose your position—and then suffer what other punishment I deem appropriate." Brinton bore his menacing eyes into hers and walked toward the door. "Wait. How could I have forgotten to mention it?" Without turning back to her, he added, "If you truly can't name another, then His Majesty will surely conclude that you stabbed the poor girl either on some personal account—or out of obedience to someone's command."

Bridget did not feel her body shaking until Brinton left the room. She collapsed in one of the chairs and struggled to breathe. It was only when she brought up her hands to cover her eyes that she realized she was still holding one of the two pillows she had just picked up when Brinton arrived. Still distraught, she pressed her fingers deeply into the pillow until she felt the outline of a folded piece of paper. She reached inside the blue and black pillow case and withdrew the note. She opened the fold and saw something written in a feminine hand.

Dearst Magesty, I have been put in fear to my life. I am afrade of her.

Bridget was sure these words were penned by Betty Keller. She used good English when she spoke lines written by the stage authors, but her own speech was imperfect—something the king found endearing. But Betty's words were written above another note she had apparently received. Bridget read it and felt her body turn cold.

Miserable child, you have no rightful place in the king's favor. Leave it now or expect your death.

This note too was written in a feminine hand—but of a most different kind.

"Please cry yourselves dry before the performance. The theatre will be full of curious and skeptical patrons expecting the worst from you Mary, and it will do us no good if you and you other women are unable to contain your emotions on the stage." Hardly composed himself, Michael Devlin gathered the female members of this afternoon's cast, who were to perform Mr. Dryden's popular *The Maiden Queen*. Mary Gibbons was to replace Elizabeth Keller as Florimel, a role Betty inherited from the incomparable Nell Gwynn when the latter stepped away from the stage and slid into the king's bed. It was one of those breeches roles that men particularly anticipated with delight, since Nell's and then Betty's shapely legs came out of hiding from under their dresses. Mary Gibbons' thighs and ankles were much thicker than Nell's and Betty's, but she knew the part and felt she deserved a chance to perform it. She was often easily agitated, and her nervousness coupled with her apparent sadness at Betty Keller's death made Devlin wonder if she could get through it this afternoon. But he also understood that some in the King's Company found Mary manipulative and deceitful—a young woman resentful of the attention other women in the company received. But she never revealed that side to him.

Devlin left the women and made his way to the empty benches which would soon be filled with patrons—most of whom attempted to listen attentively to the players' performances, while others used the occasion for social intercourse, paying no mind to the desire of those who wished to hear every word spoken from the stage. And then there were still others who would unashamedly express their opinion of every actor's abilities and laugh at every missed line or mispronunciation—as if their true joy was in seeing error and failure rather than proficiency and excellence. Sitting in the very middle of this section of the theatre, Devlin finally gave vent to his pent-up grief. "Dearest, Dearest Betty—what have I done?" He began to cry, and in a moment his tears turned to sobs.

Standing several rows behind him was Mary Gibbons. She saw Devlin in his grief, but more—she had heard what he said. Her eyes were completely dry.

Abigail Fayette concluded her tour of the Dove section of Dove-Raven House and praised her childhood friend Lady Durell for her good taste and sense of balance and order in the placement of her portraits and furniture and the miscellaneous and valuable items decorating the tables, chests, and cabinets. Glasses of wine were brought.

"Abby, now you must finish the tale of your forced exile in the land of ague and Indians. How you survived it, I can't begin to imagine."

"Easily enough. It was beautiful there. Virginia has its savage nature, but it is so varied and affecting, especially the lands west of Jamestown."

"As here. Wales and Ireland—varied and affecting, but, for me, too savage to desire a return visit. West is a direction on the compass we might do without, I'm afraid." Charlotte couldn't help giggling like the young girl she was when she and Abby were inseparable.

"You were always superior to me, Charlotte, except in one thing. I was always far more adventurous than you."

"There you lie. I married a man I didn't love." Once more the women laughed as they toasted each other with wine. "But when we were young girls and became friends in France during the exile, I was truly enamored of the fact that you were going to live in that place and experience such incomprehensible danger."

"And now I am the one enamored, Charlotte. After all, Indian attacks were very infrequent after we arrived in Virginia ten years ago, but then all of you here had to endure a plague and a dreadful fire." Abby, whose father was a member of Virginia's House of Burgesses, was deeply saddened hearing the news of London's plague in the spring of 1665, followed immediately by the devastating fire the following year. She asked Charlotte if she knew how many had died during the plague.

"Thousands upon thousands. Some have said between seventy and ninety thousand. The utter horror of that time. Those horrid bills of mortality. The city was strewn with ghastly corpses. No matter how far the distance, one could always smell death. We left the city with the king and did not return until that fall. And then the dreadful fire the following September. Three full days of houses and churches burning to the ground—including St. Paul's cathedral—burning from near Temple Bar to the Tower—but not Westminster or the court at Whitehall. God saw to it that the king would be safe, and yet my husband blames the king and his immoral court for bringing the plague and fire upon us—not to mention the war with the Dutch."

Abby nodded. She had not found Lord Durell at all congenial in the several minutes she had so far spent in his company. She thought him a man absorbed in thought and in his grievances.

"Yes, it was all horrible, Abby—with the exception that my removal from London during the plague put me in close proximity to the eligible yet deeply serious Lord Durell—and so I was able to prosper. Or at least endure well enough to live comfortably with my own set of acquaintances and relative privacy on this side of Dove-Raven House."

Abby finished her wine and Charlotte signaled her servant to bring back the bottle. "But Charlotte do you believe the plague and fire were signs of God's punishment?"

"My father drummed into my head the danger and illogic of too simplistic cause and effect—even if God's name is invoked. The king's decision to . . . well, God could not be just if he punished all of us for what a single man had done . . . although only God knows how many share the belief that he has done just that. But enough of politics, dear Abby. The subject tires me."

Smiling, Abby added, "You always despised any such talk. It always made you speak in fits and starts. You even wrote that way in your letters to me. Abby cleared her throat dramatically and reminded her friend that when they were both sixteen, Charlotte wrote to say she held hopes of being "the object of His Majesty's passion."

Charlotte waved the remark aside. "And I also wrote you when I married Lord Durell that I would pay you handsomely to burn that letter—which I fear you have not done."

"I cherish our friendship too strongly to destroy any written communication between us, dear Charlotte."

"You are kin to the devil, my pretty friend. Yes, Phoebe?" The servant had arrived with a letter. "Thank you. You may pour us another glass of wine. Do you like it, Abby? It's a southern French wine taken from a Dutch ship that strayed into the Thames. A *Languedoc-Roussillon*, I believe. Well, well. Look at this. A letter from Lady Castlemaine. She is coming to see us."

While his wife entertained her friend newly arrived from North America, Lord Durell was at table with Sir Roger Earle. The men sat on upholstered chairs, eating sliced leg of lamb with artichoke heart, stewed prawns, and scrambled eggs with anchovies. Yet their feast did not inhibit their discussion about the state of the realm; nor did it hinder them from fleshing out their scheme to use the Puritan Richard Hansall, who had parted from them an hour earlier.

Durell held up a bottle of spiced wine. "Hansall believes we'll protect him no matter what transpires. We mustn't delude him of that assumption. Would you care for more wine, Roger?"

"Indeed. It's quite satisfying. Yes, I agree we must reinforce the Puritan's sense of security. If matters go badly, no one would believe him if he implicates us. If they go well, we can dispense with him however we wish."

"I sit here and think of events sixty-five years ago and shake my head at the sloppiness of the attempt." Durell and Earle had spoken often of the 1605 attempt to blow up Parliament and kill Charles's grandfather James I in one fell swoop. Even though the chief plotter was Robert Catesby, the occasion was marked by some as "Guy Fawkes Day" in "honor" of the most notorious of the English Catholic conspirators who was discovered with the explosives in the House of Lords after an anonymous letter warned of the plot. As Durell and Earle well knew, Fawkes was arrested while the other conspirators fled to the Midlands some 130 miles from London and engaged with troops led by the Sheriff of Worcester. Those who were not killed were brought back to London and with Fawkes stood trial—and were condemned to be hanged, drawn, and quartered.

Earle stepped toward the window and gazed at the expansive lawn. "And they still celebrate November the fifth because the king was saved. You are correct, Lord Durell. There were simply too many involved. What was it—at least a dozen or more?"

"Ten more than we have, my friend."

"There will have to be one or two others to carry out the plan, and you forget Hansall."

"He *believes* he's involved, Roger, but he's not the least aware he is being used. And by the time he knows the truth it will be too late."

The men talked briefly of the irony in James I's being the target of Roman Catholic assassins. Now it was the Catholic-leaning king who posed the danger to his Protestant nation.

Durell laughed derisively. "Fawkes and his crew wished to elevate James's nine year-old Catholic daughter to the throne. At least we will propose a virile twenty-one year-old Protestant male to rule." Earle reminded Durell that since the Duke of Monmouth was a bastard son and Charles's brother James was the heir presumptive, the elevation of Charles illegitimate son would be opposed.

"James has converted—he has taken the Roman Eucharist—don't you know that, Roger?"

"I have heard rumors but those at court deny it."

"Of course they deny it. Charles has also denied he has Roman Catholic leanings. Their religious preferences have been no secret to me. Charles must die before his wife gives him a son—if she can. James's issue will be suspect because of their father's secret conversion.

Earle lifted his glass. "I toast your brilliance, Lord Durell."

"No, Roger. Let us toast our monarch."

"Very well, then. To His Majesty the King."

"Short may his life be." Other men might have chuckled, but Durell was coldly serious.

CHAPTER 5

Following five steps behind his monarch, Lord Brinton watched the king walking his dogs in St. James's Park. His Majesty seemed highly amused by the rust and white and the black and white spaniels cavorting at his heels. Brinton wondered whether they were today an antidote to the grief or concern over Betty Keller's murder—or had the king simply closed her in one of the many drawers in his expansive mind? Was Charles already planning a visit to one of the theatres to choose another mistress or perhaps sift through the faces of the wives and sisters of the men at court? Then again, the king was already smitten by the baby-faced Louise de Kérouaille, his recently-deceased sister's lady in waiting. But Brinton understood that one could depend on Charles's capriciousness when it came to his mistresses, as well as the ephemeral nature of these relationships—with the exception, that is, of Lady Castlemaine. How long would this irrepressible woman have influence on His Majesty—no matter how occasional that influence was? Charles had already promised her the titles Countess of Southampton and Duchess of Cleveland. Many thought this promise was clear evidence her influence on the king was in decline, but Brinton thought it more likely she still held a high place in his heart and that she was, for all the volatility between them, the one woman he could never dismiss or resist. Brinton found most accurate, then, the view that she had long been the "Uncrowned Queen" of the realm.

Brinton therefore considered her quite dangerous. He was confused why her conversion to Roman Catholicism seven years earlier elicited little apprehension from the king, who wittily remarked that he was more interested in the bodies of his lovers than in their souls. But Brinton knew Charles's Catholic leanings were highly troubling to many in powerful positions. That His Majesty still had deep passion for Barbara Villiers did not serve the nation well. How much better for the king and for his subjects if this woman were gone from his life—and from everyone else's.

"Henry, look at this." Charles laughed exuberantly. Brinton stepped forward to see that two of the pelicans presented to Charles by the Russian Ambassador six years earlier were attempting to mate. "Not very genteel, but let's hope effective." Charles retinue chortled along with their monarch. The king whispered to Brinton, "Male on top—entering from behind—wings flapping vigorously. My Lady Castlemaine would love it."

"You have seen everything, dearest Abby except this, my private gallery. I have only one-quarter of the portraits and paintings my husband possesses, but whereas his collection is exclusively Dutch and French, mine has only the work of English and Italian artists from this century and the last." Among Charlotte's holdings were two works by the Renaissance painter Holbein and three from Orazio Gentileschi, the Italian artist who, as Charlotte informed her friend, came to England during the reign of Charles I and remained until his death. "He was the favorite of the present king's mother Henrietta Maria. Look how elegant these pieces are."

"They most certainly are." Even when they were girls, Abby marveled at her friend's sense of and commitment to elegance.

"But even more to my taste is the work of his daughter Artemisia Gentileschi, whose work I have seen in Italy. She too came to England during the reign of the first King Charles, and I was so taken by her work depicting the strength, defiance, and sufferings of women and their revenge on men. In one piece she depicts the Biblical Judith decapitating Holofernes, whose head is forced back while Judith and her maid begin to cut it off."

Abby noted her friend's intensity of voice as she explained the Italian woman's work. "Charlotte you seem to revere her art in a way that you must always keep private."

"Oh, I do—never fear. But Lady Castlemaine is more open about the painting I have just described. She has not seen it, but was enthralled by my description of it and of other works by Artemisia that portrayed women as victims, warriors, and suicides. When I told her Artemisia might herself been the victim of a rape, Barbara said she would always carry the painter in her heart."

"Was Lady Castlemaine the victim of such a crime?"

"She has never admitted that to me, but if so it has never inhibited her desire to engage in amorous play—with the king and with other men. Still, she claims to understand what prompted Artemisia Gentileschi to paint the subjects she chose."

Abby felt uneasy at the prospects of meeting the apparently infamous Barbara Villiers. How would that imposing woman view her and the fairly innocent and serene life she had led? Abby couldn't help believing she'd be cruelly dismissed by the Countess of Castlemaine.

"Abby, there is one more artist I wish to mention—Sir Peter Lely, who has become the court's prime portrait painter. He painted during the nightmare Cromwell years, but only achieved greatness when Charles was restored to the throne. He has painted a portrait of eleven beauties of the court—the collection I will take you to see tomorrow. You will never guess who is among the eleven."

Abby smiled broadly. "I knew your beauty would be acknowledged, and now I see that—"

Charlotte dropped her smile. "Lady Castlemaine, Abby—not me. She is depicted as Minerva, the Roman goddess of wisdom and patroness of the arts."

"Dearest Charlotte, you forget I have been educated in spite of my years away from England. I also know that Minerva eventually took on the properties of the Greek goddess Athena. But tell me, how well done is the portrait."

"Oh, very. Barbara's beauty and violet eyes are well captured, and the expression suggests that this Minerva was born with weapons and armor as the Roman goddess was. And yet she also appears as a lovely Madonna in another of Sir Peter's portraits, which depicts her with her son by the king."

Abby felt even more trepidation at meeting the woman. "Do you possess any of Lely's portraits, Charlotte?"

Her friend offered a strained smile. "I was not one of his 'Windsor Beauties,' but Lord Durell has commissioned a portrait from him of his lovely wife Charlotte. It is now completed and will be brought here very soon."

"Charlotte, I am sure your loveliness is well captured. It will be a most impressive portrait to be certain."

"I asked mine to be as similar to one of the Windsor Beauties as possible. I told Mr. Lely I thought there ought to be a complete dozen beauties and that I had no objection to being the twelfth. But I shouldn't have said that. I appear in almost the exact approximation of the 'Beauties' Jane Needham—Mistress Middleton, and as she, I am holding a cornucopia."

Abby laughed at her friend's sour face. "Then why did you hold the cornucopia"

"I didn't. Sir Peter painted my head, but his pupils did the rest."

"But I still don't understand why you are unhappy by the comparison to Mistress Middleton."

Charlotte took her time in replying. "Barbara once told me that for all her beauty, Jane had an aversion to bathing. How she attracted her lovers, I have no idea."

Although thoroughly delighted by her friend's graphic depiction, Abby still had her doubts. "Oh Charlotte, I think you exaggerate."

"Don't doubt me until you meet her or until she at least passes by."

Charlotte informed her friend as well that one of the Windsor Beauties was the king's recently deceased sister, Henrietta—or Minette as she was so often called—while another was one of the king's occasional bed partners. Still another set her sights on being the king's mistress but was thwarted by the imposing Lady Castlemaine. "And then there is Frances Stuart, another of the eleven, whom His Majesty dearly wanted gasping under him but who managed to deflect his advances."

"I'm surprised she didn't agree. I wonder why she didn't."

"Perhaps you can ask Frances yourself, Abby. I have sent her a note inviting her here to meet you."

Abigail Fayette's head spun with the tales of these notable women. She thought of the many days she spent in Virginia meeting many who had only primitive appreciation of taste, manners, and beauty.

She pointed around the room. "These portraits are exceptionally fine, Charlotte. I envy your having them. And you must be so delighted to have yourself immortalized by Sir Peter Lely."

"Oh I am, but I hope to have another done of me resembling the king's favorite Lely portrait of Nellie Gwynn."

Abigail could tell from her friend's peculiar smile that there was something about Nell's portrait Charlotte wanted her to know."

"So I assume she's portrayed with full armor, wielding *two* swords?"

"With nothing on, actually."

"You jest, surely."

"I jest not at all. Charles keeps it behind a mundane landscape painting, which he takes great pleasure and mirth in pushing back to reveal his Nellie's nakedness."

"Perhaps I should not wish to meet Sir Peter, after all."

After the woman shared several moments of further amusement, Abby asked if she could see Lord Durell's collection of Dutch and French paintings.

"If you wish to venture into the Raven part of the house, feel free to do so. I choose to spend as little time there as I can. Instead, I will attend to some other matters and then meet you in the lavender room for some delicious sweet treats and perhaps another glass of that sparkling French wine we enjoyed earlier."

The women kissed each other's cheek, and Abby headed to Lord Durell's side of the house.

"So Bridget Warren, I am sure you will now inform me who you believe was responsible for the death of Elizabeth Keller."

The poor woman stood before Brinton shaking visibly, her eyes filled with tears and her hands pressed together in the attitude of intense prayer.

"I cannot know for sure because I did not see the murder, Lord Brinton. Nor did I know of any plot to murder her. I never heard anyone speak of it. You must believe me."

"But . . .?"

She understood he wouldn't allow her to escape the room without her providing a name.

"But I would imagine that—"

"Woman, I am not interested in your imaginings." His voice remained low, but the tone was cruel and threatening.

"My sense is . . . I mean, I believe that Betty Keller was . . . that one of His Majesty's other lovers had her murdered."

Brinton rose from his chair and grabbed Bridget by the back of her head, his fingers clawing at the hair under her cap. "A name, woman. Or I will break your neck where you stand." Still clutching her hair, he brought her down to her knees.

"Please my lord. Give me leave to speak."

"You have it." Brinton released his grip and Bridget fell forward so that now she was on all fours.

"I'm sure it was Lady Castlemaine, my lord."

"You mean the whore Lady Castlemaine, don't you?"

"Yes, my Lord. She."

Brinton lifted the woman to her feet. He opened her right hand and placed in it a small bag of coins. "Forgive my anger, Bridget. You are a good woman. Well deserving of reward. Continue to serve the king well."

After Brinton left the room, Bridget nearly called him back to tell him of the note Betty had written. But the note also contained another hand. Shame overcame Bridget, as she sank to her knees and prayed to a God she feared would no longer listen.

CHAPTER 6

Michael Devlin grabbed a cup of beer from the old woman who brought it to him, spilling some of the contents on his hands and wrists. "It took you long enough, damn you." The old woman shrugged and returned to her place in the Black Plough tavern not far from the theatre. This was Devlin's preferred place of refuge since he returned to London a decade earlier. Here he celebrated theatrical success and bemoaned the occasional poor performance. Always teeming with life, the Black Plough accommodated the gregarious and the odd and always resounded with laughter and the occasional scuffle. Devlin had no use for the latest rage for the coffee houses throughout the city—those dwellings where decorum was expected, the conversation often serious and political, and the mood less convivial and more scandalous. Besides, the coffee houses had become segregated bastions for lawyers, physicians, apprentices, and those holding office throughout London. Coffee wasn't the only beverage one could imbibe, but Devlin felt the taste of ale at a coffee house could never match that served at a tavern. The disenchanted Puritans had their own coffee houses and even the perverse Quakers had their dens as well. One could even be fined for swearing or gambling in a coffee house. Devlin wasn't at all surprised when insipid tea was added to the beverage list in the coffee houses—partly influenced by the king's wife Catherine of Braganza, who favored the drink. Some at the taverns even determined that she would never bear Charles a son as long as she drank tea.

Especially when he was in his cups, Devlin would often pronounce on the superiority of beer to the other social infatuation—wine. To Devlin, English beer was an honest and hearty drink, whereas wine was the soul of pretentiousness and continental, particularly French, weakness. But today Devlin would make no such arguments in favor of the beverage he held in his hand. Neither did his mood fit the environment, for he was in mourning over the death of his dear Betty Keller, dejected by the impossibility of replacing her in the short-term, and highly frustrated at the inability of the young actress he had just selected to take Betty's future roles to understand even the most basic aspects of her craft. He knew he had chosen the seventeen-year-old Anne Whitworth, who possessed a lovely freckled face and thick reddish hair. But whereas her demeanor and bearing suggested a more experienced actress, she often stood with her body turned upstage and therefore away from the patrons, and she let her voice drop, so that the end of her lines couldn't be understood. Yet even worse was her inability to ignore the remarks and wordless whistles, exaggerated sighs, and long hisses from those who sat before the stage, where rules of theatrical decorum were too often violated. And all this occurred when Anne played smaller parts. Devlin couldn't imagine what would happen to her in the larger roles Betty Keller performed, but surely Mary Gibbons would not do, even though she was to take Betty's role of Florimel. Mary's face and body simply weren't right for the parts.

In spite of these current and potential difficulties and in spite of there being another recent addition, young Elizabeth Boutell, who could handle the roles, Anne was the only actress to whom Devlin believed he could transfer his attention and emotions. Betty Keller was dead; she had to be replaced in his life—and immediately. That Anne was two years younger than Betty mattered little to him. He would train Anne as he had Betty and he would, in spite of the many years between them, have her in his bed.

Buoyed by these thoughts, Devlin finished his beer and called the old woman to him, this time offering her a coin as penance for his previous shortness of temper. He asked for a buttered-ale this time, with butter, sugar, and cinnamon mixed congenially with the ale, and the woman offered him a wrinkled and toothless grin. But before she returned with the drink, Devlin overheard two men speaking of the king and the murder of one of his mistresses.

"I should wish to bet that another of the king's ladies—perhaps even the queen herself—had the girl done in."

"No. I was told that the dead woman was an actress at the King's Theatre. I'd venture one of those new guinea coins—if I had one in my possession—that someone at the theatre—out of jealousy—had her dispatched."

The two men laughed and called on the old woman to bring them each another drink. In a moment she appeared with the buttered-ale in her hand. But the customer she had brought it for had already pushed his way out of the Black Plough.

Richard Hansall waited at the appointed place—on Magpie Lane right off Fetter Lane. He first came here with his father when he was a boy of twelve—in late August 1642. He remembered how full of spirit and hope his normally dour father was after receiving word on Magpie Lane that the first King Charles had raised his standard at Nottingham, which commenced the war between the Royalist and Parliamentarian forces for the very soul of England, as Hansall's father proclaimed. The king was determined to return to London and govern as he always had, but the opposing forces kept the royalists at bay after battles at Edgehill, Aylesbury, and Turnham Green that fall. Puritans like the Hansalls believed God had saved their country through the efforts of the Parliamentarian soldiers and their generals, even though the battles during the following sixteen months were not all victorious ones. With 1644, however, the news was more satisfying. The Parliamentarians won the field in battles at Nantwich, Cheriton, Marston Moor, and at the second Battle of Newbury.

But Hansall's hatred for the Royalists had yet to ascend to its peak. At the end of May 1644, his brother visited his uncle in Bolton, some fifteen miles northwest of Manchester and a Parliamentarian outpost within a strongly-held Royalist area. Forces under Prince Rupert attacked and captured the town, leaving over fifteen hundred dead and seven hundred more taken prisoner. Many of those dead were slaughtered after the fighting ended—resident and military man alike. As Hansall learned, Prince Rupert ignored the rules of war and had no parlay before beginning his siege. Instead the attack was sudden and in the chaotic fighting in the streets and in the plunder that followed, unarmed citizens were put to the sword—including Hansall's brother and uncle. The Parliamentarians termed the event the "Bolton Massacre," and it served to further anger and inspire those who continued to fight against the King and his forces.

Hansall was only fourteen when his brother was slain in the streets of Bolton, but his fury and hatred were ripe enough to join the fight in the summer of 1644 and throughout 1645, which found him part of the major battle of the war—at Naseby in Northhamptonshire, which destroyed the heart of the Royalists army. King Charles was at the battle with Prince Rupert, opposed by Sir Edward Fairfax and the brightest Parliamentarian star, Oliver Cromwell. Young Hansall displayed no fear or hesitation on the battlefield, but some hour into the battle that morning, he was cut down by the nails and scrap iron fired by smaller cannon. Most of his fellow soldiers had armor covering their breasts and backs to protect them from such a fusillade, but young Hansall wore only a leather tunic. His shoulder, neck, and jaw were struck by the iron shrapnel, and when he fell he screamed for assistance until he passed out from the pain. After being taken from the field and his wounds dressed, Hansall kept asking if the king had been slain in battle. He seemed to those with him that he blamed Charles personally for firing the cannon that ended his military career—at age fourteen.

The scars from his wounds—one side of his face was permanently disfigured—as well as the memory of his father's death, nurtured further contempt for the monarchy and the memory of Charles, even after the king was taken and later publicly executed on the 30th of January, 1649. Yet even being witness to the king's head dropping to the floor of the scaffold did not satisfy his hatred; nor did it lessen the memory of his brother's death in the streets of Bolton. Hansall prospered during the Interregnum, when Cromwell took power as the Lord Protector. But now in his twenties, he believed correctly that the great experiment in government would last only as long as Cromwell did. And when the Lord Protector died, and power was handed to Cromwell's politically inept son Richard, Hansall made the decision to ingratiate himself with other powerful men—all Royalists.

"Hansall?"

"I am here, Sir Roger."

Earle walked briskly to where Hansall stood and handed him three folded sheets. "Read these sheets and come to Dove-Raven House tomorrow morning at ten. Lord Durell and I think you will be well pleased by what you have there."

Earle walked back toward Fetter Lane as Hansall placed the folded pages into his boot. He couldn't risk that one or more of the sheets would drop from his hand or from his coat or the waist of his breeches. Now after the death of Cromwell twelve years and his father twenty-five years earlier, all the blood sacrificed in God's name would be sanctified with the death of the second Charles.

Abby thought lying down for a few minutes would be all she would need to get her through the rest of the day. But she had slept for over an hour. Remembering that Charlotte was presently engaged with her correspondence, Abby headed toward the Raven side of the house to examine Lord Durell's collection of Dutch and French art. As she stepped through the interior archway separating both sides of the grand house, she felt a palpable chill, as though she had stepped from a sunny early summer's morning into a chilled late autumn afternoon. Asking if she needed assistance, a servant seemed reluctant to allow her passage into this part of the house. Abby smiled and politely informed the man that Lady Durell had given her permission—even encouragement—to look at Lord Durell's paintings. The servant, still reluctant, stepped aside with an "As her ladyship wishes."

Abby was soon taken by the Dutch portraits that filled the first room she entered. Here she viewed common citizens depicted in everyday activities—drinking, eating, laboring, smiling, and grimacing. She saw the very old and very young—the inebriated, the contemplative, and the dying. The interplay of shadows and light utterly fascinated her, and she found none of the work depressing, as she assumed she might, based on Charlotte's dour assessment of her husband's collection.

Abby walked further down the hall and found another room, which she assumed was filled with French art. But before she could begin her tour of the collection, she heard men's voices coming from the room across the hall. One belonged to Lord Durell; the second she didn't recognize. At first she could barely make out what was being discussed, but soon she heard the men all too well.

"Am I to understand nothing further than that, my lord?"

Lord Durell shook his head and opened the letter the man brought from Sir Roger Earle. "No, Samuel. The less you are acquainted with the better for you."

"Then I'm not to know what it is you are planning, my lord? I have been in your service for eighteen years. I hope I have proven to you my loyalty and trustworthiness."

Abby learned from Charlotte that Lord Durell most trusted servant was a man named Samuel Greenham.

"I don't tell you what the plan is, Samuel, but, as I say, that is only for your own good. For if you were to know or seek any further to know, I would have to order you killed."

"Surely, you are joking, my lord."

Durell ignored Greenham's assumption. "You are certain Sir Roger assured that the services of two men have been secured—and that he is seeking a third?"

"Yes, my lord. He made no mention of names. Do you know who they are?"

Abby heard Lord Durell smirk. "I do not—nor do I want to know."

Greenham asked cautiously, "My Lord, can I at least understand what—"

"You have wanted three days to spend with your mother in Norwich. Take them starting tomorrow morning."

"Yes, my lord." Abby could hear Samuel's voice crack with apprehension as he uttered his reply. Her heartbeat increased as she heard Greenham walk down the hall in the other direction. She was forced to remain rigidly still until Lord Durell left the room across the hall, frightened by the promise Durell made to his man and knowing her own life might be put in jeopardy if Durell knew she had eavesdropped.

After several moments, she heard Durell walk out of the room and stop, as though he were looking into the room that contained his French paintings. There would be no place to hide if he stepped into the room. Her eye caught a portrait of a Roman mother begging for the life or purity of her lovely young daughter while a conquering soldier stood before them with his sword drawn. If Durell saw her, she would have no one there to plead for her.

CHAPTER 7

On the coach ride to Dove-Raven house, Lady Castlemaine protected herself from the chill of the early December afternoon with the same plush blanket she had wrapped around her naked body the very first night the new king returned to England after his exile. Charles was then unmarried, and although she knew he already had a son with Lucy Walter, Barbara believed she would from this point forward reign supreme in the royal bed. And she worked to remain ascendant, providing the king, she confidently believed, with sexual pleasure he could receive from no other woman. In bed, she alternated between aggression and aloofness, keeping Charles enough off balance to enhance his passion for her. He seemed equally excited whether she stared down into his eyes as he was inside her or turned her face away when he assumed the masculine position above her.

Her memory was most active whenever she rode in her coach or on horseback or strolled through St. James's and Hyde Parks, her retinue always a respectful ten paces or more behind her so her contemplations might remain undisturbed. Now as she watched the scenery pass by from the coach window, the barren trees and cloud-filled sky only deepened the memory of her time with Charles. She recalled being immediately attracted to the king's darker complexion—much more Italian than English—and his height, which made with her own a 'splendid fit, in bed and out," as he once said. She chided him whenever he claimed to be "an ugly fellow," knowing that his imperfect features only enhanced the appeal of his sensual mouth. Even at present she held that were he not king, he would have no difficulty cultivating lovers of even the highest station. The thought once more stimulated the creature inside her—the possessive, jealous, and violent presence that left literal scratches, bruises, and other marks on Charles's face and arms, along with gestures and promises that she would maim or even kill him whenever he showed interest in another young woman of the court or in one of those damned actresses.

Brushing her gloved hand on the blanket, she remembered her difficult situation right before she met Charles. She was without fortune, and her romance with the second Earl of Chesterfield ended with his decision to marry someone far wealthier than young Barbara Villiers. But Roger Palmer would take her, and when she was nineteen she and her new husband sailed to The Hague to try their luck with the man they knew would eventually be recalled to England and serve as king. But whatever charm Palmer had could not deter her ambition and willingness to claim a place in Charles's bed. Neither then nor at any time since did Barbara suffer guilt for cuckolding her husband. She only wondered if her betrayal was in some way avenging Chesterfield's rejection. She was never certain, but she vowed at the time she would become and remain the most important and powerful woman in England. As for Charles's part, he did at least make Palmer the Earl of Castlemaine and provide Barbara with the title she would carry with her for almost ten years. Even now that she was about to be created Duchess of Cleveland, she understood she would always be recalled as Lady Castlemaine. Although many whispered that her forthcoming elevation to the title of Duchess served only as a parting gift to a woman who was being fully stripped of her power and influence, Barbara was determined not to go quietly. Nor would she allow the king to dismiss her with impunity.

She banged on the coach door until it came to a stop. Her present agitation brought on dark thoughts of suppression and suffocation. She flung off the lap blanket and stepped down from the vehicle. She would walk until she once again felt in control.

"Abby, dear. Where have you been? You look almost pale." Charlotte had just completed her final piece of correspondence.

Abby waited a full minute in the gallery room after she heard Lord Durell walk past and down the hallway. He hadn't come in, although she saw his fingers wrap around the entrance way as though he were about to. Even warnings of an impending Indian attack in Virginia frightened her far less than the prospect of Lord Durell discovering her in the gallery. He would have known she overheard his discussion with Samuel Greenham—that a secret plan was currently in motion and that two men were chosen to take part whose names neither Greenham nor Lord Durell knew. Whatever the plan, Abby was certain it was nothing innocent.

"Do I? Well, I suppose I am out of breath, Charlotte."

"Have you been running?" Abby several times read in letters Charlotte's denunciation of a woman's moving too rapidly—quick walking included.

"No. I was in one of your husband's gallery rooms and I heard him coming. I assumed he would scold me for being there without you. I was therefore frightened." Abby always tried to rely on the truth as much as possible, whereas her friend Charlotte thought fabrication and exaggeration were two of a woman's most useful social tools.

"Oh, Abby. He would have been shocked to see you alone in his Raven's nest, I imagine, but he would not have been put out. He would at most have only growled at you like a dog."

Abby closed her eyes tightly as she was wont to do before making up her mind. "Is Lord Durell planning an event of some kind—perhaps even in your honor."

"Why do you ask? You heard something, I assume?"

"He was speaking to his man Samuel about the organization of some occasion—something he wanted the man to keep between them." Abby had to know if Charlotte was privy to her husband's plan.

"It wouldn't surprise me. Most likely he wants to remove part of my garden and set on the grounds some artificial ruins reminiscent of ancient Greek or Roman times. Sadly, it's becoming a bit of a sensation in and outside the city. Why brighten at a colorful display of flowers when one can darken at the sight of broken stones."

Because Charlotte displayed no concern about what her friend overheard, Abby was satisfied that Charlotte was unaware of whatever Lord Durell was up to.

"You had best change your clothes, dear friend. You'll want to look appetizing before Barbara arrives and eats you whole."

Michael Devlin was back at the King's Theatre on Bridges Street, Drury Lane watching a rehearsal, which would end in time to clear the stage for the 3:30 p.m. scheduled performance. The same actors would return in the evening and work another hour on the new comedy they were preparing. For the most part, his players were a dedicated and industrious lot, intelligent enough to learn several roles at once, a necessity given the nature of the business—the frequent to daily shift to another play with different stage movements and emotions. Fortunately the King's Company had twenty-six members; therefore some of the actors had evenings free from performance, which they dedicated to rehearsals. Devlin himself would occasionally take parts if they were brief and well spaced. As a result of the demands of his major duties over the past several years, he now lacked the stamina to act on stage more often. Nor did he have any longer the ability to memorize and then recall too many lines in an evening. He could excuse himself for this deficiency, but he was unforgiving when any of his younger actors failed to display the proper energy for the role or forgot whole lines and longer passages, thereby affecting the concentration of fellow players and damaging the play.

And a performance could be energetic with every line spoken perfectly with none forgotten and still prompt a sour reaction from the auditors in the pit, the boxes, or the galleries. Devlin had seen it all—from patrons hissing, shouting, tossing oranges and various vegetables to numerous altercations with fists, knives, and swords stemming from a dozen different complaints—personal, political, or theatrical. Other than lethargy and memory loss, the actors could exacerbate any volatile situation by performing while drunk, losing their character while on the stage or tossing in lines directed at the audience or to fellow actors which were not penned by the play's author. Devlin tried to calm heated objections from the patrons to what they heard and saw on the stage—and it took special handling to sooth the furrowed brow of Mr. Dryden, the company's major dramatist.

There was even more to tax Devlin's patience—from an orange women's stealing from those in the pit to the ladies of fashion, behind their vizard masks, flirting with gentleman sitting near or at some distance away. If the king or his brother the Duke of York wished for a favorite actor to secure a choice part, Devlin had to re-cast the play. Three years earlier, the company's popular actor and playwright John Lacy offended the king, queen, and the Duke and Duchess of York by improvising lines about the court's corrupt ways, leaving Charles no choice but to throw his favorite actor in prison for several days. That was right during the time the King's Theatre was undergoing a number of much needed improvements in its structure and behavior. With the Lacy business, Devlin came close to resigning his post. Instead he stayed on to endure the myriad of frustrations his position guaranteed. His darling Betty Keller made all of it worthwhile, but now she was gone.

"Mr. Devlin?"

Devlin looked to his left and right before responding. "Yes, Francis? Francis Gottlieb was the tallest actor in the company—as tall as the king and a favorite of the actresses, although not the audiences. He seemed too dull and plodding was the usual complaint, but Devlin could trust him to deliver a solid performance—with no forgotten lines—no matter what the part.

Gottlieb bent down and whispered in Devlin's ear. "I have made the arrangements. Tonight at 9:00 the both of you will meet at Sir Edmund Pollard's home in St. James's Square."

"Will Pollard be there?"'"

"No. He is in Spain, and he knows nothing. You will have complete privacy."

"Good." Devlin realized he would be taking a serious risk going to Pollard's, but with his dearest Betty dead, he felt he must become involved.

With his lady gone off to Dove-Raven House, Thomas Lockwood felt emboldened to stand in her dressing room and examine her dressing table and the beauty enhancements she applied. Even lying on the table undisturbed, her pearl powders and rouge enchanted him. He touched with the tip of his fingers her wash ball—the shredded soap mixed with spices and herbs that lengthened the time the soap could be used but more importantly added to her skin a lovely scent that he had the distinct pleasure of enjoying whenever she was near. Lockwood touched her rouge, lifting a small daub of red to his finger, which he brought to his lips as though he were kissing his lady's cheek and mouth. He recalled how he and Lady Castlemaine laughed at the estimation of others that women who enhanced their faces with such feminine appliances were cheats at heart, and since they could deceive with their looks, they would likely betray their husbands. "That much *is* true, Thomas" she cheerfully said. "Far truer than the belief that women actors would improve the conduct of those who came to the theatres." Rather than laughing, she offered the second comment with disdain.

But most alluring to him was the mirror in which his lady examined herself daily. Yet he felt envious of the glass knowing how often it had seen her lovely face—never adequately captured by Mr. Lely's portraits—and witnessed her in various stages of undress. Lockwood had in his possession discarded pearls that once caressed her neck, one broken pearl eardrop, several locks of her thick brunette hair, and a torn chemise she asked him to dispose of along with other articles of clothing. He had slept every night with the discarded chemise close to him. The chemise still carried her scent, and often he placed his hands inside it—where her body had been.

Lockwood returned to his duties but not before vowing silently that he would do anything she asked. He had already done much. He only wanted to do more.

CHAPTER 8

"Do you recognize this other hand?" Bridget Warren handed the note she found near Betty Keller's body to the actress Mary Gibbons, the daughter of Bridget's cousin, the retail merchant Walter Gibbons, now deceased.

Mary's eyes expanded as she read the words *Miserable child, you have no rightful place in the king's favor. Leave it now or prepare for your death.* "This is indeed an elevated hand, Bridget. A lady's hand, to be sure." Noting that she couldn't guess the author, Mary pushed Bridget's hand away when the older woman reached for the note. "No, let me hold this for a time. I can show it to others who might know the author."

"No, you cannot keep it, Mary. I'll be severely punished if it is known I have kept this from the eyes of the king and Lord Brinton. Let me have it back."

Mary smiled and placed the note behind her back as though she and Bridget were children playing a game. "Don't you wish to know who wrote this? I promise you if I find out its author, I will return the note for you to do with it as you wish. You can then place it back in the room and pretend you have only just discovered it. I only ask that you say you showed it to me and that I identified the writer. This can improve both our positions, don't you see?"

Bridget once again attempted to grab the note, but her effort was half-hearted. Perhaps Mary would find it was indeed penned by Lady Castlemaine, as Bridget had told Lord Brinton. Besides, if Lady Castlemaine was the author, it did not necessarily mean she had Betty murdered, for she had threatened many with harm during her years as the king's favorite—even His Majesty himself.

"Dearest Abby, you will see Lady Castlemaine in her decline, I am afraid. And it saddens me for reasons I cannot adequately express."

"But from what you have told me, she seems to be a woman who could never show herself in such a state." Abby was still evaluating the conversation she had overheard between Lord Durell and his man Samuel. "I wonder if the actress Nell Gwynn has given the king something Barbara could not."

"Yes, our dearest Nellie. The name suggests the nature of her pedigree, and yet I can't help liking her. Though I am, as you know, too discreet to openly admit my joy in having her here to entertain me with her filthy wit and dramatic charms. In fact, she is aware you have arrived and will come to pay her compliments. She insists on it. Just prepare to be overwhelmed. Your sea passage from Virginia will seem like a lake crossing in comparison.

Abby smiled in anticipation of conversing with the actress and mistress of the king. "Well, I look forward to meeting her. My life has now lost its drama."

"Nellie can provide you with more than you can handle. Her cunning will soon have you spreading your legs for every man she introduces you to." Charlotte laughed at Abby's reaction. "Don't be shocked. Such is all the talk now among women. The king has endorsed it through his example and the spirited vocabulary of his ladies. Now, how long have you been without a husband?"

"I shouldn't even answer you. But you well know it has been almost two full years since his death. Why? Am I more attractive being a widow of two years?"

Charlotte shook her head. "No, dear Abby. I don't think any desirable man will be at all interested in you. You have looks comely enough for now, but as a widow without a major endowment, you are getting more undesirable with each passing day. Besides your advancing age, you are too normal, too delightfully placid to intrigue the most handsome men. And you have already made your offering to the altar of Hymen; therefore, you couldn't attract that predatory aspect of many suitors."

"Such as His Majesty?"

Charlotte ignored the question. "You have my condolences, but remember I will always be here to hold your knitting and listen to your woeful tales of loneliness." Charlotte laughed and kissed her friend, who playfully resisted the attempt. Their moment was interrupted by Charlotte's woman Phoebe Clarke.

"Lady Durell, this has just arrived." Charlotte read the note and sighed with disappointment.

"Our Lady Castlemaine sends word that she will come here later this evening. It appears she was in the coach on the way but remembered she had an appointment this afternoon and had to go back. Well, let us spend the next two hours at cribbage, the way we did when we were girls."

Abby shook her head. "A game you always seemed to win. I would prefer to move to the lawn and play shuttlecock."

"A vulgar game for vulgar times. But no, I am not in the position where I can afford to leap about with a . . . What is it, Phoebe?" The woman had been trying to interrupt.

"Forgive me, but Lord Durell would like to see you for a few minutes."

Charlotte added exaggeration to her groan. "Very well. Excuse me for leaving you, Abby. The donkey brays."

"Can he not come here to speak with you?"

"No. It was part of our arrangement, remember. When I insisted on making this part of the house strictly the province of women, I did not take into account that when my husband was desirous of speaking with me I would be forced to walk a hundred miles through the halls of this demi-kingdom to speak with him. But I have the most powerful legs of any lady in the realm. Always sore but without question considerably powerful. Phoebe, keep my dearest friend company and see to her wants. Oh, did I tell you in any of my recent letters what Phoebe's real Christian name is?" With that teasing reference, Charlotte headed toward the long hallway to the Raven side of the house.

Abby smiled at Phoebe, who had her head down either in embarrassment or deference. The servant was a short and slender woman with a pleasant face and demeanor that made most difficult expressing one's impatience with her. Abby was taken by Phoebe's eyes, which seemed permanently lifted as if to say, "I hope I haven't disappointed you."

"Well, Phoebe, I am curious if nothing else. Would you tell me what your real Christian name is? Or does Lady Durell jest?"

"No, madam. She does not. My given Christian name is Silence."

Silence? Well, I would imagine that such a one would be difficult to live up to."

"I imagine it would be, Madam." The poor girl didn't change her expression.

"I take it then you are the daughter of a Puritan family." Phoebe began to reply but stopped. "No, please. Tell me. It is all right."

"Yes, madam, I belonged to a large family. I was the twelfth child of a non-conforming clergyman, who gave all seven of his daughters' virtuous names. I am afraid he had too much virtue and not enough imagination when he came to naming me."

Abby laughed. "That was very clever, Phoebe. I will not ask the names of your brothers and sisters, then." In Virginia, Abby heard many highly unusual allegorical names given to Puritan children in England, such as Diffidence, Kill-sin, Die-well, Humiliation, Fear-God, and Praise-God Barebone's son, the formally and incredulously named "If-Christ-hadst-not-died-for-thee-thou-hadst-been-damned Barebone."

"But how did you come to be called Phoebe?"

"Lady Durell gave me that name. She said Phoebe was one of the twelve Titans in the Greek mythology and that it was a strong name for a woman, because she was the grandmother of both Artemis and the powerful Hecate."

"If I remember my lessons, Artemis was the avenger of her sex and Hecate was the goddess of witchcraft, ghosts, and crossroads, of all things."

"Then you see I am hardly worthy of the name."

Abby grinned. "I cannot believe those deities reflect you—although Lady Durell . . . I am only teasing, Phoebe. Tell me, how do your father and mother take to having you called Phoebe?"

"My father is dead."

"Your mother then. Is she still alive?"

"She had twelve children, madam. What do you think?"

Abby didn't know which was more amusing—Phoebe's reply or the subservient look on her face as she delivered it. "I'm sorry to laugh, Phoebe. Forgive my insensitivity."

"There is no need, madam."

"Well, may I ask if you are content working here?"

"Oh, very. It is always a lively place, wherever Lady Durell happens to be, but especially here. So many important people come to Dove-Raven House. I feel frightened I will offend them, especially the important women who visit.

Abby thought she might learn from Phoebe what Charlotte might not share with her. "And who frightens you most?"

"Queen Catherine, though she never looks at me or raises her voice. It's just that she is so sadly regal I fear she will one day simply begin to cry and tell everyone how miserable her life is. She is childless and the king doesn't love her the way he loves other women."

"I am told His Majesty loves her in his own quiet way." She had in fact been told no such thing. It had been her believe since childhood that if a man truly loves, he can never do it quietly. "Does the king frighten you also?"

A slight smile began on Phoebe's face, but she immediately suppressed it. "Oh, no. He can frighten no woman, not even one of my humble place. He has come up to me and kissed me three times on the mouth, and I was never once frightened."

Phoebe's depiction matched the one Abby heard from others who traveled from England to Virginia. "How often has he been here?"

"Only once, madam, to see Lord Durell—but he didn't kiss me here. It was at Court when I went with Lady Durell." Phoebe looked at Abby as though she hoped to be asked more. Abby remained silent; yet Phoebe continued unprompted. "I also enjoy being in the company of Nellie Gwynn. And another one who has acted on the stage—Mary Davis, though she is better known as Moll. She has such a beautiful singing voice. I could listen for hours. She is now with child."

With a twinkle in her eye, Abby asked, "Oh, by whom?"

"By somebody, madam."

Abby was delighted to receive the impressions of the young servant. "Are there any others that frighten you? What of the French girl, Louise?

"Oh, the king's latest interest? Oh, no. She does not frighten me. She is even shyer than I am. Lady Durell says she is only being coy, and it is true I have only seen her once, so I cannot judge her well. As for others, I am made uncomfortable when another one come here, who was like Moll some seven or so years ago. Abby asked who that was. "The Duchess of Richmond, madam."

"Yes, Charlotte had written me of her. Her name is Frances Stuart, is it not?"

"Yes. My older sister Comfort and I followed her for several days trying to see who it was that the king was so desperate to bed. She was beautiful but sometimes she appeared more like a beautiful boy. She has never been mean, but only very distant. That was what made the king want her, I believe."

Abby was surprised by Phoebe's apparent sophistication regarding a man's physical desire. "I can see why you might feel uncomfortable around The Duchess of Richmond, but what of Lady Castlemaine?" Phoebe once again lowered he head. "What is it, Phoebe?"

"There is news from the court that Betty Keller, the actress, has been killed."

"Oh, dear. I don't know her. I'll have to ask Charlotte."

"Lady Durell doesn't know yet, madam. I have only just heard myself from the bottle boy who brought here a doctor's remedy for one of Lord Durell's ailments. They are saying in town that Lady Castlemaine had her murdered."

"Do you think that is true?"

"I cannot know, madam. But I . . . I must return to my other duties now." Phoebe bowed her head in deference and left Abby alone to ponder the dreadful possibility the servant presented her.

Barbara had taken the message from a rider who caught up with the carriage while she was walking some fifty yards from the road. She was now on the way back to her apartments, reading the note for a second time.

Dearest Lady Castlemaine,
You might find it advisable to come back. I have been told that Lord Brinton

will speak openly tomorrow morning about evidence proving you had Elizabeth Keller slain. I do not know what that evidence is, but it seems that Lord Brinton is convinced it is both genuine and damning. I shall prepare for your immediate return—Thomas

Barbara trusted the assessment. Thomas Lockwood was a man well experienced in evaluating the whispers he heard from others of his station. He could sift easily through salacious rumor and collect only information that served his lady. He was also quite adept at planting information and watering it with everything from an honest face to the employment, without their knowledge, of men and women who lent credence to rumor owing to their elevated positions—from men of court and the king's mistresses to military advisers and even the queen herself. As she shouted for the carriage to increase its speed, Barbara considered what "evidence" Brinton possessed to implicate her in Betty Keller's murder. Had she been betrayed by one of her enemies at court? By Nell Gwynn perhaps? By one of her former rivals? Even by the king? But she quickly swept aside these possibilities in favor of one candidate who rose to the forefront of her mind. The queen, Catherine of Braganza.

As the carriage passed Hyde Park heading back toward Whitehall, Barbara reflected on her relationship with Charles's lawful wife. Nine years earlier, the king accepted the recommendations of his advisers and agreed to wed the Portuguese princess. Barbara knew Charles would have to marry and that she would have to devise some way of maintaining her power over the king's bed and heart after he took a queen. She recalled being mollified somewhat when Charles informed her that as early as the 1640s negotiations to have Charles marry Catherine had begun and that the reason for the alliance had remained compelling after all that time. Charles also said England would be granted trading rights in Brazil and the East Indies. They would furthermore be awarded the Seven Islands of Bombay and Tangier in North Africa. Two million Portuguese crowns were an additional incentive, and England agreed to protect Portugal against Spain and to allow Catherine the free expression of her Roman Catholic faith.

"Don't be alarmed, my sweetest," Charles assured Barbara at the time. "The marriage is profitable and strategic and has nothing to do with my feelings and desire for you." Barbara could smile at the memory of the king kissing her ardently and taking her fully after he spoke his wedding vows and before he came to the marriage bed and his new wife. "I was unsuccessful, my love," he later admitted to Barbara. "My passion for you made impossible my performing a husband's duties." Barbara had no hesitation in having Charles's marital inability whispered loudly at court. But Barbara's satisfaction was short lived; Charles was to take himself and his wife off to Hampton Court for their honeymoon. Barbara confronted him with a stark declaration. "I am with your child, and I will not be separated from you no matter whom you have chosen to wed." As usual, Barbara's demands were met; she spent the period of her confinement at Hampton Court as well—a vivid reminder to the new queen what she would have to endure in the years ahead.

"I'm sorry, my lady but we must deviate from our course. Two wagons have lost wheels in front of us. There is no room to pass them." Barbara sighed as the coachman turned onto Coventry Street from the now congested Whitecomb Street. Barbara remembered riding on Coventry with the king and his new bastard son in 1662. "You will install me as Lady of the Bedchamber. I will not be cast off to be ridiculed further." Her husband Roger, facing his own humiliation as a royal cuckold, had left her, and Charles accepted that she needed income and a respectable position the public couldn't ignore. "I must have my lodgings everywhere you are," she insisted. The newly minted Countess of Castlemaine still seethed at having been told the queen refused to accept the king's domineering mistress as a lady in waiting, having been warned by many others of the "beautiful sorceress's" machinations. Barbara learned as well that Catherine simply struck her name off the list of potential candidates—a gesture that suggested the Portuguese princess's easy superiority to her rival. But Barbara would not permit the king to accede to his wife's wishes, and in desperation relied on her volatile temper mixed with her sexual charms to force Charles to choose her over his queen—at least as far as the appointment was concerned. Now, eight years later, Barbara felt the residue of the panic she experienced then and the disappointment that drove her to respond with a foul tongue and the firm pressing of her fingernails into the king's forearm, drawing blood.

She was much more in control the day the king brought her to court to meet Catherine, who had never seen her rival. Much to Barbara's surprise, the queen reacted favorably, offering a pleasant smile as she extended her hand for Barbara to kiss. When one of Catherine's ladies informed her she was in fact greeting the notorious "Mrs. Palmer," the queen lost control of her emotions and reacted with horror and panic, resulting in her being carried off from the chamber. Barbara's spirits were further elevated when Catherine withdrew from her husband and refused the request of important men of court to reconcile with the king. "I shall return to Portugal rather than submit myself to the king's unjust demands," she exclaimed, and when Barbara learned this, she encouraged Charles to "let her go."

"No, I will not. I have a better way to satisfy both you and the court," he replied. He dismissed almost all of Catherine's Portuguese retinue and allowed the queen to learn for herself that she was helpless in this situation, which others had constructed for her. Her pride and anger gave way to acceptance of her lot as a foreign queen and of her husband's devotion to Lady Castlemaine, whom she accepted as a Lady of the Bedchamber. Barbara often recollected the resentment she demonstrated when Charles spoke well of his wife's forbearance and expressed tenderness for whatever Catherine suffered—especially the queen's three miscarriages, about which Barbara felt little pity but a full measure of relief. Over the past eight years, Lady Castlemaine became annoyed whenever someone praised Catherine for establishing the new rage for having tea, which had been customary in Portugal, or making popular among many the cacophonous sound of her beloved Portuguese bagpipes. Barbara often ridiculed the queen's past secluded life in a convent—she had even asked to go on a pilgrimage to a shrine in Lisbon when informed she would marry the English monarch—and Catherine's appearance and personality. Although she realized too that Charles was not and would not be faithful to her alone, Barbara had the consolation of knowing no one pleased him sexually the way she could. Other calming factors for Barbara were as minor as the queen's being two years older than she and Catherine's difficulty in English and as significant as the queen's being disrespected at court and having royal advisers encourage Charles to divorce his Catholic and infertile wife. But these hopeful signs were quickly turned to disappointments, as the king refused to cast Catherine aside and demanded that his queen receive the respect to which she was entitled.

Even Catherine's birthday worked against Barbara in that it fell two days prior to Barbara's own. Therefore, Lady Castlemaine faced the indignity of her celebration with the king being much more subdued than the one he shared with his wife. And even worse, over the past eight years Catherine had won the loyalty and favor in the eyes of Charles's subjects for her patience, gentle manner, and genuine affection for the king. Much to Barbara's chagrin, Catherine even began to shed some of her virtuous and stilted demeanor in favor of dancing, card playing, picnicking, shooting arrows, and even fishing. And she developed an interest in fashion at court, speaking well of shorter dresses that would show off a woman's feet. More than once Charles infuriated Barbara with praise of his wife's fashion sense.

By the time she returned to her residence, Barbara's suspicions turned completely toward Catherine as being the one behind Lord Brinton's implication that Lady Castlemaine was responsible for Betty Keller's death. Brinton adored the queen and she him. Catherine's hatred for Barbara had not abated in eight years, and the queen had the power to inspire many to right her wrongs. Catherine well knew how many despised Lady Castlemaine and how many would be willing to think the worst even without appropriate evidence. "Dearest Charles, will you save me now?" Barbara whispered as Thomas Lockwood opened the door of her coach.

Chapter 9

As Charles strolled with his entourage and dogs on Horse Guard's Parade near Whitehall, the site of jousting tournaments during the reign of Henry VIII, Lord Brinton broke from the other courtiers and spoke with the man responsible for keeping his eye on the king's small spaniels. Brinton had previous occasion to speak with the "dog man" Burgess at Whitehall Palace, where Charles permitted his favorite spaniels to roam at will, even during important occasions. More than once, Brinton complained that the king spent more time petting his spaniels than paying attention to matters of state. "His damned mistresses and dogs," Brinton often muttered.

Brinton signaled one of his retinue to bring him a cloth sack. "Here Burgess. You have been told what to do with this, I assume."

"Yes, my lord. I'm to have what is in this sack placed at Lady Castlemaine's residence, but not in a conspicuous place."

"You are certain you can do it?"

"I will entrust the job to no one but myself, my lord. And I will speak to no one else about it. I will confess nothing to any living soul."

"Good. You will be rewarded generously."

"Thank you, my lord."

Brinton nodded to Burgess and walked rapidly to rejoin the king. Burgess walked in the opposite direction some hundred feet before he stopped and opened the sack. It contained an impressive ornamental silver box of some ten or eleven inches in length. Seeing that the clasp was not secured, Burgess opened the box. Inside was a red felt bottom which contained a depressed outline of something that rested in it. The item was missing but Burgess could easily see the box had contained a splendid knife of some kind. Closing the top of the casket, Burgess noticed an inscription *Carolus Rex* and a date "1640." The silver box and knife were presented to the king's father, Charles I—before Civil War tore apart his country.

Richard Hansall joined with eleven other religious dissenters for late afternoon prayer. Leading them was one of the non-conforming ministers who had been chased from the pulpit eight years earlier for his refusal to accept the preeminence of Anglican worship, including the use of the Prayer Book of Queen Elizabeth. The minister lost his privilege to teach and was imprisoned for his refusal to take an oath never to resist the king or attempt in any fashion to undermine the Anglican Church or to interfere in matters of state. Hansall used his influence to free the minster, although the man continued to risk further imprisonment by meeting with other dissenters in the basement of homes, as he was doing at present. Representing only a small handful of those who met similarly throughout the city, Hansall and the others at this conventicle risked the loss of their freedom, but they were unafraid and undeterred. Hansall revealed to the others only his devout side, but his mind always dwelt on matters of his own survival, influence, and revenge.

"Remember that the word of God comes to you from God alone and not *through* man, even if he wears the ostentatious cloth of a bishop." The minister's words struck Hansall as amusing in that this man of the true God was indeed sending God's word to this small conventicle, though he wore the unostentatious garb of a dissenter. Hansall needed no teacher or guide. He relied on his own intelligence and determination to shape all his thoughts and decisions. When he was younger, he could find much to laugh at in some of the dissenting sects, with their Saturday, instead of Sunday, worship; the nude worship of the Adamites, the surreptitious and insular ways of the Familists; the outlandish verbal attacks of the Muggletonians, who cursed all those who derided their faith; the "God in all things" beliefs of the Ranters, with their dismissal of both church and scripture; and the strange ways of the Seekers, who rejected formal religious services, church hierarchy, and clergy, choosing to wait in silence at their gatherings until God inspired them to speak out.

But Hansall did find satisfactory a woman's fuller participation among those who trembled at the word of God—the Quakers. That women would be encouraged to speak up in church or even to be ministers themselves was the most fervent wish of his own mother, who died before she had a chance to witness the radical acceptance of women among a few of the dissenting sects. Yet it was the fate of Hansall's father that influenced more his perspective on his independent faith and hatred of the monarchy.

When Charles assumed the throne in May of 1660, he promised to show mercy to those who fought against his father and contributed significantly to the government of Cromwell. The passing of the Act of Indemnity and Oblivion, with its provisions for amnesty, relieved Hansall, who feared his father Stephen would be put to death upon the restoration of the monarchy. The son convinced his father not to flee England, because he received word from one of Charles's advisers that Stephen Hansall would be allowed to go on with life, as had Cromwell's son Richard. But a provision of the act allowed for exceptions to the amnesty. Although it was Parliament who determined who would be excluded from the Act, Hansall always believed they were simply doing the bidding of the new king. They even had the dead posthumously "executed," namely Oliver Cromwell, whose rotting corpse was exhumed over two years after his demise and hanged in chains at Tyburn for a day before being beheaded and thrown into a pit. His severed head remained on constant display on a pole outside Westminster Hall, the place where the present king's father was condemned to death in January of 1649.

But it was the execution of Hansall's own father in October 1660 that shaped his hatred of Charles II and prompted his attempts to assassinate him. Stephen Hansall was quickly arrested along with others who directly participated in the execution of the old Charles eleven years earlier. Stephen was a minister, faithful to the established form of religion, although an enemy to the men who guided that faith—the bishops particularly. Later, the elder Hansall found Puritan politics far more to his liking, and he served as one of Cromwell's chief propagandists. Educated at Cambridge, Stephen was adept in his preaching not only God's word but also in convincing men to enlist in the Parliamentary army against the king and in providing a rousing sermon for the troops on the eve of several battles. He also used his oratorical gifts before the vanquished Royalists to convince them to see the wisdom in turning their backs on the king and his army. The generals employed Stephen Hansall to speak to the Parliament on the actions, condition, and needs of the Parliamentary troops, making him valuable as both an advocate and a historian of the army.

The Elder Hansall's influence and reputation placed him at the head of the force bringing the captured king to London for his trial, and he spoke in his sermons of the justice of punishing the monarch to the upmost. Accepted as a valuable counsel to Cromwell and other leaders, Richard's father was said to have been the first to argue for Charles I's trial and subsequent execution. Charles II knew of Stephen Hansall's skills and activities long before he came to London in May of 1660, and Richard believed the new monarch only waited five months to have his revenge in order not to appear bloodthirsty. But over several days in the middle of October 1660, Stephen Hansall, along with several others equally responsible for Charles I's beheading in 1649, suffered the ultimate form of punishment. With his son in attendance at Charing Cross on the 17th, the elder Hansall was briefly hanged, and then was, while still alive, placed on a table and drawn"—his abdomen cut open and his intestines and sexual organs removed and immediately burned. Now dead, the elder Hansall was "quartered"—his arms and legs were cut from his torso and, finally, his head was severed. His son Richard never averted his eyes from his father throughout the latter's horrific death and mutilation. He knew his father's spirit required his son to avenge his death—and that it would only accept the death of the present king as fit payment.

Twice before Hansall made an attempt on the king's life—the first in the late spring of 1662. Early in the morning, as Charles bathed nude in the Thames as was his habit, Hansall elicited with two bags of coins the support of two simple-minded boatmen, who piloted their small craft some fifty meters close to the king. Hansall was in the water on the far side of the boat so he wouldn't be seen. The men dropped an anchor when they were parallel with the king, and Hansall raised half his body into the boat and took the musket lying inside the craft and aimed it at the king. The weapon was a new flintlock recently adopted by the army with accuracy promised up to one hundred meters. With one of the boatman holding Hansall's torso steady, Richard fired and the recoil drove him back into the water. He had no idea if the round lead ball had hit its mark, but his instincts told him to stay under water and swim as far away from the boat as possible. When he lifted his head for air, he heard shouting from the shore and the cry to capture the men in the boat. By the time Hansall swam far enough away and returned to shore, he saw the king's guard react instinctively by hacking both the boatman to death with their swords. Charles watched the execution, as he dressed.

Three years later during the Great Fire in London, Hansall tried once more as the king was assisting others in fighting the blaze. Hansall followed Charles, knowing the chaos in the city would serve to mask his attempt. He had a pistol with him and vowed to get as close to the monarch as possible so that his second attempt on the king's life would be successful. Equipped with a bucket and a spade, Charles's feet were submerged in the mud, making him even more vulnerable. As the king moved toward a house, which he would help pull down, Hansall made his way behind him, acting as though he was distraught over losing his property to the flames. Charles turned to speak with him, and Hansall reached for the pistol. He dearly wished to see the king's face as he shot him in the chest. But as Hansall reached for the weapon, the king sprung upon him and dragged Hansall away from where he stood. A section of the house fell on the spot Hansall had just vacated. Hansall forced himself to thank the king and move away from the area, seething that the man he so hated may have just saved his life.

Five years had passed and there had been several decisions made to try again but none ever came to fruition. But now, ten years after his father's execution, Hansall believed he found his moment to act. He had earned the trust of powerful men through the role of go-between and informant, and he ultimately found two in particular who shared his desire to see Charles dead—Sir Roger Earle and Lord Durell. This time Hansall would not have to risk his life with water and fire.

"Mr. Devlin, sir."

"What is it, Francis?"

"They want you to see this."

Gottlieb pointed to the now empty stage at the King's Theatre, and Devlin waited until five of his company came out to rehearse a scene from Mr. Dryden's latest effort, *Almanzor and Almahide*, the first part of which—the first five acts—the King's Company would perform in a few weeks. As Devlin watched the actors take their places on the stage, he immediately headed toward them. "Where is Nell?"

Gottlieb followed a step behind. "She has sent word that she feels ill, Mr. Devlin."

Devlin sighed in frustration. "Thank you, Francis. I hope she is not again pregnant with the His Majesty's child." She delivered the king a son only six months previously, and many marveled that she would return to the stage so quickly or at all—since she was now the mother of a royal bastard child. Still amazed that Nell achieved such success on the stage and in the royal bed at the age of twenty, Devlin depended on the public's curiosity about Nell being an incentive for a successful run of performances. Indeed, Devlin promised the playwright Dryden that both parts of this play about the late fifteenth-century conquest of Granada would reap much financial reward. But Nell, portraying the heroine Almahide, needed every one of these rehearsals—and she had already missed two of them.

"I told Anne to take her place today. I hope that is all right, Mr. Devlin."

"Yes. Thank you, Francis." Devlin smiled as his latest beautiful young protégé walked on the stage. She wasn't a member of this cast, but Devlin wanted her to gain as much experience as she could with the company's better actors. Betty Keller had been rehearsing the role of the virtuous Benzayda in Dryden's play, but her murder now cast someone else in the part, much to the objection of Mary Gibbons, who assumed she would get the role if Betty were re-cast as Almahide, assuming Nell would decide not to act it. But just an hour ago, Devlin refused Mary the part, fully aware that the audience would not accept a woman of Mary's appearance and manner to play half of a wholesome and noble couple. Instead, Devlin gave the part to the seventeen-year old Elizabeth Boutell, another of his favorites, whose short height and childish face were perfect for the role. Mary Gibbons was awarded the part of a female slave, which she accepted without complaint, even though Devlin easily detected her bitterness over the minor role he assigned her.

Devlin spoke to young Anne and encouraged her to read the lines of Almahide as if she were actually to perform the part. She displayed a refreshing earnestness in the passages

What dismal planet did my triumphs light!

Discord the day, and death does rule the night:

The noise my soul does through my senses wound.

Ah, Esperanza, what for me remains

But death, or, worse than death, inglorious chains!

But Devlin was not pleased by her constant fidgeting on the stage— even with the text in her hands. She possessed grace in her movements, but she needed to stop walking during her speech. She needed to heed better his lesson to keep her face forward for the audience, rather than turn and look directly at another character, a habit the lesser actors had difficulty breaking. Anne never arched her head upward as did some; rather, she tended to drop it toward her right shoulder. But at least she avoided the infuriating habit of several of the players, particularly Mary Gibbons, of licking or biting her lower lip during a performance.

All in all, Devlin warmed to Anne's beautiful face, perfect skin, and lovely height. With the loss of Betty Keller, Anne would do much to comfort him and ease his mind in the days and weeks ahead. He could see himself in love with her as he had been with Betty. At least Anne had no relative connected to the regicides of 1649, as had Betty Keller, whose father was one of the men who fled to the Netherlands in October of 1660, narrowly escaping the fate of those who were hanged, drawn, and quartered. As Devlin learned only a week before her murder, Betty's father was Henry Kneller, one of the commissioners who signed Charles I's death warrant. As Devlin also learned, Betty's maternal aunt, who took her in after her father fled, was responsible for dropping the letter "n" in her niece's surname— the only compromise the seven-year-old girl agreed to, because she loved her father and would not agree to change her family name more radically. Betty would not admit to the identity of her father when Devlin confronted her with what he had learned, but the expression on her face told him the account was true. That he had shared with Lady Castlemaine's man Thomas Lockwood, while the men consumed several pints at the Black Plough Tavern, what he learned about Betty's parentage—her mother had died when she was only four—may well have cost his dear sweet girl her life. But of that he couldn't be sure.

CHAPTER 10

"Did you have ill words with Lord Durell, Charlotte?"

"Why do you ask, Abby?"

"Your face is flushed." Charlotte brought her hand to her face as if she could rub away the offending color.

"I did, but our battles have no effect on me—or on my face. If I have added color in my cheeks it is because I am embarrassed to say that Lady Castlemaine will not be joining us this afternoon or evening. Here, read this. It has just been delivered."

Charlotte handed Abby the note, delivered by the same man who brought Lady Castlemaine the message to return to London. Abby read Barbara's apology claiming a sudden stomach pain and a promise to visit the following morning.

Charlotte laughed. "Barbara couldn't have more stomach pains if she was stabbed in battle. It is her most often employed excuse."

The women were discussing how they would entertain themselves in the absence of Lady Castlemaine, when Phoebe entered the room.

The appearance of the girl triggered Abby's memory. "Oh, Phoebe. That reminds me. Charlotte, have you heard about the young actress found dead at Whitehall?"

"Yes, I have Abby. The same messenger informed me. What's that, Phoebe?" The servant whispered into Lady Durell's ear. "Yes, by all means have her come in. Well, Abby we will have to wait until morning for Lady Castlemaine, but part of our evening will be spent in the company of someone else of considerable significance."

"There is such a look of triumph on your face, Charlotte. These gatherings and introductions feed the fire of your life now exactly as they did when we were girls. The military would have been your sphere had you been a man, for your life is in flanking maneuvers, surprise attacks, and explosions. God should have given you a chin beard and a moustache, not a sparkling mischievous eye and pretty face."

Charlotte seemed much pleased by Abby's compliment. "No, dearest friend, there are no chin beards now."

"Indeed, I have noticed. And what of those long periwigs?"

"It started when His Majesty came from the continent wearing one ten years ago. Before long they became the general fashion of the men. Wigmakers have enjoyed immense profits ever since."

Abby demurred. "Still, the chin beard elongates the face when the chin is weak. And beards hide the evidence of scars and pox marks, which are often better left unseen. And I am still not in favor of the periwigs. Let the man continue the custom of growing his own hair long if he wants it so."

"It's too late for that now, Abby—except among the vile Puritans. The king and the French have determined the man's look at least for the time being."

Both women were laughing as Phoebe returned to the room with a breathtakingly lovely young woman, whose only blemish were some inoffensive marks of smallpox on her features. Charlotte dragged Abby toward her guest. "Abby, I want to introduce you to Frances Stuart, the Duchess of Richmond. Frances, this is my dear friend, Abigail Fayette."

"I am pleased to meet you, Abigail. I understand that you and Charlotte have been friends since you were young girls."

"That is quite true, . . . um." Abby was unsure how to address the woman.

"We are at Charlotte's sanctuary for wayward women; therefore, there is no need to stand on any pretense. I should like you to call me Frances."

"Very well, thank you." Abby was struck by Frances's pleasant yet pronounced aloofness.

"Phoebe, we will no longer need you."

"Yes, Lady Durell." Phoebe caught Abby's eye and did a quick "aloof" impression of Frances before leaving the room.

"Frances, before you arrived, Abby asked about the history of the king's love affairs, and we were about to turn to your section of the book."

Frances rolled her eyes and sighed with a mixture of playfulness and inevitability. "I should not have been included in the text, Charlotte. For as everyone knows and as I have told you often enough—and as I *hope* you have told Abigail—His Majesty's entreaties were all in vain."

"And that's why I adore you so." Abby was confused by Charlotte's meaning. "But as you know, others have claimed that the king's long war to defeat your resistance and then his sudden withdrawal—if I may use such a vulgar yet appropriate term—were surely the result of your finally consenting to his entreaties." Charlotte winked at Abby, who assumed her friend had often teased Frances this way.

Frances walked to Abby's side "Abigail, if I can depend on one thing, it is Charlotte's incessant probing on this weary topic."

"Incessant probing indeed!" was Lady Durell's retort.

"Oh, Charlotte." Abby's frown failed to disguise her delight in Charlotte's bawdiness, which showed its first signs when they were girls and came upon two dogs mating.

"I speak only truth, Abby, and she knows it. Frances, despite your refusal to consider her worthy of your attention, I think you and Nellie Gwynn speak the same language."

"We are quite different continents, dear. We have nothing, not even language, in common, though common is a more than apt description of your illiterate actress friend. Unlike you, I would be completely horrified if one knew I had entertained that woman in my house."

"Now, Frances. You must see that Nellie is now more than in the same country as the king—in the same sheets, to be accurate—and is that perhaps why you have no use for her?" Charlotte's voice lost some of its teasing quality with this remark. Abby thought Charlotte was coming closer to interrogating the Duchess of Richmond, who took her time to answer.

"The king sought me, and I profited because of it. What I did *not* give him is what is unique, and I shall forever be famous because of it. Eight years have now passed, and my fame shows no sign of fading." Abby was surprised by France's giggle—it seemed so out of character to her bearing.

Charlotte extended her hands as if she were presenting a portrait. "Ah, yes. *La Belle Stuart* now and for always. She whose beauty is and will long serve as the face of Britannia." Charlotte explained to Abby that following the Dutch War, Charles had a commemorative medal struck featuring Frances's face as the model for "Britannia" and that later her visage was also stamped on the new coins of the realm.

"And the king rewarded her in this manner when he was most angry at her."

"Why was that?"

"Because I married, Abigail." Once more, Frances giggled as might a twelve-year-old girl.

Charlotte recounted further events from Frances's relationship with the king. In his attempt to bed her, Charles offered her money, land, and title, but she continued to refuse.

"My choices were either to submit my body to the king or to marry, I'm afraid."

"Yes, and how fortunate you were, dear Frances. She chose one of the king's distant relatives—who was also named Charles Stuart—the Duke of Richmond." Charlotte's face beamed with more pride than amusement.

Frances added, "My new husband spent his money foolishly and drank inordinately, but he served my purpose well."

"Oh, but His Majesty was furiously jealous when he learned of the planned marriage." Charlotte revealed that Charles had laid out several schemes to prevent the marriage, but that only prompted Frances and her new Charles to elope.

"The king vowed never to see me more, Abigail, but last year when I became very ill with smallpox, he came to my bedside and forgave me for refusing and then deceiving him. When I first knew him at age fifteen, I served the new queen as Lady of the Bedchamber, and then seven years later after my recent illness, he gave me that position again. We are now friends—His Majesty and I—and his conversation with me never turns to the matter of our past. Besides he has his new interest in Ellen Gwynn and of course most recently with the girl Elizabeth Keller. Oh, dear me, Charlotte. You do know of the child's death?"

"Yes, I heard of it but minute ago. What more have you heard?"

"It was a deliberate act, but no one yet knows who committed the horrible crime or who might have ordered it done. But you may guess who many feel is the leading suspect."

"I cannot begin to think who."

"Oh, come now, Charlotte. The soon-to-be Duchess of Cleveland—our dear Lady Castlemaine."

Charlotte's face registered sadness but then quickly altered to playfulness. "You may wish that she was responsible, Frances—only because of your sour relationship with her."

Well, I cannot debate that point with you. But it did not start out as such."

"Indeed it did not." Charlotte explained to Abby that Lady Castlemaine once brought the king to her bed, into which she had a short time before deposited young Frances. "It was rather a playful spaniel of an idea of Barbara's, but it completely turned and bit the poor woman on the nose."

"This is true, Abigail. The result of her displaying me in bed was that the king found a compelling need to possess me. But why would I have given in to him then? I could see and hear the wars he and his Barbara fought in and out of bed. Besides, I was made to believe that if his queen died, he would only marry a virgin like me—though I made sure to let him imagine always what I would be like the day my virginity was no longer a hindrance to his passions. My face read virginal and aloof, even when I let the king see me undress before him.

Abby marveled at the tale. "Did you and Lady Castlemaine quarrel about the king?"

"Not at first. Barbara thought of me as an inexperienced puppet to whom she was attracted because she felt my friendship and virtuous manner would make her look charitable and liberal-minded to the king. She dressed me from time to time in boy's clothing and literally placed me in chairs and, as Charlotte told you, in bed. But when His Majesty demonstrated a desire for my person, as a woman, not as a beautiful boy, Barbara revealed her insecurities as rapidly and violently as she was so very capable of doing. We fought with quiet fury very often and once with such volume that her shrieking and howling were heard throughout the palace, awakening all who slept. When the king made his amorous play for me, Lady Castlemaine threatened me in a host of ways—from ruining my reputation court to seeing me bludgeoned to death."

Abby was surprised by the graphic threat. "Are you serious?"

"Most assuredly so. And when she didn't threaten me, she called me many sorts of names—from 'silly' and 'childish' to 'ignorant' and 'cowardly.' I would answer back that she was 'old' and 'lewd,' which she hated—

especially when the king would defend me and laugh at the insults I threw at his favorite mistress."

"You called her old?"

"Yes, Abigail. You must remember that when I was fifteen and drawing the attention from the king, she was twenty-two—and to me that was old. Of course now that I am twenty-three, I have a different view on what is old."

The three women shared a sustained laugh before Frances continued, "I for a moment lost my famous reserve. However, when Charles took my side in one of the disputes between me and Lady Castlemaine, I was forever again in control of both my emotions and my voice, something Barbara knew painfully she was incapable of doing—and that more than any other reason is why she hates me to this day."

"And do you hate her as well?"

On the contrary, Abby. I only pity her. She is a woman Charles no longer desires as he once did. For her, there can be no greater punishment. Why should I wish anything more—or less—on her?"

Several minutes of further conversation included Frances's compliment to Charlotte. "It was never fair that you were born with such a gift for drawing the notable women and men to your side." Frances then reintroduced the matter of Betty Keller's death.

"Charlotte, I should like to talk more about this dreadful event the next time I come, but in the meanwhile, I think you should bring up the matter the next time Lady Castlemaine visits you. I would be most curious to see how she reacts."

Charlotte shook her head. "I cannot think I will, Frances. Barbara would know I was only seeking an indication from her that she knows something about Betty Keller's death no one else does. I'm sure she's already heard talk of her involvement."

"You are most likely right. Well, I am certain all will be revealed in due time."

"Oh, I almost forgot. I have a special treat for the Duke, your husband. Phoebe?"

"I am here, Lady Durell."

"Bring that bottle of that *Pontac* wine—the *Haute-Brion.* Frances, I promised your husband a bottle three months ago. I can present him with more if he likes it well enough."

Frances thanked Charlotte for the wine and expressed her pleasure at meeting Abby. Immediately after she left in her coach, Charlotte poured herself and Abby a glass from another bottle of the *Haute-Brion* and shared other details of Frances Stuart's history with the King.

"Even at fifteen, Frances was charming and graceful—and few could match her in her choice of clothing. I remember being so jealous of her ability to dance and attract the eyes of so many, while I . . . But most of us shook our heads at how easily she laughed at the king's witticisms without always understanding the joke. Unlike Barbara, she had no interest in politics and agreed to everything he said about the subject. The French Count de Gramont supposedly said about her that it would be difficult to image in a young woman less brains combined with such beauty. Even so, I truly despised her for all she possessed that I didn't, but soon enough I saw that she only enjoyed the thought that the king wanted her, which encouraged her flirtations and her teasing him with her sighs and kisses. Often in front of the Court, Charles and Frances would kiss in corners for a full half an hour without any shame. You will be surprised to know that I then began to be on her side in the sense that I encouraged her to maintain her virginity and refuse the king. I say that because I feared for His Majesty's heart."

"I understand what you mean, Charlotte. It only testifies to your kindness and affection for your monarch. Did his subjects approve of her desire to put the king off the way she did?"

"Oh, I came to determine that Frances was smarter than I gave her credit for. She had all the advantages of being a favorite of the Court and especially of the poor queen, who would protect her should she fall out of favor with Charles, and Frances knew she could continue to enjoy all the dances and parties and the advances of so many men at Court. What would she gain, since she truly did not love the king, if she became his mistress? Yet many of us were disappointed that Charles continued to claim she was his favorite." Charlotte went on to speak of the speculation during Queen Catherine's serious illness in 1663 that Charles would marry Frances upon his wife's death.

"Would Frances have married him, do you think?"

"I do, Abby—for then her fortunes would have been more secure than if she were merely a royal mistress." Charlotte added that during the plague in 1665, Frances fled with many others to Hampton Place and sat for her "Windsor Beauties" portrait painted by Peter Lyly. "That was when I returned to hating her."

"As I said, you deserved to have been included in the series, my dearest friend."

"Again, I thank you for that compliment, but two years after the end of the plague, another rumor swirled that Charles would divorce Catherine and marry Frances, who we supposed made clear she would never give herself to the king unless she was his wife. Whether she ever said such a thing, I don't know, but it sounded quite plausible to many of us. It was only after she and the current Duke of Richmond eloped that my affections and admiration for Frances returned to where they are at present." Abby shook her head and laughed, and the two women drank a toast to the absent Duchess of Richmond, and after another hour of girlhood reminiscences, they separated for the evening.

Later, while lying in bed, Abby considered further the possibility that Lady Castlemaine was responsible for the murder of Elizabeth Keller. Abby decided she would take the measure of Barbara when the woman visited in the morning, but then her mind turned to the secretive discussion she overheard earlier in the day. Could Lord Durell and his man Samuel have been speaking of Betty Keller's death—and if so, did they know more about the event than they should have? Abby considered the possibility of her dear friend's husband having something to do with this murder as too horrifying to ponder.

Chapter 11

"I trust the performance went well this afternoon, Devlin."

"Yes, my lord. It was well attended, and the patrons behaved fairly well throughout."

Devlin's voice betrayed his nervousness. But such was always the case when he was summoned by Lord Brinton. Devlin arrived at Brinton's apartment ten minutes before his appointed time—fearful he would be delayed enough to be late. And one was never late when Brinton summoned.

"Have you any guess as to why I asked you to meet me tonight?"

"No, my lord. Forgive me, but I do not." Devlin fervently hoped it wasn't to discuss Betty Keller's death.

"Come and look at what I have just received from His Majesty." Devlin followed Brinton to a dining table, on which lay a detailed drawing of the king touching one of his subjects for the King's Evil—the contemptible scrofula that swelled the neck and revealed ugly growths that enlarged over time. "Have you ever witnessed the king's touching of his subjects, Devlin?"

"No, my Lord." But Devlin recalled losing one of his most talented actors to the disease. The man was touched by Charles, but to no avail.

"For some reason, His Majesty touches more of his subjects than does the French King Louis *le Grand, le Roi Soleil.*" Brinton's dislike of the French monarch was evident in the derisive way he said, "the grand, the Sun King." "Last year alone, our king laid hands on some five thousand of his subjects, some of whom had no trace of the King's Evil but who disguised their necks with cloth stuffed bandages and some with sand and mud applied to their necks, which they tried to keep together by pressing the side of their chins on their shoulders."

Brinton laughed, but Devlin could only wonder why His Lordship wished to share this matter. "I suppose some desired the king's blessing, even if they were deceptive, my lord."

"Yes, you have it, Devlin. Deception. What I must both use and discover in others in order to best serve our king. And that brings me to you. Do you know why our friend Lowther has been sent to Spain?"

"My lord, I am not sure." In truth, Devlin felt certain William Lowther was in Spain to be certain the Spanish Court maintained its agreement to recognize England's occupation of the island of Jamaica in the West Indies, which the English had seized sixteen years earlier. "But I imagine he is there to be sure the Spanish boy king has not been convinced to reject our claim to Jamaica."

"He has been instructed to make sure that is not so, but I have given him a more important assignment than to keep an eye on the incestuous issue of the Spanish king and his equally incestuous caretakers. Did you know the lad has been cursed with a hideous face and a deformed jaw that makes difficult his speaking and chewing? He is physically debilitated and has a barely-functioning mind. They still treat him as an infant. They even refuse to bath him."

"So I have heard, my lord, but . . ." Brinton's delight in denigrating the Spanish Court caused him to delay the point he wished to make with Devlin.

"But Lowther has a more significant purpose. I have charged him with finding two or three young and beautiful Spanish women and seeing that they are sent here. He will look first for those who perform on the stage, but if none are available or beautiful enough, he will select those who can be trained to be given roles here in London."

"Trained, my lord. By whom?"

"By you of course. You excel in the teaching of your craft, and I have every confidence you can do what is necessary."

"But if they speak no English?"

"You will teach them enough to get by. The roles may be small ones—that should not matter. It's only important that the king sees them and wants them in his bed. His Majesty's love of the female actors should be of no surprise to you."

Devlin managed to keep his expression merely quizzical. "But why must they be Spanish? There are more than enough—"

"Because they *are* Spanish and not French. The king has set his fancy on a young woman from France—Louise de Kérouaille, who accompanied the king's sister earlier this year. Charles then appointed her Lady in Waiting to the queen, whom Louise treats with great respect and deference, unlike that whore Castlemaine. But Louise is French—and France is always our enemy, regardless of what agreements and treaties there may be between us. The king will soon tire of the slut Nell Gwynn and other of his older mistresses. With your actress Betty Keller dead, I wish His Majesty to make a sexual alliance with a Spanish girl—preferably two or three. The balance of Europe demands that Spain side with us against France—in any way it can. I must protect his majesty and this nation from unnecessary French influence. The child Louise will surely be employed by the French to provide information about our king, our government, and our military. I greatly fear that if she is made the king's favorite, all of us will suffer greatly for it."

"I understand, my Lord."

"Good. Be ready to train these Spanish beauties for the stage. I will see to it that they end up trained for the king's bed."

Unsettled by his meeting with Brinton, Devlin walked east on the Strand and turned to his right, making his way to the Savoy Stairs, which, along with similar structures on the riverbank, led down to the boats tied up on the Thames. It was here several years earlier that he watched his young actress Betty Keller frolic on a frozen section of the Thames. She had fallen hard on the ice and was in evident pain by the time Devlin reached her, after slipping twice himself. She buried her face in his chest and cried from the pain, squeezing him tightly and shivering in his arms. He felt more than a father to his young apprentice then; his emotions distorted his perspective to the point that he fancied they were contemporaries and that he was the noble suitor who had rescued his lady from distress. Devlin knew he loved her at that moment in spite of her having just turned fourteen. From that day forward, he wished away the time until she would reach seventeen or eighteen and be more acceptable as his wife. Devlin was married twice before—unhappy unions which ended in each spouse's death two years before and two years after Charles returned to England in 1660. Both his wives were only two and four years younger than he, whereas Betty was almost thirty years younger than her mentor. Devlin well knew that many an older man lusted after young women and not infrequently married them—often to the derision of friends, relatives, poets, and writers of plays. Devlin had both appeared in and agreed to stage several comedies featuring such men—and he hated to think he'd be so portrayed when he married Betty Keller. But he wouldn't be swayed from his desire. He loved her too much to save himself from the ridicule he knew would come.

It took Devlin well over three years to accept his foolishness. Betty Keller would never be his wife—even though she had never rejected such an offer, which he had yet to extend. Devin said nothing about their future together beyond the theatre—choosing to wait until she reached her eighteenth birthday on the first day of November 1670. Staring into the darkened waters of the Thames and hearing only the inconsistent rhythm of the water, Devlin's thoughts returned to the early October night six weeks earlier when Betty asked to see him after a long rehearsal. The day had been otherwise splendid; the performance that afternoon had gone well, with the king in attendance and thoroughly enjoying the play. Betty came to Devlin's room at the theatre with grave concern on her face. She had this night received a "proposal," she said. Devlin's body tensed. Another had asked for her hand. Who was it? One of her fellow actors? A nobleman who had admired her on stage?

"The king, sir."

Numbness swept over Devlin's body at hearing the name. "What?—I don't understand. What do you mean a proposal?"

"To visit him, sir." Betty had always addressed Devlin formally—something he didn't mind, but would of course direct her to change once they agreed to marry. "Should I go, sir?"

Terrified at what he was certain were the king's motives for extending the invitation, Devlin thought of Frances Stuart and her widely-known refusal of His Majesty's sexual advances. He had spoken to the Duchess of Richmond briefly on two occasions. Could he invite her to counsel Betty? How would he go about asking? No, the thought was absurd. "You must go,

I'm afraid."

"Then I will. But you need not fear, sir. I cannot think of myself ever serving at court. I want to remain here as an actress."

Her words offered some comfort, but Devlin barely slept knowing that Charles had asked Betty to see him at ten in the morning. She returned in time to perform that day, but she wasn't herself and twice forgot her lines. Devlin chose not to speak with her afterward as he would have ordinarily done. He didn't want to know the reason why she seemed so distracted.

The following morning he kept away from Betty until she finished her rehearsal for the next play she would do. She was only slightly better than she was in performance the afternoon before. He came to the stage to speak with the actors and asked Betty if he could see her privately—not wishing to embarrass her in front of the others. As he approached, a messenger brought her a sealed note from Whitehall. Betty opened the seal and read. Her eyes expanded, and a look of concern swept across her lovely face.

"Please forgive me, Mr. Devlin. I cannot stay. The king has asked to see me immediately. I must go." After she departed, the other actors stood on the stage with their mouths agape. Some were shocked, some were amused, and one actor was gleeful his prediction had seemingly come true. Only Devlin remained in silence—with his heart broken. He knew the king had already or would soon cuckold him—as it were. Betty wasn't his wife, lover, or even daughter, but these facts did nothing to sooth his pain.

Devlin couldn't bear to watch Betty Keller on stage the first two weeks after she became the king's latest mistress. Charles had been to the theatre on two occasions in that time and asked to see Devlin on his second visit.

"Your Betty has so improved as an actress since I first saw her, Devlin. You must be proud that your efforts have so handsomely paid off."

Devlin reacted visibly to "Your Betty" but managed to compose himself quickly. "Thank you, Your Majesty. She has a splendid chance to be among the very best London has seen, provided she . . ." Devlin knew better than to complete his thought.

"Keep up the fine work with my company, Devlin. I've frankly grown tired of hearing my brother boast of his theatre having London's best actors and performances. I'm afraid I'm to blame for my generous permissions to them when our theatres first opened. And it's true that we have in this theatre no male actor who even approaches the talent of Mr. Betterton at the Duke's playhouse. Yet I believe you have put more attractive women on the stage—and for that I am most grateful to you." The king's wink and smile slammed deeply into the pit of Devlin's stomach. It was a miracle he could articulate his reply "Thank you, Your Majesty."

With each day, Devlin sunk more into despair whenever he saw a smile on Betty's face or heard her laugh. That she tried to avoid him as much as possible hurt deeply until five days before her death when it came to him that she only kept from his company because she understood he did love her dearly and therefore didn't wish to sadden him by being exuberant about her new relationship with the king. Another might have told him she avoided his company because she didn't wish to hear Devlin rail against her decision to be the king's mistress, peppering her with reasons why she made a serious mistake—based on purely moral grounds. But Devlin's sudden shift from resentment and emotional despair prompted a more hopeful scenario in which he might have his Betty back again. He had only a few days before learned of her family's past and her father's actions during the trial and execution of Charles I. Now he felt emboldened to use that information and effect a change in the present king's feelings for his new mistress.

A reminder of what he did the next day made him shudder in the chilly December night air, causing him to feel as though he was about to lose his balance and fall into the Thames. He dropped to his knees on one of the Savoy Stairs and once more whispered, "Dearest Betty. What have I done?"

Chapter 12

"Your Majesty, forgive the interruption."

"A perfect time for it, Henry. I am losing the match."

Lord Brinton had broken up play at 6:45 in the morning—the very early morning being the king's favorite time for his tennis and swimming. Brinton regretted nothing more about his service to the monarch than having to rise at such an ungodly hour.

Standing in the tennis court at Whitehall, Brinton explained to Charles that he had "difficult news" relating to the murder of Betty Keller.

"Well, what is it?"

"Your Majesty, I would prefer to speak with you in private."

Charles stared at the racquet in his hand. "Very well. I'll finish this match, and if I lose it I'll demand another of dear George here." Charles used his racquet to point to George Villiers, the Duke of Buckingham, who was breathing hard and ingesting several swallows of water. "He's two years older than I am, Henry, and he's beating me. If I don't exact my revenge on my dear old friend and valued minister, I'll end up despising him the way his enemies do."

The king laughed, and Brinton smiled at the irony. Buckingham was a skilled intriguer, who had encouraged Charles to divorce his childless wife. Brinton never trusted the man and agreed with the court observer who noted that although the handsome and fashionable Buckingham was "courteous, affable, generous, magnanimous and adored by many people," he was also "an atheist, blasphemer, violent, cruel and infamous for his licentiousness"—keeping company with the most notorious of the Court wits, the young poet John Wilmot, the Earl of Rochester. Also an exceptional mimic, Buckingham earned Brinton's contempt when he did a withering impersonation of Brinton's voice and mannerisms which entertained the court and especially the king. But Brinton saw the most irony in the fact that George Villiers was the cousin of Barbara Villiers,

Lady Castlemaine and soon to be Duchess of Cleveland—the very woman, Brinton would shortly convince Charles, who was responsible for the death of Elizabeth Keller.

Arising at 7:00 and assuming Charlotte wouldn't stir until at least 10:00. Abby dressed and made her way to the labyrinth behind the Dove House side of the estate. Entering, she found the maze-like structure a perfect representation of her thoughts during the night. What was Lord Durell referring to in the conversation she overheard? As her father said, one of the pleasures of living in Virginia was the freedom from the intrigues at Court and that a return to London would re-immerse him in the world of "nods, smiles, and whispers." He grew to appreciate the direct, if at times brutal, ways of the native Indians. Abby was like the others there who concluded the natives were more like her kind than those in England assumed. The native Indians married, raised and educated their children, and entertained themselves. But Abby missed the world she knew as a younger girl—the world she shared with her friend Charlotte. To Abby, London and the world of the privileged and powerful was even more appealing in its dangers than what her father found in the wilds of Virginia.

Moving further inside the labyrinth, she recalled that in Greek mythology the master craftsman Daedalus constructed the maze for King Minos—its purpose to hold the Minotaur eventually dispatched by Theseus. But the labyrinth was so shrewdly made that Daedalus had difficulty extracting himself from his artful construction. Abby appreciated that the tale of the labyrinth served as a warning to ponder the possible dire consequences of one's clever inventions. Daedalus's efforts, after all, only made the task of slaying the Minotaur even more problematic. Abby understood that her intent to discover the meaning behind Lord Durell's words of the previous day might well lead to nothing, in spite of her effort to ascertain their import. She had also learned from her lessons that Socrates cautioned against entering labyrinthine argument, noting one might well end up after exhaustive search no closer to the goal of comprehension.

Abby took only five more steps into the labyrinth before she heard the voice of man coming from the center of the structure. It was neither Lord Durell nor Samuel Greenham. She leaned her head against the seven-foot tall hedge.

"Lord Durell, I have come earlier than planned because I received this message at half past six this morning and I needed an answer from you immediately."

"I don't think well this time of day, Hansall. And I don't like meeting without Sir Roger in attendance."

"As I said it could not be helped, my lord."

"Very well. So why must the date be changed?"

"I've been informed that the king is not going to Gray's Inn tonight. He'll remain at Whitehall until tomorrow evening."

"Then simply postpone it until tomorrow night."

"It's not that simple, my lord." Abby heard Hansall explain that "the men chosen" had to leave for Scotland with the others being sent by the Earl of Lauderdale at noon tomorrow and therefore would not be available.

"Then we have no one to do it?"

"I will secure the services of two others today, and I myself will make a third."

"Don't be absurd, Hansall. You . . ." Abby's eyes broadened at Durell's hesitation. "You are certain you are up to it, Richard?"

"Yes, my lord. It is better this way, believe me."

"Very well. Then I need not hear from you until sometime tomorrow night."

"A message will be sent, but you will never see me again afterward."

"As it must be. God bless you, Richard. Now, come to the house and . . ."

Abby heard nothing more. She waited another thirty seconds before she left the labyrinth silently and quickly toward the west side of the house so she wouldn't be seen by either man. After they were more than half way to the house, she came from behind the other shrubs flanking the labyrinth and noticed that Lord Durell wore a robe and slippers, devoid of wig—with Richard Hansall in somber brown clothing, wearing his own hair in the long style of the previous generation.

"Do you really believe Barbara killed my pretty Betty?"

"Or had her killed. Yes, Your Majesty, I do. I regret being forced to make that conclusion, but this note seems the kind of proof I sadly cannot ignore."

Brinton lowered his eyes as Charles read a second time the note Bridget Warren discovered in the bedroom at Whitehall. "It looks much like her handwriting."

Brinton sighed as if in pain. "It clearly is, Your Majesty."

"But it does not confess to *having* killed her, does it?"

"Well . . . no, but you must see that—"

"If I presented you a guinea for every time my Lady Castlemaine threatened to kill me or one of her competitors, you could retire from service a very wealthy man."

Brinton forced a smile as his anger welled inside. Was it possible the king was going to dismiss Barbara Villiers as being responsible for Elizabeth Keller's death? Whether she had anything to do with it at all mattered not a bit to Brinton. It was vital that the king believe she did or at least accept that it was likely or at least possible she was responsible.

"She and I both lost our fathers, and she was as witty as I was. She also understood my allusions and moods. At times we felt as though we were the opposite sex of the same person. Do you understand my meaning, Henry?"

"I do, Your Majesty." Brinton couldn't believe it. The king was getting wistful about that whore Castlemaine.

The king laughed. "I recall that at first we tried to be discreet about our relationship—always putting ourselves in the company of my brothers, but discretion was soon cast aside for our mutual passion. She was not only the most intriguing beauty I ever saw but she was intelligent and, as the poet Shakespeare said, 'saw quite through the deeds of men.' She is also the mother of my children, Henry. Surely you can understand that for all the problems she has caused me I am loath to consider her a murderer."

"I certainly understand."

"Good. I thank you for showing me this. Charles handed the note back to Brinton. "You are a special friend to me, Henry."

"I am more gratified by your words than you can ever know."

"Well, let us take a walk around Whitehall and into St. James's Park. See to it that Burgess has my spaniels ready to accompany us. Now I will change into more proper clothing."

Alone with his thoughts, Brinton decided to instigate another plan to implicate Barbara in the king's eyes. He still had use for Bridget Warren's "testimony." He would later today call on his own mistress, the actress Mary Gibbons, who had given him the note, and further the new scheme.

Abby walked further away from the labyrinth until she reached the west side of the Dove House section of the estate. Her head felt the effect of every step she took. What had she just overheard? Her mind shaped it in outline form. Mr. Hansall had delivered to Lord Durell a message that was important enough to wake him early in the morning. A response from Durell was sought, and Durell regretted that Sir Roger was not there to hear it. The date of something had to be changed because the king would not be leaving for Gray's Inn tonight but rather not until tomorrow evening. Something was to be done that required the services of three men, who were scheduled to leave for Scotland tomorrow with the Earl of Lauderdale's representatives. Hansall assured Lord Durell that the plan could still go forward because he would hire two others and make up the third himself. Durell had initially seemed opposed to Hansall taking part but he within seconds changed his mind. Whatever Hansall planned to do with the other two men would result in Hansall's leaving London, if not the country. And it was evident from his appearance that Richard Hansall was a Puritan or religious dissenter of some kind.

No possibility Abby seriously considered could be innocently explained. There could be no chance Hansall was to oversee a delightful surprise for the king when he reached Gray's Inn in the north of London. The tone of both men's voices and their having met away from all eyes in the center of Charlotte's high-hedged labyrinth informed Abby that something foul was afoot. When she combined what she overheard in the gallery the day before, Abby felt the onset of fear and considerable agitation. Assuming King Charles might be at some danger on the way to or when he arrived at Gray's Inn, Abby knew she must speak to someone and quickly. But who could that be? Charlotte? Would her friend give any credence to the possibility that her husband intended through others to harm the king? It was impossible Charlotte would. Abby regained control of her emotions when she remembered that His Majesty would not be leaving for Gray's Inn until tomorrow evening or late afternoon. She had to get to Whitehall and speak to someone there—perhaps even the king himself. She would just need a reason to break away from Charlotte before 3:00 tomorrow afternoon.

"Please, Mr. Devlin, don't kiss my mouth. Here." Young Anne Whitworth offered her cheek to the theatre manager, who lowered his head in apparent embarrassment.

"You must forgive me, Anne. I am sorely pressed of late and I suppose I need the sweetness of your affection to comfort me."

She reacted with sympathy, taking his hand and lifting his chin. "I know the death of Betty has hurt you deeply. I should not be so selfish. Here." She offered her lips to Devlin, who kissed her more sweetly than ardently, allowing his lips to remain on hers only briefly.

"Thank you, dear girl. I was simply in need of your kind touch—that is all." Devlin stared into her eyes and saw she believed him. Satisfied she did not attempt to break their kiss before he did, Devlin realized he was indeed transferring the desire he had for Betty onto Anne. This time he would do all he could to keep her from the embraces of the king, even though her tender age of seventeen would not deter His Majesty from calling her to Whitehall. She was, after all, only a single year younger than Betty was, and Charles had begun his liaisons with Lady Castlemaine and the song-bird Moll Davis when they were both nineteen—and Nell Gwynn when she was eighteen. And Devlin and many, many others knew that Charles wanted to bed the even younger Frances Stuart, even though he was not successful. But Devlin did not wish to remind himself that Charles was in his early thirties at the time he first desired Frances, not in his later forties as Devlin was now. After all, there were prostitutes playing their trade in London who were two or three years younger than Anne, who seemed by her manner and intelligence even younger than her years. Devlin concluded her sympathy and kindness and her theatrical ambition would serve him well in his seduction of her.

"Sir, I must go and study my part, but first let me kiss you once more to show I am sensitive to your feelings." She kissed him on the side of his mouth, touching his lips enough to encourage inadvertently his hope for her physical love. Devlin felt disappointed she did not look back when she departed.

"I think she's a most pretty one, sir. She'll be yours for the having soon enough—in a year or two, I should think."

"What . . .?" Devlin turned to see standing behind him the homely Joan Pegge, one of the theatre's orange women. The king remarked that the woman, whose age was guessed as anything from thirty-five to fifty, had according to Nell Gwynn "one of the most disagreeable faces" she had "ever beheld." Devlin could not challenge the assessment. Joan had the widest jaw he had ever seen on a woman, although it held up her expansive mouth with a mere seven teeth inside it—three widely spaced at top and the other four in a straight row across the bottom. Joan's nose dipped below her top lip as if it had been made of hot wax and dried accordingly. Her eyes were also widely spaced and above the left one was only half of a brow—the other half burned off, she revealed, when someone pushed her face into a fire. Joan's bulk was more solid than soft and no one doubted her strength or willingness to trade blows with women and men alike. And yet the actors and most of the theatre patrons loved her and the tales she told before and occasionally during a performance. Her job was to sell oranges and she never minded being called an "orange wench," whereas the orange girls generally took offense at the appellation. Along with oranges, Joan also sold or dispensed such items as ribbons and pig-bladder sheaths for the prevention of pregnancy, and she was often a go-between for those wishing to have their pregnancies ended or diseases prevented. Devlin was set on expelling Joan from her duties when she brought a dildo to show several of the male patrons and slipped it under her dress, simulating the insertion of it. But the hue and cry of the men against her dismissal convinced him she should remain selling oranges, as long as she demonstrated less of a willingness to perform sluttish activities. Joan was simply part of the spirited ambiance of the King's Theatre, along with the wits, the fops, and the ladies of questionable vocation.

"Why do you have that, Joan?" She was carrying an elegant lady's fan in her right hand.

"I've been sent back in the theatre to retrieve it for one of the ladies who lost it yesterday afternoon, Mr. Devlin. You know how often I am sent to collect such items." Devlin did know—from fine jewelry and lace handkerchiefs to soiled snuff boxes and notes from willing women to and from their ardent male pursuers.

"Joan, what are you doing?" Devlin couldn't help smiling at Joan's manipulation of the fan as though she were a beautiful lady of quality.

"I know the language well, Mr. Devlin. I glide it through the air to suggest my pleasure and assent—and shake it madly like this to reveal my anger and embarrassment. Watch how I slide it opened under my eyes. That's to show my lustful suitor I am interested. But if I move it away only slightly, I will inform him that he will not do." Devlin could easily see why the male patrons—and indeed some of the women—would be saddened to see Joan go. "I place it next to my heart like this to show that I love the gentleman—and with it only half opened against my lips I tell him he may kiss me." Devlin laughed at the thought of no man taking up such an offer. "But if I place the fan against my nose, I am saying that I don't trust you. I yawn behind an open fan—meaning you bore me. But If I draw it through my hand like this I am saying I hate you. And if I place the fan behind my head like this it is to say that you shouldn't forget me."

"Trust me, Joan. There can be no fear of that."

"But I say again, sir, that young mistress Anne will look excellent in breeches the way Nellie does and pretty Betty did." Joan paused to gauge Devlin's reaction to the recent murder, but he showed no emotion. "Yes, she has pretty legs and feet and will delight in all such roles you give her."

"Thank you for your assessment, Joan, but I'm sure you now have other business to carry you away."

"So I do, Mr. Devlin. I must deliver this fan. I will return this afternoon to peddle my oranges."

When she left the theatre, Devlin made his way to the stage and imagined Anne not only in breeches but also in "couch scenes" which revealed the lovely actress asleep on a couch or bed in some state of partial undress. How beautiful Anne would appear in such a scene—although Devlin imagined it more in private chambers than on the public stage. This time, however, he could contemplate the moment without visualizing the king's intrusion on the scene, as he was forced to do when the woman lying on the bed was Betty Keller, not Anne Whitworth. Those agonizing thoughts would not leave him for some time to come. To be cuckolded by the king—by this king, who he knew would shortly take Nell Gwynn from his theatre. By this king, who had stolen Betty from his heart, an act that resulted in her brutal demise.

CHAPTER 13

After leaving Charlotte a note, Abby requested a coach to make the short journey to London and Whitehall Palace. She hadn't made up her mind to speak with anyone about what she overheard in the labyrinth, but she simply couldn't remain further at Dove-Raven House until she resolved the matter clawing at her conscience. She had only spent one evening in London before coming out to stay with Charlotte, but that was at her uncle's home on White Cross Street in the northeastern part of the city. When the vehicle reached Charing Cross before its turn onto King's Street, Abby's ears drunk the sounds of the street traffic and the high-pitched whine of a street seller shouting, "What d'ye Lack" at everyone within fifty feet. Abby was pained when she saw one merchant shoved to the ground in front of his shop by a man whom the seller tried to prevent from going in. The language the men shared was distasteful its vulgarity and violent threats, even if some of it was unintelligible. Looking on the other side of the road, Abby viewed a collision of two wagons, a pair of boys running dangerously in front of horses, a poorly dressed woman blowing from her nose the contents of one nostril unto the wall of a shop, and a chamber pot being emptied onto the street from above. But more to her satisfaction were the bright colors of the clothing worn by men and women alike and the playful exuberance of the children. The morning was a marvelous one, sunnier and slightly warmer than most at this time of the year.

When the coachman helped her from the vehicle at the north end of Whitehall, he explained that the extensive palace had well over a thousand rooms, and from what she could determine from her perspective, Abby believed the palace could have passed for a small town given its size. The coachman added that Whitehall included "an indoor tennis court, a bowling green, and pits for cock fighting."

Abby frowned at what she deemed the barbaric sport of pitting cocks against each other, but thanked the man nevertheless for his kindness and information. "I'll be here waiting for you at our appointed time," she cheerily remarked. Abby informed him she wished to traverse by foot to the front of the palace and to St. James's Park across the way. She dismissed the coachman's concern that she shouldn't walk alone. In Virginia she had walked most often unaccompanied, and she found that a habit she didn't wish to break in spite of any dangers with which the city might confront her.

As she passed in the front of the palace, Abby thought of other places inside besides the tennis court and bowling green. Here were several beds, she guessed, in which the king entertained his mistresses—in addition to the one his wife Queen Catherine reposed in. Perhaps Charles had one bed he had chosen for Frances Stuart and perhaps kept unoccupied since he had given up on her. Did Moll Davis and Nell Gwynn lie under him in the same bed? Did Lady Castlemaine have her own—empty now that she had moved to her own lodgings? And inside was the bed where the young actress was found slain yesterday morning. If Whitehall possessed more than a thousand rooms, there had to be many places the King could be attacked if not killed. Charlotte informed her last night that Charles infuriated his ministers, especially Lord Brinton, because he made himself too accessible to those who might wish him harm—whether swimming in the Thames or walking through St. James's Park.

Abby smiled as she thought of Charlotte's correspondence going back many years, which talked about Whitehall and her desire to live there "regardless of status." When they were last together as girls, Charlotte playfully vowed to marry the exiled Charles and return to England with him as queen. Abby wondered how many other girls and young women conceded to similar fancy. Now she was glad she had come without Charlotte's jostling her senses with bawdy predictions about how she would have satisfied the king in his bed. "Pardon us, please." Abby stepped out of the way of two gardeners carrying a long section of a fallen tree. She asked what had happened. "It fell over in the Privy Garden three days ago after a storm," one of the gardeners replied. "It just toppled over. Quite unexpected."

"Will you plant another like it?"

"We must do so. When a tree falls like that, it brings foul luck to plant another unlike it."

The men moved on, but Abby was struck by the metaphoric relevance of the gardener's comments. England's monarchy was toppled by a Parliamentarian rebellion—its king publicly executed. What could have been more unexpected than that? But the martyred king wasn't replaced—at least not immediately—by another monarch but rather by a different species of ruler, which most assuredly brought bad luck to the country. But now Charles II ruled as king. Would he suffer the same ill luck of his father? The commotion behind her chased away these serious contemplations. "There he is!" shouted several men and women at the same time.

Abby turned and heard the barking of several dogs before she saw the king. He came out of the park holding his arm forward, not to ward off those pressing upon him but rather to allow them to touch his coat. Abby moved briskly toward the king and noticed he was speaking with many of those who approached him. Soon she heard them laugh at something the king said. She finally came close enough to hear him clearly.

"The best thing you can do for your husband's condition, madam, is to insist he take early morning swims in the Thames."

"But Your Majesty, the weather isn't good for that now—it's December, after all."

"Nonsense. A man comes alive the second he immerses himself in cold water. Believe me. I know. And thank you for informing me of the correct month. It is so mild today that I woke up believing it was April." Again the gathering laughed at the king's good-natured bantering.

At the insistence of those in his retinue, Charles started toward the palace, wishing his subjects a pleasant day. His path took him directly to where Abby stood. She bowed as she was taught as a child and when she lifted her head, the king's eyes met hers. He slowed his stride and nodded, keeping his eyes on her even after he had picked up the pace of his walking. Abby saw him whispering to one of his men as he turned his head toward Whitehall.

She was certain her heart stopped for the entire time His Majesty looked at her. Now she was able to breathe again. As she expected, he wasn't handsome in the way many judged an attractive man to be. But his eyes, mouth, and demeanor were utterly captivating. Yet there was something else she could not define—that which pushed aside reason and judgment and appealed to something more intimate in a woman. She grinned imagining what Charlotte or that actress Nell Gwynn might call such intimacy. Charles had gone another thirty feet toward Whitehall when Abby recalled the disturbing words she had heard in the labyrinth. She took three rapid steps toward the palace with the compelling urge to warn the king of what she heard and ask him to stay away from Gray's Inn this evening. But she halted as others pushed past her to see as much of Charles as they could. How could she tell him? What would he think if she did? What of poor Charlotte's fate if her husband was arrested for treason? Could it be that murder was not Lord Durell's intention? Could it be something less sinister?

At the moment the king disappeared into the palace, Abby turned and stared into St. James's Park. But she was not admiring the view. Her eyes were completely shut, as though she were attempting to resist with all her might what her conscience demanded of her. A moment later, she opened her eyes and headed toward the palace.

"But I cannot say that to His Majesty. It would be a lie. I never saw or heard Lady Castlemaine say any such thing. Isn't it enough that I have said the writing was hers, my lord? Even though—"

"It *was* hers, and no, it is not enough." Lord Brinton forced Bridget Warren against the wall of his apartment at Whitehall. "Need I remind you what I can have done to you, woman?"

"No, my Lord, please don't harm me. I beg of you, please don't." She placed both hands on his forearm and began to sink to her knees. Brinton jerked his arm free and she fell prostrate.

Brinton bent down and pressed her head to the floor. "Do what I tell you and you can keep your position and live in Whitehall as you have. If you refuse I will keep pressing down until I break every bone in your miserable face." He took both hands and commenced pressing her head into the floor.

"I will do it! I will, I swear it, my lord."

Brinton held her head against the floor until she began to cry. "Good. Now dry your eyes and come with me."

Sir Roger Earle arrived at Gray's Inn and began his inspection of the immediate area where the king would spend his time the following evening, instead of this evening as originally planned. His Majesty would come ostensibly to discuss the declining importance of this Inn of Court, a precipitous drop of significance from the days of his father and grandfather, James I. To Charles, the Civil War and the Interregnum halted and then altered the method of legal training. The king would speak with dignitaries there and listen to suggestions for reversing the course Gray's Inn had taken the past thirty years.

But Earle and Lord Durell knew the king was mainly coming to Gray's Inn to gamble at cards and then meet, as he did periodically, with the wife of one of the senior benchers, Sir Joseph Willet. A devotee of Lanterloo, the card game that arrived in England from France when the monarchy was restored, Willet was easily swayed into games lasting through the night—especially by four members of Charles's court who accompanied His Majesty to his visits to Gray's Inn. They would keep Willet occupied for as long as the king was in the company of the man's wife. Most often, Charles would stroll with her along the Gray's Inn walks, eat a sumptuous meal with her, and then enjoy her companionship in bed. No one dared mention to Sir Joseph that Charles and Willet's wife were sharing affections. Whether Willet realized or guessed he was being cuckolded by the king, neither he nor anyone else would say.

Earle knew Charles and Amanda Willet had their sexual liaisons in one of the houses across Holborn Street near Lincoln's Inn Fields, where stood the rival theatre belonging to the Duke's Company. Charles had first attended the public theatre at Lincoln's Inn Fields nine years earlier—and it was then that he first met Amanda Willet, then only recently married. She was but seventeen and her husband twenty-two years her senior. That night she impressed Charles with her intelligent estimation of the excellent actor Thomas Betterton of the Duke's Company as well as she did with her dark hair and penetrating brown eyes—and in the aftermath of a tempestuous argument with the newly minted Lady Castlemaine, the still-unmarried king came to Gray's Inn and spent two nights at the home of Sir Joseph and his wife. One the second night, Charles stole his first kiss from Amanda, who assured him she was less than satisfied with her husband's attentions. Two years passed before the king saw her again. Even more beautiful and more disenchanted with her husband, Amanda willingly agreed to Charles's suggestion that they further their intimacies. It was at this time she allowed the king to touch her sexually, and on his next visit they enjoyed each other fully, as Sir Joseph spent the evening winning at Lanterloo—his good fortune coming at the orders of the king. Given his marriage, his obsession with Frances Stuart, and the possessiveness of Lady Castlemaine, Charles saw Amanda only once between 1664 and 1667, but for the past three years he had come to Gray's Inn at the rate of once every six weeks to two months to be with Amanda, who, as Charles told Lord Brinton, provided him a particular pleasure none of his mistresses—not even Barbara—would agree to perform.

Earle came to Gray's Inn to make sure the entrances and exits at the house across Holborn had not been altered. Three men would enter from the rear passageway to the bedroom where the king and Amanda Willet would be lying alone. No one else would be inside the house. Charles would be run through as he was copulating with Willet's wife. From the beginning, Earle and Lord Durell planned to implicate the Puritan Hansall for planning the murder. The fact that Hansall was actually going to be at the house near Lincoln's Inn Fields—as Durell informed Earle—only gave their plot a better chance at success. Charles would be dead; his more compliant brother James would ascend to the throne until his Catholic leanings were fully revealed, and then Charles's bastard boy Henry, the Duke of Monmouth would rule the kingdom, with the assistance of men like Lord Durell and Sir Roger Earle, of course.

"Yes, Your Majesty, I speak the truth."

Charles stared at Brinton, who wore the expression of one grieved at having been doubted. The king returned his gaze to Bridget Warren, whose head was down and eyes were closed. "You are telling me that you heard Lady Castlemaine promise to remove Betty Keller from my bed forever by killing her?"

"Yes, Your Majesty."

"And that you said nothing because you have heard her speak similarly for many years about other women and that you believed she would never actually harm any of them in that way—that is, to have them murdered?"

"Yes, Your Majesty."

Charles again glanced at Brinton, who stood close to Bridget as though he feared she would swoon. "And you say you saw Thomas Lockwood and Lady Castlemaine examining the bedroom where Betty was found and speaking low to each other?"

"Yes, Your Majesty." Her voice gave away her fear.

The king sighed. "Bridget, you will not be punished for keeping Lady Castlemaine's comments to yourself. I have always believed as you did that such eruptions of her temper were only releases of her many frustrations. But I won't truly believe until I learn more. I trust you understand the penalty if you are lying to me, Bridget."

She kept her eyes closed until she no longer heard the footsteps leaving the room. When she opened them, she was alone. She was now free to sink to her knees and begin her tearful prayers to a God she feared had abandoned her.

Chapter 14

"And where, may I ask, have you been?" Charlotte greeted Abby in the hallway on the Dove House side.

"You were asleep and I was restless—and curious; therefore, I went into London and enjoyed several minutes outside Whitehall. I also spent a few moments in St. James's Park."

"Well, you have then ruined my desire to take you myself."

"You can still do that, Charlotte. There was much I didn't observe." Abby did not mention seeing the king.

"Well, this has in fact worked out better, because now I can present you with a surprise." Please go inside this room.

When Abby stepped into the "Red Room," as she called it, owing to the prominent color of the furniture, she saw standing by the window the woman she had most longed to meet. The Countess of Castlemaine, Barbara Villiers.

When Barbara turned, Abby saw a woman who more than equaled Charlotte's description of her beauty. But it was not so much an inviting beauty as an intimidating one. Abby couldn't visualize anyone simply walking up to Lady Castlemaine with a broad smile. No, one would halt and wait for permission to come forward.

Charlotte made the introductions, and Barbara extended her hand to Abby, who obeyed what she felt was a summons to speak. "This is so much a pleasure for me, Lady Cas . . ." She halted in embarrassment. Should she address her as Duchess, even if the formal elevation had not yet taken place?

"You may call me Barbara, Abby."

Relieved she hadn't insulted Lady Castlemaine by failing to address her properly, Abby also felt exhilarated, as though she had been accepted into this formidable woman's special circle.

As she stepped closer, Abby examined Barbara's still exquisite face. The eyes were an intoxicating violet and her lips were full and moist. Now that Barbara had turned thirty, Abby tried to imagine how she looked a decade earlier when the king made her his mistress. The subtle though visible lines around her eyes and to the side of her mouth suggested the passage of time, but what age took away it also replaced with a look of slight weariness yet one nonetheless attractive in a way a younger face could never duplicate. Barbara's alluring features radiated knowledge and experience in the romantic arts of pleasing and enticing. Hers was a beauty that no future age would find passé. Not even seeing the king earlier this morning left Abby feeling as awestruck as she did this moment.

"Abby, Charlotte has told me about you, and I would be interested to hear your impressions of Virginia." The sincerity and friendliness of Barbara's voice surprised Abby.

"It is a remarkable place. So much natural beauty. Frightening in many respects, and yet almost regal in the way it beckons those who cannot ever hope to change it. It maintains its sense of wonder and loneliness, while still offering its riches to those who would venture to it." Abby felt tightness in her throat. She had spoken of Virginia, but her words were reflective of how she saw Lady Castlemaine.

"Yes, I should like to go there someday."

Charlotte laughed. "I cannot imagine that, Barbara. You of all women were made to live here and in this time."

"No. Not at this time, Charlotte." Barbara's pensiveness struck Abby, but before she could go further, Phoebe entered the room.

"Phoebe, it is not yet noon, but I am sure that Lady Castlemaine wouldn't mind some wine. I know I wouldn't. Or Abby, for that matter.

Yes, Lady Durell. I assume the Bourgogne will be sufficient."

"Very good, Phoebe. For a girl raised in the wrong religion, you have acquired considerable knowledge of what truly pleases."

"Thank you, Lady Durell." As she turned to leave, Phoebe offered Abby a knowing smile.

Barbara shook her head, "She never once looked at me. She fears me, I know it. Yet have I not always been civil to her in this house?"

Charlotte smiled. "Civil to her, you have been. Others, I must say, have not always been so fortunate."

"I am always disappointed when members of Phoebe's class fear me. I don't want that. I have attempted to be kind to them, and they either mock me when I ride past them or look down and walk away when I come towards them."

Again, Charlotte attempted to pull Barbara from her dour reflections. "But my Lady Castlemaine is much less concerned when she is feared by members of the higher class. In fact, it is reaction she more than cultivates."

Abby winced at the apparent insult. "But Charlotte . . ."

"No, no. I have just now paid her the highest compliment. True, Barbara?"

Barbara broke free from her contemplations and laughed, which surprised Abby, who somehow imagined the infamous and beautiful woman was incapable of such overt expression.

Charlotte enjoyed her ability to delight her notorious friend. "Abby, you will prefer the wine as a morning drink far more than that piss the queen has made popular."

Barbara laughed once more. "Abby, a gentility of discourse in this house is often non-existent. At times I can tolerate Catherine's drink well enough. But this is not one of those occasions."

"Then you and Nellie Gwynn have more in common than you might think." Abby realized her friend had seized her opening. Ever since they were girls, Charlotte enjoyed "dropping a frog in the stew," by introducing topics that ignited warfare among her elders.

Barbara elevated her chin. "I have nothing in common with that vile little slut."

"That she may have been."

"And is, Charlotte."

"But I believe she has had no more than three lovers, perhaps four or five if all rumors are to be believed."

"You misunderstand me then. A slut is not measured by the number of men she has taken inside her. Sluttishness is a public manner, the habitual depravity of mind, a lack of intelligence and respect for what it truly means to lie back and receive. Nell Gwynn is a slut, even if she has had no more than one man."

103

"I am sorry you feel that way about her, although I do understand why. And yet I recall your telling me just a few short years ago how much you enjoyed her performance as Florimel in Mr. Dryden's play. I can still remember exactly how you praised her voice and her movements on stage."

Part of Abby wished she could find refuge in Charlotte's labyrinth; the other part wished she could add something to this potentially incendiary conversation.

Barbara waited until the wine was poured before she responded. "Yes, I did enjoy her performance. She came out and captivated everyone in the theatre without having to say a single word. But when she spoke and walked, she held them firm for the entire time she was on the stage—then, and for every other performance she would subsequently give. And yet, unlike the others, I preferred her in more serious parts, for that is what I like best to watch, but the crowd demanded her in comedy, and she obliged them exceedingly. It is her way, you see, to oblige whatever anyone wants. But it was when I saw her the second time that I marked the king's expression as he looked upon her. And then I knew, for I had seen that look much too often before, with those cunning whores Frances Stuart and Molly Davis, and others I refuse now to name. But with Nell Gwynn the look was even more determined. She would be his, and he would not be denied."

Barbara's words and pained expression stirred Abby's sympathy. In spite of her reputation for selfishness and cruelty, this was a woman who felt considerable personal hurt—born from love for the king. Charlotte, however, felt that the moment was worthy of being continued.

"You mentioned Frances. I am sure the two of you have by now ceased all hostilities."

Barbara turned to Abby, who saw anger and cruelty encroach upon her lovely features.

"I will never forget those years, Abby. Frances, the former Maid of Honor to Queen Catherine, the cunning harlot to many, and yet so much the "Chaste Diana" painted by Sir Peter Lyly. The beauty who favored the look of a boy—who found recreation in playing Blind Man's Buff and building card castles. The object of powerful men who wanted the king's eye turned away from his whore Castlemaine. Utterly childlike whenever it suited her purpose. Laughing so insincerely at all of the king's attempts at wit. The young girl for whom His Majesty organized a 'Committee for the Getting of Frances Stuart for the King.'"

"A committee, really?" Abby was both flabbergasted and amused.

"Yes, really, Abby. Really."

Charlotte encouraged Barbara and Abby to taste the wine. When the women voiced their approval, Charlotte continued. "But Barbara, it was you whom everyone looked at before and throughout the performances. Your box, whether you were next to the king or not, was often the stage to which they directed their attention."

"It was for so long, it seemed—for so very long. For all they said about me in the streets, I felt not their hatred in the theatre but only their amazement, their desire, and their fear. Charles has often been praised for his frequent patronage of the theatre, but it was I who so often insisted on his going. For there I knew I performed more brilliantly than any of actresses on the stage. It was I who dispensed the royal favor. The men actors sought a sign of my approval before they looked to His Majesty. And the actresses always demurred in their looking at the king, for fear of me."

Abby asked if Barbara approved of women performing on the English stage. "I champion my sex and I saw no reason why they should not perform the parts written for their sex. Besides, I knew it would infuriate the Puritans, so why not? When I first saw the actresses then, I never believed they would be rivals for the attention of the king, but I was so very wrong."

Phoebe entered and asked Lady Durell if they were satisfied with the wine.

"We are, Phoebe.

Barbara smiled at Phoebe. "Tell me, my dear. Do you have good recall of the times you went to the theatre these past several years?"

Abby found the question most surprising. "You have gone to the theatre, Phoebe? With the parentage you had?"

"Yes, Madam. That is in fact why I went. My mother even insisted on it."

"We can trust that our pretty little Silence was not silent then."

"No, Lady Durell, I was not."

Barbara sighed with exasperation. "I will ask again. Do you recall vividly your times at the theatre?"

"Yes, Lady Castlemaine. Every occasion I recall vividly."

"And what most vividly?"

Abby believed Barbara was expecting Phoebe to mention the times Lady Castlemaine sat in the theatre boxes.

"I remember most the carryings-on. The arguing and kissing. The slaps to the face and pinches on the arms. The touching and grabbing. The shouting across the whole theatre. But I was always bothered by the men who would shout out their own comments or repeat lines when they had no business doing so. There was also the—"

Barbara interrupted, "And you have seen me there?"

Phoebe lowered her eyes. "Yes, Lady Castlemaine. Two times."

"And?"

"I . . . I truly mean to tell you, Lady Castlemaine, that you were the most beautiful person I had ever seen."

"Thank you, Phoebe." Barbara's appreciation was sincerely expressed. Abby was taken by the woman's need to hear Phoebe's compliment.

After Phoebe left the Red Room, Barbara took another sip of wine. "Have you been married, Abby?"

"Yes, I have, Lady Castlemaine."

Charlotte reminded Abby that she had permission to call Barbara by her Christian name, but Abby hesitated, still not feeling comfortable with the familiarity. Barbara read her new acquaintance's discomfort. "Well, I am soon to be the Duchess of Cleveland, or so the king says. But, you say you have been married then?"

"Yes, my husband died two years ago."

"And mine still lives. Yours was named?"

"Thomas."

"Mine is named Roger. Roger Palmer, Lord Castlemaine. But he owes his title to his wife's having been in love with the king. Was your husband an idealist?"

"No. A practical man."

"I should not know what that is. Mine was an idealistic and honorable Royalist, who had one practical idea in his life and it cost him dearly."

"And that was?"

"To bring his wife, as well as gifts, to the soon-to-be king, then at Breda in the Netherlands. He wished me to humor Charles so that we might be given preference when the monarchy was formally restored. This is fine wine, Charlotte. I will have another glass when I finish this one. And must I wait for Phoebe to return to have it poured? Abby, your dear friend Charlotte has an aversion to anything approaching domestic drudgery, except, I suppose, groaning in feigned passion under her husband during their twice-monthly couplings."

Charlotte feigned insult. "Barbara! Besides, it's now only once a month now, though the groaning is still feigned."

Abby was delighted by the bawdiness of the two women. "I will pour another glass of wine for you both before the discussion takes even more of a Nellie Gwynn turn." Abby's eyes expanded at the realization that she might have erred in mentioning the king's present mistress, but Barbara expressed no offense.

"Thank you, Abby. Do you know what this means? It means, as Charlotte knows, that I am committing myself to some serious discussion about the state of my life and serious questions about the state of everyone else's. But I am not quite through interrogating you, Abby. Have you any children?"

"I had one, but she died in the cradle and I have not had another. Perhaps if I marry again . . ."

"Then you have lost a daughter. I am most sorry. Tell me. Did you truly love your husband?"

"No, I did not really love him, although I did find him a pleasant and thoughtful man. It was a marriage of convenience—for each of our parents, I mean." Abby's wit failed to elicit a smile from Lady Castlemaine.

"I did not love Roger before, when, or at any time after we were married. He was a husband like so many others. I did not hate him; he simply bored me. I am guilty of using him once, when we first married, but I have more than made up for the ridicule I have caused him since. He has received a title, a living, a home in Ireland, and a place in the Irish House of Lords."

"Do you see him often?"

"No, Abby, Not often. But I have seen him during these past several years. We have at best been coldly formal, the true reflection of my heart as far as he is concerned. His eyes show the humiliation of a spurned man, not that of a husband who has lost his only love. There is a difference. It was Charles he hated, not me. Charles's disloyalty he simply could not forgive. He had drunk many a health to the exiled king and gave him gifts and a pretty wife to feast his eyes on. In fact, I was convinced he wanted me to be one of the several wives offered and then accepted by His Majesty before he returned to England to take his crown. Had I been sampled by Charles and then discarded as were the others, Roger would have been content, as it would have made his reward all the greater. But when Charles took me for his own and would not discard me, my husband found that aspect of his cuckoldry too horrendous to bear. I could no longer be his property to dispense when the occasion called." Barbara offered a weak smile. "His father told my husband, 'If you marry that woman, I predict that you will live to be the most miserable man in the word.'"

"Roger Palmer was never the man for you, Barbara."

Barbara's smile was now more natural. "What you say may be said of nine of ten marriages now, Charlotte."

Abby continued to feel uncomfortable noticing the pain in Barbara's violet eyes. Barbara stepped toward her. "Abby, after the monarchy was restored and those miserable Puritans removed from power, what one might have been put to death for only a few years earlier was immediately practiced and flaunted. The city and country took back their spirit, and the excesses that resulted in the aftermath purged the land of its malaise and discontent. The Virgin Mary could again be invoked, though the times were uncongenial to her memory. Men could again wrestle on the green; both men and women could drink a health now. All could once more wear velvet, red-heeled shoes, silken hose, ribboned garters, and jewels on their fingers. Women now flirted in church and passed unattended into taverns, verbally jousting with men as never before."

"And the theatres."

"Yes, the theatres, Charlotte."

"And you were queen of it all." Abby detected a slight emphasis on "were," making her wonder if Charlotte was deliberately tormenting Lady

Castlemaine with a reminder that she was no longer the king's favorite. Charlotte's voice dropped to a near whisper. "And to think he now prefers Nellie Gwynn."

Barbara stood and walked to the window where Abby first saw her. "Nell could sing better than I, and, even though I am more than an accomplished dancer, the king would rather *watch* her dance than dance with her. What is worse, I wonder? To have His Majesty refuse to dance with me or to witness his admiring another's dancing?" Now Barbara seemed to be talking to no one in particular. "I vowed then that I would never again be wounded or humiliated by another actress."

CHAPTER 15

Devlin found the report distressing. The attendance at the rival Duke's Theatre for the past week had easily surpassed that at the King's. Whereas he took comfort in the fact that Nell Gwynn's forthcoming return to the stage in Dryden's *The Conquest of Granada* would surely swell the numbers in his favor, Devlin also knew she might fully retire from acting, at least for the foreseeable future, to spend whatever time she had left as the king's favorite mistress. And now that Betty Keller was gone, there was no woman who could replace either Nell or Betty in the hearts of his patrons. It was therefore all the more important that young Anne Whitworth build a following, but again Devlin understood she wasn't quite prepared for the kinds of roles both Nell and Betty excelled in. Thomas Betterton was now in charge of the Duke's Company, and soon they would have an elegant new theatre in Dorset Garden, which would allow for further scenic capacity and the opportunity to stage more ambitious and opulent productions.

"You seem agitated, Michael."

"Richard?"

"I hope you will forgive me for not meeting with you at Sir Edmund Pollard's—and I trust you received that message before you went to St. James's Square—but I realized the time to meet wasn't right. I think it is now, however,"

Hansall sat next to Devlin in the upper gallery, but Devlin insisted they leave the theatre in silence and walk up Drury Lane toward St. Giles's in the Fields. Neither man spoke until they reached the church. But each considered the irony of their acquaintance. A man of the theatre and a man whose kind despised the theatre and its ungodly associations. They had known each other for almost thirty years ever since Devlin's father harbored the Hansalls when Richard's father was sought for speaking out publicly against the corruption of Charles I shortly before the Civil War commenced in 1642. Although he professed loyalty to the king, Devlin's father also criticized the monarchy and while in Oxford made some of his opinions known to the king after spending several hours in a local tavern. The king knew his enemies were about to lay siege to the city and had no patience for anyone expressing criticism, especially within his hearing. With a dismissive swipe of his hand, Charles ordered Devlin's father arrested, but when his antagonist resisted, one of the king's guard ran him through.

Remembering the senior Devlin's kindness to them, the Hansalls took in Devlin and his mother, and the boys grew up as brothers. Hansall's father ignored Michael's theatre experience and treated him like a son. But Devlin was cajoled by other actors to flee to the continent in the late 1650s, and there he came to the realization that if the late king's son was invited back to rule England, theatre would recommence with many new and exciting changes. But soon after his return, Devlin witnessed the execution of his adopted father—the elder Hansall—and he developed a hatred for Charles, although he never displayed anything but loyalty and appreciation when the king gave him control of one of the two theatres established at the restoration of the monarchy.

When the men arrived at the churchyard, Devlin finally spoke. "Here there are buried over three thousand souls who were victims of the plague."

Hansall smiled at what he deemed was the perfect summons to speak about the subject at hand. "Five years have now passed, and still the king remains unpunished for his sins. God has sent both plague and fire to punish us for not doing his work. But there have been other, more personal punishment as well. The murder of your actress may be deemed one of them.

Devlin took a moment to compose himself. "What is it you want from me, Richard?"

"Now is the time, Michael. I am to be God's avenging angel." Hansall explained the plot to assassinate Charles the next evening, when the monarch arrived at Gray's Inn. "Fate—or rather, God—would have it that those set with the task must travel to Edinburgh. Now the responsibility is mine."

"But you will not make the attempt alone, will you?"

"Two more are needed."

Devlin looked more intently into the churchyard. The wind, which had blown vigorously, bringing in cooler air, calmed to a soft breeze. Devlin thought nothing of Hansall's invitation; rather, his mind unfurled the image that had for months tormented him unceasingly—that of His Majesty lying above Betty Keller and thrusting inside her until she cried out in pleasure. But now he visualized the satiated Charles leaving the bed and nodding to a shadowy figure who came forward and covered the naked body of Betty. The figure then disappeared, leaving the sight of young beauty with a knife buried into the place where the king had been.

"Yes, Richard, I will assist you. What will you have me do?"

"Good, good, Michael. You will be doing God's work. But we will need a third."

"Francis Gottlieb will go with us."

"You trust the man?"

"Yes. He has already brutally attacked another for me."

"Lady Castlemaine expressed a desire to acquire one of the male issues of the king's favorite spaniels, and I have brought the dog here as instructed."

Thomas Lockwood petted the dog Burgess brought to Lady Castlemaine's home. Yes, he recalled both her desire to have this dog and her payment in advance to Burgess to secure an animal sired by the spaniel Charles called "Pudding."

"What do you have in the bag, Burgess?"

The dog handler explained that he carried other items to deliver nearby. "Here, take the dog, Lockwood."

Lockwood scooped the young spaniel in his arms and bobbed his head to and fro to avoid the dog's attempts to lick his face. When Lockwood left the room, Burgess removed from his bag the ornamental silver knife box Lord Brinton had given him. Burgess stepped inside one of Lady Castlemaine's receiving rooms and hid the box behind the wood in the fireplace Lord Brinton assured him was never used.

Lord Durell and Sir Roger Earle began their meal with soup made from ox tongue spiced with nutmeg and followed the dish with sliced leg of lamb with artichoke heart and topped with raspberries and red currant. Durell wanted just enough food to dull their hunger before they talked of the king's visit to Gray's Inn the following evening. Accordingly, Lord Durell left off the plates some of his other favorite accompaniments—scrambled eggs, kidneys, anchovies, and stewed prawns. As for Earle, knighthood had not been bestowed on him until 1664; therefore, he had plenty of experience eating in chop houses along with tradesmen and common citizens, where grilled chops and steaks, accompanied by beer and wine were the favored fare. Earle still recalled his boyhood when he daily fed on staples of cheese, bread, onions, and the disgusting pottage he was forced to ingest. On rare occasions some meat or vegetables helped make the pottage more bearable, although Earle swore that when fortunes turned his way, he would never take another mouthful of the rude concoction. And now fortune had indeed smiled upon him. Earle presently dined at the home of a Lord—a powerful one, whose influence was most often unseen and unheralded. If their plan to dispatch the king was successful, Earle would find himself in a position of considerable power, the likes of which he couldn't have imagined when he dined on that miserable pottage and scraped the maggots from his cheese.

When Lord Durell ate, he didn't wish to be conversant—a preference that infuriated his wife and forced her to keep the number of large dinner gatherings at Dove-Raven House to a minimum—that is, when members of both sexes were invited. Earle was now used to Durell's silence when they ate together; besides, Earle knew His Lordship's mind was active regardless of his silence. After the meal concluded and the wine glasses were refilled, the men walked to Lord Durell's small library and returned to the topic that was foremost in each man's thoughts.

"Roger, you realize that it would serve us best if Brinton suffers the same fate as the King."

"I had thought the very same thing, my Lord. But I cannot be sure he is accompanying Charles to Gray's Inn tomorrow evening."

"No, but I know where he will be if he does not go, and it will be an easy matter to kill him."

"Excuse me, my Lord, but will it not be difficult to blame Hansall for this murder as well—since he'll be near Gray's Inn at the same time?"

"You assume Charles and Brinton will die at the same time. That is not what I have in mind."

"I see. If I may attempt to reason this out, they will die at different times so that Hansall may be blamed for both deaths. Am I correct to make that assumption?"

"Very good, Roger. If we see to it that Sir Joseph Willet is blamed for murdering the king because Charles has made love to his wife, Hansall can still be accused of killing Brinton."

"I am anxious to learn how that will achieved, my lord."

"For all his intelligence and resolve, Brinton has a weakness easy to exploit. He is man with his own special needs. And . . ." Durell halted and called out, "Who is there?" Phoebe stepped into the library. "What are you doing in this part of the house, woman?"

"Please forgive me, my Lord, but Lady Durell has asked me to inform you that she and her friend Abigail are going to the theatre and will return before nightfall."

"Thank you."

"Is there a message you wish to return to her, my lord?"

"No."

Phoebe left the room and quickly made her way down the hallway to the Dove House side of the house.

"You continue to amaze and horrify with your poetry, John.

John Wilmot, the Earl of Rochester, bowed ceremoniously. "I could not ask for a better reception of my scribbles, Your Majesty." Charles and Rochester stood at the edge of St. James's Park watching a series of foot races, one of the recreational activities recently popularized.

"What were your lines about the lady's fair ass that you recited at our last gathering?"

"With low-made legs and sugared speeches, / Yield to your fair bum the breeches."

Charles laughed. "That's it—that's it exactly. You also said something about starting a poem about St. James's Park that would bring more ladies to the place at night."

"I have. I think it will be a hundred lines or more. I am sure copies will be made and handed out to every member of the Court."

"And what happy images do you imagine to include in it'"

"Since you asked, my couplets so far include such blissful glimpses of nature as 'Whence rows of mandrakes tall did rise / Whose lewd tops fucked the very skies' and this humble observations about the Park—'And nightly now beneath their shade / Are buggeries, rapes, and incests made.'"

"Ah, examples of your gift for subtlety, I assume?" The king indulged a boisterous laugh. "What are other poetic subjects you hope to examine, John?"

"Well, I hope to devote verses to some of the ladies you have known."

"Be careful, my friend."

Rochester ignored the warning. "I'll certainly do something on the horrors of marriage. Well, I have some lines already on that subject."

The king continued to smiled, "You have my leave to quote them."

"Very well. 'If you needs must have flesh, take the way that is noble; / In a generous wench there is nothing of trouble.' Hmm. I cannot remember the next couplet but it says the worst that can happen is that you catch a disease. Then comes 'And diseases, you know, will admit of a cure, / But the hell-fire of marriage none can endure.'"

Charles again laughed and marveled at his young friend's talent with the bawdy phrase.

"Oh yes, I haven't written a line of it yet, but I will eventually write a poem about Signior Dildo."

"And am I to receive copies of these?"

"It depends on whether you are included in the lines, Your Majesty. No, I am in jest. I will leave you out of it. I don't wish to spend another three weeks in the Tower for my transgressions."

The king nodded at Rochester's reference to the time the young man in essence abducted his eventual wife, after her relatives objected to her marrying the financially destitute Rochester, even though it was the king who suggested the eighteen-year old marry the beautiful and wealthy heiress, Elizabeth Mallet. Rochester had her coach stopped, and she was transferred to another and driven off. When Charles heard of the abduction, he sent Rochester to the Tower, and after three weeks the young man was released only because he wrote a thoughtful apology to the king, who had been especially angry because he had acted as Rochester's benefactor—conferring on him on annual pension and sending him on a three-year Grand Tour of Italy and France when the boy was fourteen. Some informed Charles that young Rochester had become completely debauched at thirteen.

"But after I released you from the Tower, you went on to make yourself worthy of my affections." The king was most pleased when Rochester proved himself as a warrior at sea in the Dutch War of 1665—so much so that Charles increased the young man's pension, provided him with lodgings in Whitehall, and granted special license for Rochester to enter the House of Lords, even though John was not yet old enough to serve. "And you ended up marrying the woman I approved of after all." So he had, but still without the approval of Elizabeth Mallet's father.

The races being over, Charles and Rochester returned to Whitehall, where they were met by young Earl of Mulgrave and Sir Charles Sedley, two members of the often drunk "Merry Gang," to which Rochester belonged. Most notoriously, as the king knew, Sedley once stood naked on the balcony of a London tavern jocularly selling to the crowd a powder that would make all "the cunts" in town run after him. One report claimed that a thousand people watched Sedley's antics, which crested with his taking his penis and washing it in wine, after which Sedley downed the beverage and did it again, only this time drinking to the king's health. That added flourish turned many in the crowd against him, not to mention the Lord Chief Justice.

Rochester pulled the two men away from Charles and explained that now wasn't the time for planning their next debauch. The young Earl's face lost its gaiety as he returned to the king. "I have debated whether to mention this to you. At first I thought not, but now I feel I should."

"You have my permission. What is it, John?"

"Some tavern talk, relayed to me by one of my spies, who heard it yesterday afternoon. A besotted merchant claimed that one of the men being sent to Scotland by the Earl of Lauderdale told him in the same tavern that he heard a new government would soon 'save the kingdom.' I thought you should know."

Charles shook his head. "I should know that you *heard* from one of your spies that he *heard* a drunken man say that he *heard* from someone headed to Scotland that this man *heard* that a new government was soon to save the kingdom."

"So I heard, Your Majesty." Rochester's droll delivery set the king to laughing again.

"John, do you know how many such warnings I have received these past ten years? I even heard them before I returned to England. If I were to respond to every hollow threat made by tavern dwellers, I would never come out of Whitehall."

"Nevertheless, I would take special care when you travel out."

The king placed his hand on Rochester's shoulder. "It is nothing, I am sure, but good thanks for your concern. Now I have some business that demands my entire afternoon, I'm afraid. I'll leave you to ponder other lewd metaphors and verses."

CHAPTER 16

"I am simply amazed. All I have heard about this place has failed to prepare me for what I see here."

Abby sat with Charlotte in one of the side boxes at the King's Theatre and glanced at all sections of the structure. A green woolen cloth covered the benches in the pit below them as well as adorned the boxes where the more affluent would view the play. Abby wondered if the backless benches would become uncomfortable for the patron and whether those down there stood up and stretched their backs while the play was being performed. She witnessed several men of noble bearing in the pit area, and Charlotte informed her that such well-off men enjoyed watching the play from that vantage point. "There is more bantering and masculine behavior there, as you can see." Two men were in the midst of an altercation about something, with one of the men grabbing the other by the cravat while others laughed and encouraged further battle. "Do you see that woman, Abby?"

Charlotte pointed downward to an unattractive female tossing an orange to one of the male patrons. "I assume she isn't one of the actresses."

"No. She's what the men call an 'orange wench'—too homely and old to be given the title 'orange girl.' Her name is Joan Pegge and she's a sly one. Picks pockets with as much dexterity as she tosses oranges."

Abby's attention was next drawn to five men wearing what she assumed was the height of male fashion. Each man's coat was of a different color—white, light blue, green, pinkish red, and silver. Each touched another's article of clothing—coat sleeves, cravats, hats, and periwigs.

"Charlotte, look at those men fondling each other's clothing. I find it rather amusing—and peculiar."

"So do we all. Where they are standing is commonly called 'Fop Corner,' for obvious reasons."

Abby spent the next few minutes observing men and women

shamelessly interacting in the boxes and gallery, with a number of men in the pit shouting words to the women above them. The more privileged women, including Lady Durell, employed their fans to their advantage, but Abby never lifted the fan Charlotte had given her. She had not yet been schooled in the art of communicating with one. Finally, the play began.

Today the King's Company staged the tragedy *Othello* by Mr. Shakespeare, a play written, as Charlotte informed Abby, nearly seventy years earlier but still popular with London audiences. Abby was immediately absorbed in the drama, even though Charlotte made matters difficult by commenting on almost all the actors who played the parts. As soon as the villain Iago took his place to begin the performance, Charlotte whispered to her friend that the actor Michael Mohun fought in the Civil Wars and was shot. "He's superb at playing the villains, Abby. Just watch." Abby was trying to do just that and listen to his speeches at the same time. "He's not tall or now young enough to play the hero. He is over fifty. But he moves so gracefully. There. See?"

The actor assaying the role of the Moor Othello was Nicholas Burt, whom Charlotte said did the part when the theatres first opened ten years earlier. "He's lost some of his magic, I'm afraid, but the part will soon go over—so Mr. Devlin has told us—to Mr. Hart." Mr. Burt also fought in the Civil War and was "about sixty years of age."

But of the male actors, Charlotte had the most to say about Charles Hart, who tonight took the role of Cassio, the wrongly-perceived lover of Othello's wife. Other than the character's speeches, Abby heard Charlotte's opinion about "my favorite of the King's Company actors." First, she noted that Hart and Nell Gwynn had excelled in a type of comedy that emphasized equal power between the sexes—with each proficient at flirtation and verbal warfare—and that Hart had trained Nellie in her acting. Abby judged Hart to be a man in his forties, yet she had to agree that he possessed a magnetism his role this afternoon did not require. Charlotte made her next point most exuberantly. "Mr. Hart and Nell were lovers before the king decided she would be exclusively his. They are also to appear together in Mr. Dryden's new play next season, and many of us are of the opinion that she and Hart will renew their affections at that time." Abby smiled at the image of Charlotte sitting at table with her friends making wager as to when the renewed lovemaking would commence, as well as betting on the fate of Mr. Hart when the King discovered he was betrayed by Nell.

The woman playing the Moor's wife Desdemona was Margaret Hughes, whose appearance on stage prompted Charlotte's most animated remarks, for which she was twice hushed by those nearby. Charlotte revealed that ten years earlier—in the same role—Margaret was the first woman to act on the English public stage. "She was thirty then and is forty now, but she still handles the part well, don't you think?" Charlotte's question came after Hughes had spoken but ten lines. The next hundred lines were lost to Abby because of Charlotte's quick catalog of Margaret's history.

"Charlotte, please. I'm trying to listen to the play."

From behind her fan, Charlotte continued to whisper gossip about court and theatre figures before finally leaving Abby in peace for the next several minutes—that is, until Margaret Hughes reentered the stage. "Margaret was such a beauty with her dark hair and attractive legs, which drew men into her trap. She followed the example of Frances Stuart, but did give in when she was satisfied with the bargain. Now she is with the King's Company and has been painted several times by Mr. Lely." Having exhausted the pertinent facts about the actress and her passionate experiences, Charlotte permitted Abby to enjoy the rest of the performance without interruption, although not without aggravation, as one of the young men in the pit kept looking up at Abby and blowing kisses. He then decided to make particular movements with his fingers that Abby deemed utterly vile—until the orange woman, Joan Pegge, slapped him forcefully on the back of his head, causing him to stop his rude behavior.

After the performance and as the women began to enter the coach taking them back to Dove-Raven House, Charlotte looked behind the vehicle and saw someone she apparently recognized. "Abby, get in and I will join you in a moment—after which she walked toward the man standing some twenty paces behind the coach. Abby looked out the window and strained to see who was conversing with Lady Durell in the shadows. After less than a minute Charlotte climbed into the carriage and began speaking of the play. Abby put up her hands. "Charlotte, who was that man you were conversing with?"

Her friend smiled. "Someone I hope you never meet."

"Why?"

"Because if you did, you might tell Lord Durell that his wife is not the faithful turtledove he thinks she is." Charlotte laughed softly, but Abby thought there was something insincere in the expression.

"Thomas?"

"Forgive me, Lady Castlemaine, but I have just been given this note from Lord Brinton."

Having just returned from Dove-Raven House, she took the note. "He didn't bring it himself, did he?"

"No, My Lady. It was delivered by one of the messengers from court."

"I abhor that man."

Lockwood hated to see agitation mar his lady's beautiful features. He watched as she opened and read the note. Lockwood adored seeing her face express everything from sheer joy to utter disgust. There was nothing about her by which he wasn't enthralled. His secret collection of items she had discarded more than proved his fascination and devotion. Now her agitation gave way to concern. "What is it, my lady?"

"Brinton wishes to visit me here. He is coming with the Earl of Lauderdale. I cannot think of two men I would wish less to see."

"Does the note say why they are coming, My Lady?"

"It does not. Only that it is important we meet."

Lockwood knew Lord Brinton despised Lady Castlemaine in spite of what he might have said to the king. Previously, she felt immune to Brinton's censure and influence on His Majesty, but now she seemed most disconcerted if not frightened by the impending visit. But Lockwood knew less of Lauderdale's views of Lady Castlemaine. "Why do you think he's coming with the Earl of Lauderdale, my lady?"

"I don't know. Only heaven understands how much I loathe that man as well. Even though he was involved in the Scot's delivery of the first Charles to the Parliamentarian side, the king's son has for some reason included him among his favorites at court. Lauderdale only changed his view of monarchy when he saw the wind had shifted against his views. Charles told me he liked the man and thought he would serve as the fittest secretary for Scotland."

"And His Majesty apparently still finds him useful in that office."

"Yes, Thomas, he does. He stays close to the king's ear. Although smart enough, Lauderdale is one of the ugliest wretches of the kingdom, a foul-mouthed licentious character of little merit otherwise. A haughty, imperious man without cause to be either. You have seen him, haven't you, Thomas?"

"Never at any close distance, my lady."

"Then you will be in for a treat when they come tonight. He's large of bulk, with a full mound of flesh under each eye, and a tongue far too large for his mouth, which sprays spittle onto anyone he is conversing with. So try and keep your distance." Her concern was effaced from her features by the boisterous laugh she expelled.

Lockwood was captivated by Barbara's joyous reaction. How he wished to see so much more of it. "My lady, can any man be that unappealing?"

"That one is. And yet the man still managed to find a wife and beget a child, who ran off to Paris last year after learning her father had begun a romantic affair with another woman." Now Barbara offered a derisive laugh, which Lockwood mimicked.

"He has a mistress? How old is she, my lady? Surely not of a tender age."

"Heaven's no. His mistress is in the middle of her forties, only ten years younger than the Earl—so the affair isn't completely absurd, I suppose."

After she excused Lockwood, Barbara opened the drawer to her wardrobe and pulled from it a box in which was a chemise with a wide flounce and daring slit in the front. It was not something she wore for the king; rather it was the garment she wore three years earlier when she stepped out to the balcony and jeered at one of the most powerful men of the day—Henry Hyde, Lord Clarendon, whom she fully detested and worked very hard to destroy.

Clarendon's influence on Charles was considerable. He was the chief minister and Lord Chancellor. His daughter Anne married James, the Duke of York soon after Charles began his reign. But it was Clarendon's efforts to bring Catherine of Braganza to England as Charles's wife that pitted him against Lady Castlemaine. Barbara soon learned that Clarendon publicly complained about the king and his sexual dalliances—especially Charles's relationship with Lady Castlemaine. Barbara recalled with pleasure the hours she spent displaying her hurt over Clarendon's "cruel" remarks about her morality, until she knew Charles would share her indignation and occasional fury at the Lord Chancellor. With her prompting, Charles told Clarendon his private life would brook no interference, and when Queen Catherine failed to produced children, Barbara hinted to Charles that Clarendon sought an infertile woman to wed the king because he wished to see one of his grandchildren eventually inherit the throne. With no legitimate child, Charles would be replaced by his brother, the father of Clarendon's elder granddaughter, who would then be the heir presumptive upon James's death.

Hearing of Lady Castlemaine's machinations, Clarendon refused even to mention her name or allow his wife to speak to her. Finally, the loss to the Dutch in 1667, for which Clarendon was blamed, led to his dismissal by the King. Clarendon was then impeached by the House of Commons, but fled to France before he suffered further harm. Now holding the chemise, Barbara recalled her words to Lady Durell the day before Clarendon gave up the Great Seal of office.

"Clarendon thought me nothing but a bewitching harlot, whom he could replace in Charles's heart with a modest and virginal Portuguese princess. Seeing I still held the king's interest even after he married Catherine, the Earl castigated me using every foul epithet he knew. But he learned I could not be trifled with and that when I am insulted or underestimated I will have my revenge. This whore's 'luck' cost him his position and his place as an Englishman."

To Thomas Lockwood, Barbara once boasted, with the aid of her third glass of wine, that the King's attachment to her was stronger than to anyone else, with the exception of his sister Minette. "But she was his sister, and naturally there could be no contest between her and me. Did you know that His Majesty once excused himself from talks with the French delegation about the serious matter of avoiding war just so he would not keep me waiting for our dinner? The king always preferred my company to that of his ministers, and he often held meeting on matters of state in my apartments at Whitehall."

But that was some time ago now, and things had changed. Barbara held the chemise to her breasts and recalled the night she wore it last. Clarendon was just leaving Whitehall after the king stripped him of all power when she stepped out to the balcony and showered the Earl with abuse, reveling in his misfortune. She remembered tears running down her face because she was shouting so fiercely at him. When he lifted his head to look at her, she suddenly stopped. For as long as she lived, she would never forget his words.

"I pray you remember, madam, that if you live on, you too will grow old as I am now."

Clarendon walked away as Barbara groped for something more to say in refutation of his words. Nothing came. And now she was thirty—she was, as the lover of a king, now old. But she would not concede to a retirement. She would not be put into a wardrobe as a memory of the woman she was. She still had powers to employ. And even if she could no longer do it openly, she still had the intelligence and passion to influence events and to remain in favor with the king, whose desires she felt confident she could still satisfy.

CHAPTER 17

Hansall ripped apart a folded sheet of paper, collapsed the torn sections into a ball, and threw it into a fire pot at the edge of a cobble-stone alley off Bow Street. The two men using the pot to keep warm on this cloudy and windy afternoon reacted angrily to Hansall's encroachment on the fire they had constructed. Hansall tossed the men a coin and moved toward the Strand. The fire was welcome now that the calendar had turned to December, but never had it been to Hansall more so than in early September four years earlier. When the flames spread from a bakery in Pudding Lane in the middle of the night, Hansall was awake, unable to sleep because he could not drive out of his mind his bitterness over the fact that God had not punished the king and his city for their decadent behavior and retribution against Hansall's father and other men who had done their best to rid England of a corrupt monarch and establish a government of decent God-fearing men. After his father's execution, Hansall entertained frequent thoughts of retribution against the king and members of his court and council. But it was soon apparent that the citizens of London preferred licentiousness to sobriety and had no reluctance to vilify and humiliate those who remained nonconformists in religion, dress, and behavior. On that September night, Hansall believed God had finally gotten around to setting matters right.

London had experienced a ten month-long drought following the plague of 1665, leaving the dried-out wooden buildings vulnerable to the flame, and Hansall believed the lack of rain was also God's will so that the city could be purged by fire. The updraft of winds, which spread the flames, also seemed a sign from the Almighty. The following morning when Hansall saw the fire moving westward toward Whitehall, he went as close to it as he could, dodging the fiery debris that blew toward him. It was unlike anything he had witnessed before—a malevolent and avenging force, yet still purposeful and judicious. Those who passed him on their way out of the city with as many possessions as they could carry on carts or on their backs encouraged him to flee, but Hansall knew he would not leave the city until he saw the fire engulf Whitehall—the very seat of immorality and corruption.

Hansall witnessed much of the city's destruction—over ten thousand houses, many official buildings, and some eighty churches—including St. Paul's Cathedral, but much to his dismay the flames did not reach the palace at Whitehall. How could God destroy so much and leave the king's residence unscathed? There were but two miles the fire had to travel from where it started on Pudding Lane to consume Whitehall, but that part of the city remained as it had been. Whereas others speculated that the fires were deliberately set by agents of the French or the Dutch, leading to violence against foreigners throughout the charred streets, Hansall reluctantly concluded that God sent a message that to finish the work of just retribution righteous men would have to perform the office. He tried to do so the evening he came upon the king throwing water at the implacable flames, but his attempt was thwarted by the king's actions, leaving Hansall to severely castigate himself for his failure. Soon he found comfort in his reading of Romans 13:4: "if thou do evil, fear: for he beareth not the sword for nought: for he is the minister of God to take vengeance on him that doeth evil."

Other men's plots to kill the king in the following three years failed, which only convinced Hansall further that he was chosen either to plan or to perform the attempt—this time successfully. Although he let Lord Durell and Sir Roger Earle believe they were orchestrating this latest plan to assassinate Charles, Hansall fed them information and several courses of action they both consumed willingly. Durell and Earle initially rejected Hansall's desire to take part himself, but the recent change in the king's schedule now provided the Puritan his opportunity to murder the monarch and recruit Michael Devlin in the plot. He wanted someone who truly hated the king—someone still burning from the loss of Betty Keller to Charles's bed and her subsequent murder. Hansall took one more look toward the fire pot spitting flames, into which he had thrown the ball of torn-up paper note outlining the latest plan to murder of the king.

Sir Roger Earle finished his letter to Sir Walter Browne, "And let me know immediately how you would break the news of his father's death to the king's son—assuming of course that illness takes down the king unexpectedly." Earle's reference to Charles's assassination was barely disguised, but at this point Earle's arrogance pushed him to believe he could deny plausibly that he was referring to such a heinous act. The king's eldest illegitimate child, James, the Duke of Monmouth—now twenty-one— was presently serving as Colonel of His Majesty's Own Troop of Horse Guards, a post he held for the past two years. Yet, the young man had been encouraged to believe that he—and not Charles's brother, the Duke of York—should become king if his father died. That raising an illegitimate heir to the throne would violate both law and precedent was dismissed by those who saw in the Duke of York a man with pro-French leanings, and whereas many thought he favored Roman Catholicism and argued for its toleration, Earle and Lord Durell knew what the country did not—that the Duke of York had already converted to the Roman faith. They feared that if he assumed the throne he would strive to be an absolutist king and attempt to diminish the power men like Durell and Earle had gained since the restoration of the monarchy ten years earlier. Other aspects of the Duke of York were also troubling. He was married to the daughter of the now disgraced Earl of Clarendon, and whereas the couple raised eyebrows with their affectionate displays of kissing and nuzzling at court, James was almost as bad as his elder brother in the keeping of mistresses. One wit observed that James was "the most unguarded ogler" the country had ever seen. In truth, his young and lively mistress Arabella Churchill had just delivered their second child, also named James.

The popular Duke of Monmouth, Earle and Durell believed, would ultimately be accepted over the flawed James by most of the populace. Several men, including Earle's correspondent Sir Walter Browne were to see that Charles's son would be ready to claim the throne after the death of his father. Those insisting on the Duke of York as successor could be defeated with argument and force, if necessary. Earle folded his letter, sealed it, and handed it to his messenger. "Go immediately to Sir Walter.

Make no stops along the way and keep the letter secure."

"I will, Sir Roger."

"Oh, and leave me one of your oranges."

"Very good, sir." The orange woman Joan Pegge pulled the largest one from her bag and gave it to Earle, who placed two coins in her meaty hand.

"I'm most satisfied with your reports, Joan. Be sure you keep your ears and eyes open at the theatre for anything else I might find of value."

"I have done so and will continue to do so, Sir Roger." Joan bowed her head, disguising any indication that she hadn't always told Earle everything that he might wish to know.

Grimacing from discomfort, Lord Brinton placed three coins into the hand of the actress Mary Gibbons. "There's an additional coin for your troubles."

"And for your pains, my Lord."

Brinton frowned at her attempt at humor. "No such allusions when it is over and done, Mary—remember our agreement."

"Forgive me, my Lord." Mary placed the three coins in her purse and rubbed her right hand, which had become fatigued and chaffed by the activities of the past several minutes. His Lordship had been arranging these periodic visits for the past eight months, soon after he had allowed himself to drink too much before and during a performance of the King's Company and then to be seduced by Mary Gibbons in the tiring-house at the theatre after her fellow actors dispersed for the night. The following morning, as he shared his breakfast with his wife, Brinton burned with a guilt he felt he must somehow expunge. Accordingly, Brinton arranged a meeting for Mary Gibbons to join him at one of the vacated homes he owned a mile north of the city. When she arrived, Brinton asked her to sit and served her wine, but took none himself. He spent no time in idle talk.

"Before I speak of my sinful behavior, I must insist that you say nothing of what occurred between us and what may happen between us from this time forth."

Mary was perplexed by Brinton's allusion to their future interactions. If he felt remorseful over their sexual encounter, what did he plan for them from this night on? Did he expect her to seduce him while he muttered ineffectual protestations?

"Do you swear your discretion, Mary?"

"Of course, my lord."

"Then follow me."

Brinton led her to a near empty room at the back of the house, bringing a dining chair with him. The room was empty, except for a dust covered side-table and a baby's cradle, devoid of linen. But in the corner of the room on the floor was also a three-foot wide coffer, without ornamentation. Mary thought the chest contained nothing of significance, but her curiosity was nevertheless aroused.

"What is in the coffer, my lord? Is it something you want me to see?"

"No, but it will have its use."

Mary tensed. She was certain he wished to take her while she sprawled face down over the chest. The sex act would be dreadfully uncomfortable, she knew, but she would accept the position if it kept alive Brinton's interest in her and her chance for betterment and financial gain.

"But first, dear Mary, I need to speak of our recent liaison. Here." Brinton extended his hand and seated her in the chair he had brought with him. As soon as she sat, he knelt in front of her, bowed his head, and commenced an emotion-laden apology for taking advantage of their differing situations, for betraying his wife, and for behaving most unlike a close confidant of the king. Initially startled by Brinton's obsequious behavior, Mary soon concluded he was feeling guilt over more than his dalliance with an actress of the King's Company. She wondered as he went on whether Brinton had wished to follow his monarch's example and take advantage of an actress, even though it was she who was the aggressor in their sexual encounter. Finally, Brinton daubed the tears from his eyes and stood.

"And now I require you to complete my penance." Brinton walked to the cradle and removed from it a leather strap of some two to three inches wide. Handing it to her, he went on. "You will use this on my body between this place and this one. Brinton placed his right hand behind him and touched a spot at his lower back and then right above his knees. No lower; no higher. Do you understand?"

"Yes, my lord." Mary's shock soon gave way to concern. That this powerful man wanted to be physically punished might be well and good, but what if she struck him too vigorously? What if he changed his mind after the first blow or two and then avenged his pain in some way? What if he took his beating and then arrested her the following day—or the following week—leaving her to rot in prison?

"I will turn from you and remove my clothing. You may turn away as well." The two of them stood with their backs to each other as Brinton removed his periwig, coat and shirt and dropped his breeches below his knees. In moment, Mary heard the sound of wood moving across the floor. "You may begin."

Mary turned and saw that Brinton had knelt in front of the coffer and grabbed with each hand the handles on the side of the chest. He was almost exactly in the position she imagined herself to be when she first saw the coffer. She dangled the strap and debated where to strike him first. She decided on the buttocks and inflicted a healthy but not brutal blow.

"No, no, not hard enough. Not hard enough." Brinton seemed to be imploring her rather than complaining. Mary increased the ferocity of the next blows until she reached ten. Out of breath she waited to hear what Brinton would say—whether he would call an end to his punishment or ask for more. Having said nothing so far—only wincing and slightly articulating the painful effects of the strap, Brinton now let a torrent of emotion pour from him. He asked for five more, and Mary no longer felt concern or fear but rather intense delight at her mastery over such a powerful man. The flush of vanity and power she experienced when she had seduced him could not compare to this new experience.

When she finished the fifteen lashes, she hesitated. Did her penitential lord now require comfort? Indifference? Further cruelty? She was amazed he held on to the coffer's handles throughout the ordeal, never letting go even for an instant. "Turn your back, Mary." Briton rose up and began to re-dress. "I will require this again at other times. I will reward you handsomely for your service to me and protect you from all harm."

"Yes, my lord. Whatever you command me to do." She curtsied to him, still with the leather strap in her hand."

"Return the strap to the cradle and leave."

She took several steps toward the front of the house before she turned back to him. "My lord, may I ask you one thing."

"What is it?" Brinton had just replaced his periwig, remarkably looking none the worse for what he endured.

"Won't your wife see the welts and bruising when you retire at night?"

"On those infrequent occasions when I copulate with my wife, I insist on entering her from the rear with only my breeches lowered. She never sees my unclothed body."

With each visit made to Brinton's abandoned house outside of London, Mary learned more about him—his interests, opinions, and secrets. After their second meeting, they shared wine afterwards—Brinton behaving as if nothing had happened between them—and soon Mary volunteered to share information and serve Brinton's intrigues in any way she could.

CHAPTER 18

Abby watched Charlotte leave the room before she rose from the sofa and allowed her agitation some release. She walked to one of the ornate cabinets and opened the first of twelve small drawers. She might be able to open them all before Charlotte returned. Phoebe had come into the room and whispered in Lady Durell's ear. Charlotte nodded and excused herself. "I have to tend to something, Abby," she said. "When I come back I'll bring you something sweet and delicious." Abby's first assumed Charlotte was going to her husband to speak about whatever plot was afoot. Abby hated entertaining such a thought, but now she severely doubted Charlotte's protests that she and Lord Durell were keeping to themselves except for social and the occasional sexual gatherings. Abby feared Lord and Lady Durell were both conspiring against the king, but she couldn't be sure until she had more proof.

She explored five of the small drawers in the cabinet—finding nothing incriminating—before she heard Charlotte's laughter in the hall. Abby made it back to the sofa as her friend re-entered the room.

"I hope I haven't been too long. I promised you something sweet and delicious, and here it is." In a dramatic sweep of her left arm, Charlotte beckoned someone to enter. "May I present to you the sweetest *and* tartest treat of them all—our dearest Nellie." Charlotte laughed as Nell Gwynn took an actress's bow. Abby stood and felt her mouth drop open. Her face flushed, partly in surprise but also in shame at having falsely assumed Charlotte's motive for leaving the room earlier.

Instead of offering her hand or a salute, Nell rushed to Abby's side and whispered. "Please don't tell me you are a Puritan girl like little Phoebe. Just looking at you, I know that the king would love to kiss you—fully on the mouth too. But take care, my sweet Abby—you don't know where that mouth has been."

Abby's sputtering could barely be heard above Nell's raucous laughter.

She clearly delighted in the effect her words had on Abby, who could only look at Charlotte as if pleading for assistance. Finally, Abby squeaked, "I am happy to know you, Nell."

"But perhaps not to be seen with me, I fear."

"Oh, no. Not that at all."

"Do you know that this month at Oxford they made me their jest and put their hands on my coach?"

"Were you hurt?"

"Not at all. I merely opened the door and said, 'Pray, good people, be civil. I am the Protestant whore.' They immediately calmed and gave me three rousing houzas!"

Charlotte seemed dubious. "Is that true, Nellie, or are you telling another broad tale of yourself?"

"Would I lie to you, Charlotte? Besides, when it comes to me, there is hardly a difference between the truth and a broad tale." Nell sniffed. "What is that fragrance? Not yours, Abby. Yours, Charlotte?"

"No. It is the remains of the Duchess of Richmond."

"So Frances was here recently? Abby, I fear Lady Durell is manipulating us all on that elaborate chessboard of hers. She wants *all* of us in this room together, at the same time. I am right, aren't I?"

Abby laughed, now beginning to feel comfortable in Nell's effervescent company. Her face revealed her true age of twenty, but her mouth suggested someone who had lived many, many years in ill company. "I wouldn't know that, Nell."

"Call me Nellie. Well, now to important matters. Do you both like the color of this dress?"

Charlotte handed Nell and Abby a glass of wine. "I do. I have not seen you wear that color before."

"No, because it is new. As part of the 'Harem Money' His Majesty puts in my coffers. I have had made for me new dresses of scarlet, sapphire, orange, emerald, rose-pink, sliver, green, gold, and white—though I must point out that my clothing money amounts to far less than others I might name, such as Barbara the Main Castle and the new French Catholic whorish slut, Louise. But then I was always a modest girl—except for my silver things, which I always deface with my initials. It's all I can read anyway, so . . ."

"We have long pitied your misfortune, Nellie. That is why I invite you to visit me. I want to see up close how the downtrodden live."

Charlotte and Nell laughed at her witticism, but Abby could barely raise a smile. She had seen many of the downtrodden in Virginia, and when she went to St. James's Park earlier she viewed many on the fringes of the Park and on the streets who looked ill, displaced, and desperate. Did Charlotte ever think of these men, women, and children who populated London and the countryside? From what she was told, Nell Gwynn rose from the downtrodden to become the King's favorite. Had she too forgotten from where she came?

Nell tightened her face. "Abby, you are looking serious. That will not do. I have made it my business since I first came to the theatre to make others smile and feel overcome with admiration for me."

"I think that is what some call 'ambitious,' Nellie." Charlotte gestured for Abby to sip her wine.

"So I've heard. Abby, you must wonder if I feel myself exalted merely because I have been loved in the theatre and have shared the king's bed."

Charlotte added her assessment. "Perhaps not exalted, but surely modest."

"You are too witty for my tastes, Charlotte. But allow me to finish. Abby, I have no title other than the Darling Strumpet of the Land. I don't set myself up as anything better."

"Abby, did you know Nell Gwynn has the prettiest foot in England?"

"Now I am blushing—with pride at your truthfulness, Lady Durell. Although you might have added that I also have the loveliest legs on the stage." Abby deemed her lack of modesty completely inoffensive. Perhaps it was Nell's smile as she praised herself that suppressed any resentment or jealousy. Perhaps it was that she was just so likeable.

Charlotte pulled Abby toward her. "She has special dresses designed for some of her stage parts. Those that are really too short of length to be respected in polite company—wide and divided so that they may better fly up when our Nellie dances."

"The town has demanded it. I am a slave to their whims. That's what being an actress means."

Charlotte's face lost its gaiety. "But surely His Majesty will not want you acting now that he has moved you into Whitehall."

"I will soon stay away from the theatre—at least for a time. But I shall not stop doing what I do best." Nell punctuated her remark with a wink at Abby. She put the wine glass to her lips. "Rather nice, Charlotte. Much better than that imported urine you serve to your guests. Tell me. Are they as wild about tea drinking in Virginia, Abby?"

"No, not as it is here, Nell."

"I said to call me Nellie. You have passed my test and qualify for more familiarity."

"Well, I am most honored, . . . Nellie."

"To continue, of all things England has embraced since the restoration of the monarchy, this foul drink is the most repulsive. It has no taste, and only a woman of such pretense as Charlotte here would insist on coating one's palate with such piss." Charlotte could only grin at the teasing insult. "Everyone believes that 'The Bat' is the one mainly responsible for the import of such an impotent drink.

"The Bat?"

Charlotte gestured for Nell to speak more softly. "She means the queen, Abby. Queen Catherine. Nellie calls her 'The Bat.'"

Nell took Abby's hand. "True, but it is Charles's coinage. The queen is Portuguese, and most of their women are short, ugly, and for some reason proud—in their hideous black farthingales. His Majesty received a miniature portrait of her before she came to England, which did not, and I say again *did not*, reveal her pug nose and protruding front teeth." Nell pushed in her nose with one finger and thrust forward her teeth, to the delight of her companions. "She couldn't even close her lips because of her over-hanging front teeth." When he first saw her, the king told me he exclaimed, 'Odd's fish! I believe they've brought me a bat instead of a woman!'"

"Abby, the queen does not look that horrendous, nor do her ladies. Nellie is simply doing her acting again."

"Hardly that. Your friend Abby here will have opportunity to see for herself and judge the accuracy of my portrayal. But for all that, the queen is a good woman."

Letting go of Abby's hand, Nell asked her to speak of her years in Virginia and seemed enraptured by the account, whereas Charlotte was impatient to move the topic to something more interesting—especially because she had heard much about Virginia already.

"I wish I could have visited you there so you could have shown me the wilderness and the native inhabitants. I have only seen one of them. He was displayed here in London and drew so big of a crowd that I became envious. But since it is too late for you to show me Virginia, I would like to be your guide and show you the exotic areas to which respectable ladies like your hostess Lady Durell refuse to go. Delightful by-ways off the Strand and Fleet Street. Then down Tower Street to Tower Hill. Then back by way of Thames Street. Then down to the river itself and Puddle's Wharf. Places where any anxious woman may have all her anxiety washed away with a brew and a fuck."

"Nellie, please. That is too vulgar—even for you."

"Ah, there you lie. Nothing is too vulgar for me. Vulgarity provides the excellent flavoring to life. A dash here—a sprinkle there."

"And where did you learn that piece of wisdom—from the young Earl of Rochester?"

"I made it up myself, Charlotte. In any event, Abby, there are walls near the Strand if you prefer not to do your fucking lying down in a ditch near the Thames."

The last remark was too much for Abby's sensibilities. She put both her hands over her face and turned away. Nell came up behind her.

"False modesty and shame is the sure sign of a whore, you know—whether she be a wife or a lady—isn't that so, Charlotte?"

Being used to this lewd banter, Charlotte was unfazed. "Just imagine what she'd say to you, if she didn't like you, Abby."

Nell moved in front of Abby. "Forget about Whitehall and St. James's Park. Spend your time at London's many cock-fighting pits."

Charlotte wagged her finger at Nell. "You love both Whitehall and St. James's Park. You cannot deny that."

"Well, I will amend my recommendation somewhat and say that Abby must allow me to take her to St. James's Park in the middle of the night, for there she will see the God Dionysus and his five thousand devoted worshippers. There you will witness such grand ins and outs going on under every tree."

At that moment, Phoebe entered the room—her face revealing she had heard Nell's lewd remark. "Is there anything else you need, Lady Durell?" Phoebe refused to look at Nell, who had likely embarrassed the girl on other occasions.

"Nothing, Phoebe. You may go."

"Give up your Puritan gods, Phoebe, and let me show you the pleasures of worshipping Dionysus."

Phoebe turned and walked briskly out of the room, holding her hands in front of her face. Nell grinned in triumph.

"Is it your ambition to corrupt that poor girl?"

"As a matter of fact Charlotte, it is. So tell me, Abby. Did you have theatres in the land of tomahawks and two-headed serpents?"

"None that I knew of. Theatrical performances have been done in spaces resembling something like a theatre, but . . . no, I saw nothing of the kind myself in Virginia. Have you done your acting in several theatres or in just one?"

Charlotte had an answer at the ready. "Our darling Nellie has been the exclusive property of the King's Company . . . and of the King's Company."

"My, so damned witty, Charlotte. So very, very damned witty." Oddly, Charlotte appeared surprised and then almost disappointed in her witticism. She quickly lifted her smile as Nell continued. "I have not acted for the Duke's Company—meaning the king's brother—old dismal Jimmy, as the Scots call him." Abby asked how long Nell had been acting. "Six years now, which would make me old enough to know better and to know how better."

"She may be illiterate, but she does not lack for intelligence otherwise."

"Was that a compliment, Charlotte? Oh, but what a damned serious state I have put all of us in. I am an actress of the comedies; I do not favor the serious parts."

Charlotte winked at Abby. "Nellie, wasn't it Moll Davis who was last year immortalized by the poet Mr. Flecknoe as the "pride of the stage and darling of the court."

Nell's face turned sour. "Flecknoe is an idiot and an ass. Yes, Moll was *once* thought of in that way. But she, like Frances Stuart, is part of the king's past. I, on the other hand . . ."

Charlotte held up her hand. "But dear Nellie, you once truly hated Moll, didn't you? I seem to recall an incident in which you slipped a laxative substance in her food right before she was to see His Majesty."

Abigail's eyes expanded. "Did you really, Nellie?"

"Another of the many tales about me too good to deny. The story is that I found out Moll was to share the king's bed one night, and I offered her sweetmeats that I filled with jalap so that she would have to purge herself during the night. Charles told me his fiery pole soon dwindled to a dead cinder when she began farting uncontrollably."

"But the story is not true?"

"I would never say that, Abby."

After Nell and Abby shared yet another laugh, Charlotte continued her attempts to manipulate Nell's reactions. "Was it not also noted that on one occasion the loutish Sir John Coventry insulted you, for which the king rewarded him by having his nose slit to the bone?"

Nell's smile left her lovely face. "That is true. I was so surprised by the king's encouragement of that act. But I was more troubled by such a demonstration of violence from him than I was pleased by his courtly defense of my honor. I had not then, nor have I since, asked him to defend that which cannot be defended."

Abby's curiosity sought more admissions from the irrepressible Nell. "So His Majesty no longer sees Moll Davis?"

"The king has seen her since the brief time she was the major thorn in dear Lady Castlemaine's side. His Majesty is perhaps the world's most peculiar lover. To love and then leave is totally foreign to him. He will love and then promote, reward, visit occasionally, and sometimes even again poke and tickle, as if to verify that he had once done it more often. I have told him these charitable acts are simply his belief that the poor woman has so missed his regal scepter that in pity he reunites it with her lonely cunny. Besides, the king was never truly enamored of Moll's dancing, which was unequalled by any of us."

"You are the queen of the breeches roles, Nellie."

"Thank you, Charlotte. I was about to make the same claim. Although you did neglect to point out that other than my legs and feet, my ankles have been deemed the best on the stage—whether at the King's Theatre or the Duke's. Abby, I have often thought how much I wish we could tie down all the sour- faced Puritan men on those benches and force them to watch me in breeches. That would kill them or convert them to the English Church surely."

"May I ask something else about Moll Davis, Nellie?"

"Of course you may."

"How do you feel knowing that Moll has one of His Majesty's children?"

"Having the King's child is not an exclusive privilege by any means. My boy Charles is now almost seven months old and is already showing the king's features. Having one of the king's children is a shared occupation—except by the queen his wife. I believe His Majesty has now and will eventually have enough natural children to populate a small city. Besides I have no need to feel inferior to Moll Davis, now that I am again wishing to carry the king's child."

"Is your lady at home, Lockwood?"

"No, my Lord. She is off with her children. Exactly where I do not know."

Lord Brinton stared into Lockwood's eyes, searching for any indication the man was lying. "When do you expect her to return?"

"Late afternoon or early evening, my Lord."

"When she returns, be sure she remains here until I revisit her at eight tonight."

"Very well, Lord Brinton."

Brinton and the two men accompanying him returned to their carriage. Behind it was another carriage, inside of which, where Lockwood could not see them, were Burgess the dog handler and Mary Gibbons.

Lockwood watched both carriages drive off, but without one of the two men who had arrived with Brinton. He was standing not fifty feet from Lady Castlemaine's residence—waiting for her to return and likely instructed not to let her leave again."

"What did he want, Thomas?"

"He didn't say, my lady."

Barbara's face wore an expression of concern, which clashed with her lovely dark red dress and the deep red coloring of her cheeks and lips.

"I suppose I must be here when he returns. If only I maintained the power I possessed when I dispatched Lord Clarendon, I would see to it that Brinton was sent abroad. I often speak to the king about him, but His Majesty laughs at my complaints and believes the man really adores me but knows he could never have me in his bed. Therefore Brinton reacts to me with aloofness. I tell the king it is with malice and not aloofness, but then he only laughs again."

Lockwood's sense of chivalry turned his thoughts to protecting his lady against the machinations of Brinton, whatever they might be. Lockwood had recently become convinced Brinton was intent on destroying Lady Castlemaine, either by having her banished from London and the king's company or by something more dastardly. After all, Lockwood knew of others who wished his Lady dead or facially maimed—as the only ways to pull her hands free from the king.

"What is it, Thomas. You look frightened. Do you know something I should know?"

"No, my lady. Forgive me. I just cannot abide those who displease you or would interfere with your serenity."

"You are very special to me, Thomas." When she stepped toward him, Lockwood hoped she would reward his loyalty with a kiss. She did not, but rather brushed his cheek with two of her fingers as she walked past him and out of the room.

Tears welled in Lockwood's eyes as he responded to her gesture of affection. Her stepped to the window and whispered to the man keeping watch outside, "If you harm her in any way, I will kill you."

Chapter 19

"You lie!" Charlotte's reaction to what she believed was Nell's claim to be carrying another of the king's children was more animated than any reaction Abby had ever seen from her friend.

"Of course I lie—that's how I ended up with my first child."

Abby was more delighted than surprised by the admission. "It's appropriate, is it not, to offer my congratulations?

"As an actress, I accept all thanks, praise, applause, and congratulations, whether legitimate or not. But in this case you have both misunderstood. I said I am *wishing* to carry another of the king's issue—not that I am presently. Of course, perhaps I am and don't know it yet."

Charlotte tensed the muscles of her face. "Do you fear the king will disown the boy you do have?"

"I have of course thought of that possibility. Therefore, I am determined that, should his father refuse to own him or give him a title, I will call the child not Charles, but rather "The Bastard," and I will do so in public, wherever I am, until His Majesty does what is right."

Abby noticed that Charlotte's playful demeanor had altered to the point that she was casting troubled looks toward the labyrinth visible through the window. Was she worried about what business her husband and Sir Roger Earle were involved in? Abby made up her mind she would invite her friend to share her concerns and listen to hers as well. But now wasn't the time. The irrepressible Nellie Gwynn still commanded the room. Abby asked about her relationship with the writers of plays.

"I hold that a poet's play writing is the way he makes love to his favorite actress. That way he feels he can make her do and say whatever he desires. A sad substitute for issuing his commands in the sweet cool darkness of a bed, but the play writer takes pleasure on whatever sheets he can."

Charlotte turned back to her guests. "Do you think Abby would make a good player, Nellie?"

"Indeed. We can use more actresses to play the abused wife and jilted-lover parts anyway."

Abby sighed. "I have already played those parts in my life. There is no need to play them again." Nell laughed broadly as Charlotte accused Abby of exaggeration. "The abuse I received from my husband was exaggerated, but not the second part. And, no. Before you inquire, I am not at liberty to name the man who rejected my affections. Suffice it to say that it happened in Virginia several months after my husband died. So, can we know more about the beginnings of your relationship with His Majesty, Nellie?"

"He enjoyed my acting and singing and especially the fact that I liked to sit in the tiring-house conversing and entertaining men and women while in a state of partial undress. Since I always have to be witty, I told him if he wished to come behind the stage, I would dismiss all those men and women and receive him in a state of complete undress. He laughed at almost everything I said, but his eyes were smiling at me in a much more interesting way. To speak truthfully, I was disappointed I was not in his bed that very evening. But I remember the mighty Barbara already made a prior claim for that time. I would see His Majesty often after that, and he once took me to a tavern after he attempted to disguise his identity. He said he wanted to observe me in my other kingdom, the one into which I was born. My father was a tavern keeper, you see. Charles and I have always taken much delight in insulting as well as teasing each other. In fact, he never gets more amorous than after I have mimicked him to his face—his speech, his gestures, his general way. He always makes light of my devotion to gambling and my inability to read. And he knows that I will leap upon him and wiggle like a weasel whenever he pretends to find more interest in a book than he does in me."

Charlotte once more returned to the window. Abby was tempted to ask what was on her friend's mind, but she didn't wish to put a halt to Nell's entertaining admissions. "Nellie, is there a pet name you call the King?"

"I often call him—and sometimes in public as well—My Charles the Third."

"But he is Charles the Second of England. Is there something I don't understand?"

"I call him Charles the Third because he's the third in a line of men named Charles that I have spread myself for. I mention these men, and the king accuses me of being a bold, merry slut, but he loves my indelicate ways and one of our little jokes is for me to call out to him when he is with others, 'Charles, I hope I shall have your company tonight, shall I not?' And he calls out at other times, 'Nellie, you impudent, ill-bred tom-rig.' Everyone is so put off by that, and I do regret that the king is judged by many as lacking the proper seriousness of a monarch. But these are our own little intimacies. Even though there is fucking he does with others besides me, these insulting and shocking games he does *only* with me. I call him the 'black boy' because of his complexion and he showers me with 'damned little slut' as he kisses me all over my body, down to each toe on my perfect feet."

Abby realized her eyes had expanded to the size of large olives. "And do you share *other* enjoyments with him?"

"Of course I do. I share the king's affection for music. He and I sing often together, although I tell him his deep bass voice doesn't complement mine."

"Your bass voice?"

"Ha. You know what I mean, Abby. And we share an appreciation of portraits, especially those of me without even scarf or stocking on my body. Mr. Verelst has just finished his—but I am not totally naked. I am only showing an open front down to my waist. Besides, I don't much like it, as it makes my body smaller and more youthful than it really is. The king says the painter must have imagined me at twelve years of age. The Lely painting is closer to what I really look like, and His Majesty adores it, truly. I am only covered around my cunny and a little cherub boy is painted in staring at the prize, as if he would know what to do with it. His Majesty would visit me while it was being painted, and it was he who suggested the cherub boy, saying that when he was a little one of that innocent age, he used to stare at all the ladies' cunnies."

Charlotte had by this time moved to a side table and poured herself another glass of wine. Whereas Nell seemed oblivious to Lady Durell's preoccupation, Abby had become more convinced that her childhood friend knew her husband was planning something dangerous and was

143

deeply concerned it was something against the king. But Nell wasn't yet finished entertaining her new acquaintance.

"Abby, I assume Charlotte has told you about Charles's new delight— the little French pastry Louise de Kérouaille."

"I have heard of her, yes. You must be fearful she will replace you."

"'Little Catholic Carwell,' you mean? No, I have the English people on my side. I am after all the true-blue Protestant royal whore, not the Popish one. And Charles will listen to his people. He will fuck her and find her as dull as she is beautiful. She has no wit I have seen. She is no match for slutty Nell, and I am determined she will never be. Louise is but a child, though my own age. And yet at fourteen, I knew so much more and could even then have pleased the king more than she can now. It is only this need of his to construct a firm alliance with France that makes him pursue her. Besides, she was the king's dear sister's Maid of Honor. And she is presently one to Queen Catherine. I have called Louise the 'Weeping Willow' because she is quick to show His Majesty her pathetic tears. But now I have a new name for her. Her false airs and her fidgety emotional flights, in addition to her habit of cocking her head and squeezing her eyes half shut, as if she has brains enough to sift through whatever is said—has led me to call her Squintabella."

Abby thought the name especially humorous and looked at Charlotte for her reaction. Lady Durell immediately offered a smile, but there was nothing joyful about it.

"Then you think the king's interest is only political."

"Oh no. Not *only* political, but it is mainly so, I believe. His sister Minette would not let Charles near Louise when she first brought her here, but that only tempted him more. He has promised her a title already, and now that Minette is gone, he will certainly bed little Squintabella. And when I am in her company, I will not show my heart. I will be Nellie the laughing tom-rig, and let her deal with it. Barbara has had to. Well, I must go. I hope to see you again very soon, Abby. I have liked you much better than I expected to. Thank you, Charlotte for introducing us. Abby is not half as dull as you said she was."

Laughing at Nell's teasing, Abby embraced her. "You have met every expectation I had before meeting you and surpassed many of them."

"The next time I come, perhaps Lady Durell will serve lobsters and oysters and my favorite mulberries. But I will come only if the bill of fare does not include that dredge water you call tea. Perhaps when I return I too will have a new title, as does our Lady Castlemaine. The king has promised to make me Duchess of Whoreshire."

"Oh, Nellie."

"It's the title I deserve, Abby. Now your duchess must take her leave."

It was only minutes later that Abby wondered why Nellie failed to speak about the murder of her fellow actress Betty Keller at Whitehall.

The King's Company delivered another exuberant production this afternoon. The audience was for the most part decently behaved and receptive to all the performances—save that of young Anne Whitworth, who elicited laughter and jeers during and following her early entrance a third of the way through the play. What compelled her to make her appearance in the middle of a spirited father-son scene Michael Devlin couldn't fathom. The two male actors were in the middle of a comical discussion of dogs and cats, each man bragging on his respective domestic beast, when Anne came out immediately following the line "I wish I had my handsome bitch here to devour your vile feline." Anne's lack of experience caused her to sputter an apology to the audience and to her two fellow actors and stumble backwards off the stage. Devlin witnessed the catastrophe and knew Nellie Gwynn would have squeezed from the embarrassing moment every drop of bawdy humor. Even Devlin's darling Betty Keller would have come up with something that made the wrong entrance seem to work. But Anne was too young and had no chance to salvage the moment. Her subsequent entrances were met with boisterous barks and growls from both the pit and the boxes. Devlin thought it a miracle she managed to deliver her lines in the secondary scenes in which she appeared.

After she begged for his forgiveness and cried on his shoulder, Devlin realized it might take him longer to bed his young apprentice than he assumed. Emotionally, she was so much younger than her age, whereas he thought the opposite of Betty Keller, whose face, voice, and sweet breath came back to him and fueled his hatred of the king and his commitment to taking part in Charles's murder. Francis Gottlieb assured Devlin before the performance began that he would "gladly help to rid" the nation of its irresponsible monarch the following night. Gottlieb had no use for Richard Hansall and his Puritanism, but he swore to Devlin that he would set aside his feelings for the sake of England's future. Devlin wondered what his and Gottlieb's responsibilities would be when they approached the king near the home of Sir Joseph Willet. Would one of them stab Charles to death, or would they all take part as had Caesar's assassins. Which of them would say, "Speak hands for me," as Shakespeare's Casca did in the play? Devlin felt his stomach tighten. If his nerves so reacted tomorrow evening, he would simply whisper "Betty" and his body would do what he asked it to without hesitation.

"It's Lord Brinton, Lady Castlemaine. Shall I tell him you are still out?"

"No, Thomas. Let him in and I will greet him." Barbara's emphasis on "greet" suggested to Lockwood that she would gladly take a sword and run the king's counselor through the heart.

Brinton did not enter with the Earl of Lauderdale, as Lockwood anticipated, but rather with two other men, both of whom Lockwood didn't recognize. Each man was surely over seventy years of age, and Lockwood assumed Brinton brought aged associates who would be immune to Lady Castlemaine's charms. The three men formally nodded to Barbara, as Brinton encouraged her to sit, but she remained standing.

"I am here on the king's advisement to ask you a few questions regarding the murder of Elizabeth Keller." Barbara doubted he had come on the king's "advisement"—whatever that meant. Brinton once more gestured for Barbara to sit, as one of the older gentlemen took his place behind Lady Castlemaine's chair, while the other stepped toward the fireplace.

She now sat. "Before you begin, Lord Brinton, I have no knowledge relating to that bitch's death—neither how it was done nor by whom. I am highly insulted that you have come here to ask me about such things."

Brinton ignored her protestation. "I wonder if we might have a fire. This room is uncomfortable in its chillness."

"I never have a fire in this room, Lord Brinton. I do not like the smell of ashes or the view of a dirty fireplace in my receiving room. If you are cold, we can move to another room."

Brinton waved his hand. "No need. I think this room will do with a little warming. I see there are several pieces of oak resting on the andirons."

Barbara fought her impatience. "I prefer to have wood in the fireplace—for display only."

"Of course." Brinton addressed one of the elderly men. "Nicholas, is there enough wood and kindling to begin a fire?"

"There is enough wood, Lord Brinton, but the kindling is . . . Wait, what is this?" The older gentleman bent down and picked from behind the logs a black casket. "This was in with the wood, my lord."

"Bring it here, Nicholas." Brinton took the item and placed it on the table. "This is a very fine box, wouldn't you agree, Lady Castlemaine?" Barbara was surprised and confused at the discovery. "Yes, it is most ornate and seems to have held something very valuable. Let's open it and see what it contains." Barbara strained to see the contents of the black casket before Brinton picked it up and showed her the inside. "Nothing here now, but obviously a knife once resided in the casket."

Barbara's face displayed more fear than confusion. "I have no idea how that ended up in the—"

Brinton stood with dramatic flair. "Wait. I know this casket. His Majesty possessed this. It held a knife once owned by his father, the first King Charles." Barbara sighed involuntarily; she too had seen the casket and the knife. "The knife that was found thrust into the body of Elizabeth Keller—the 'bitch' as you called her, Lady Castlemaine. As it turns out, I believe I have no need to ask you any questions at all. We will take our leave and allow you to enjoy your unheated room."

Having remained seated until the men left, Barbara finally stood, ignoring Lockwood's offer to bring her something warm to drink. She walked to her bedroom with her head elevated and her lips clamped together. Only after she locked the door behind her did she allow her emotions their expression.

CHAPTER 20

"So we agree that Lord Brinton's death can be delayed at least for a time. Good. I have decided we will not meet tomorrow, Roger. When we receive word of the king's death, we will come together to testify against Hansall." Lord Durell finished his French brandy and ushered Earle to his carriage.

"I am still fearful, my lord. He will surely implicate us."

"But who will believe him? Our word will carry weight, not his."

"Someone might testify that he has been here to Dove-Raven House on several occasions."

"That is doubtful. If so, we will say that he came here to supply us with information about the radical dissenters. We will then express our horror over having been misled by one of the most radical dissenters of them all. At most, we will be guilty of naiveté. Never fear, Roger."

"I wish I had your confidence, my lord."

"Of course, we can always have him killed before he can bring testimony against us."

Earle's eyes broadened. "Will that be possible?"

"I will see it is done, if it makes you more comfortable."

Earle left Dove-Raven House relieved and more confident of the plot's success. With the weaker James assuming the throne, until Durell and others revealed his secret conversion to Roman Catholicism, Earle's power and influence would be considerably expanded and buttressed by his political connections.

When Earle returned to his residence near Whitehall, he alighted from the carriage to find a most attractive young woman standing near the entrance. She was unaccompanied, yet was certainly not one of the city's many prostitutes, so many of whom took advantage of the theatre-goers— the association of the theatres with such illicit behavior influencing both his and Lord Durell's decision to avoid being seen there, even though Lord

Durell made no attempt to dissuade his wife from attending. But this woman was dressed too fashionably to be one of the so-called "Covent Garden Nuns." Earle wondered if she was in distress.

"Can I be of any assistance to you, young woman?"

"No, sir. But I can be of assistance and pleasure to you."

Earle was immediately suspicious, but he still could not take his eyes off the young woman's face, which suggested her intense interest in him. After looking to see if anyone was noticing, Earle resisted the urge to ask the price for having her, leaving the possibility that she had a sincere, not a financial, interest in having him sexually. Earle was handsome enough to win the affections of several women he had courted, and the one he married responded to him eagerly. That she and the infant she attempted to deliver died in her bed had so far committed him to a life without another spouse. But he had periodically engaged in affairs with wives and sisters of men he dealt with politically, but no one as young and attractive as the woman standing before him.

"You imply that you would please me, but your motive escapes me. We don't know each other." Again, he refused to mention any motive that might embarrass or insult her.

"I have seen you many times and have been pleased whenever I did. When I mentioned that fact yesterday to someone you know well, he said he would like to reward you for your loyalty and counsel with something other than money or the more familiar gifts. I was the one who hinted that I might serve as adequate reward. I swore to keep secret the man's name, but I am sure you must know."

Earle smiled. Lord Durell—who else? "Then I accept his gracious gift and yours, my dear. Please come inside. It's too cold to stand out here any longer." As they stepped inside, Earle whispered, "May I know your name, my pretty lady?"

She whispered in reply, "Lucy, Sir Roger."

"Your name means 'of light, of the dawn,' and you are as welcome as a bright morning, my girl."

"Thank you, sir. Now will you do me the honor of allowing me to see your bedroom? Let us go quietly so we may not disturb your servants."

"My man is away. There is no one inside the house." Earle touched her neck and soft hair as they walked to and then entered his bedroom. She allowed him to step ahead of her to the side of the bed, while she remained near the closed door. "For the sake of propriety, may I request that you turn your back while I undress, sir? I will then go to the bed and go under the sheets. Then you too may undress and come to me."

Earle felt his sexual passions aroused as they had not been since his wife was alive. He turned his back and watched, with amusement, the alteration of the fabric on the front of his breeches. He would not ask her to hurry; he would say nothing until he felt her unclothed body in his bed. His next carnal thought was interrupted by a sensation against the back of his neck. At first he believed it was the bite of a spider, but a moment later he felt the thin blade making its way through to the front side of his neck. As he collapsed, he saw the shadow of something being lifted above him. He looked toward the door and saw it was still closed, but Lucy was no longer in the room. As he grabbed for the blade in his throat, he found that it had been suddenly extracted. Feeling his head pulled back against the thighs of another person in the room, Earle sensed the thin blade entering the side of his head in front of his left ear.

"It's unfortunate you will be away tomorrow evening, Your Majesty. I am meeting with several of the Merry Gang—including Sackville and Sedley, for a scintillating game of All Fours, and you would have been heartily welcome company, especially if you knew how I have spun the name."

Charles couldn't help smiling at young Rochester's expression. For all the young man had done to earn his ire, the king couldn't help forgiving him and himself for tolerating what he knew were Rochester's private and public satire of the monarchy. Charles too much adored the young man's joking, fine-edged wit, and intelligence to banish him forever from his company. "So how have you spun the name All Fours, John?"

"The one who plays his six-card hands the best every hour—with his trumping and capturing—will receive five minutes of time trumping the young woman who will be *on* all fours, while the rest of us watch. Of course, I plan on doing most of the trumping. If I manage to hold out for each five-minute period, I should be able to fuck until the dawn breaks."

"And you wanted me to be there and deny you such pleasure?"

"Oh no, Your Majesty. I wanted you to be there to watch and applaud your loyal subject's trumping for crown and country."

Charles laughed and rubbed his finger across his top lip where his narrow moustache resided. "Have I told you that you are prone to false statement, exaggeration, and immodesty, my good Earl of Rochester?"

"You have, my king. But it would be well to remember that I prepared sweet Nellie Gwynn's channel for you to sail into as often as you like."

"And I remember that you only recently and for the hundredth time insulted the Countess of Castlemaine, for which you will pay handsomely when I inform her of that you have said."

"She will long be the subject of my satire, sire. I already have lines for a poem I'll get around to putting on paper.

Charles couldn't resist. "Your king orders you to share them at once."

"I always—well perhaps I haven't always—obeyed His Majesty. Let me see. Here are a few I can cite exactly. She says to a counselor knight:

I'd fain have a prick, knew I how to come by it.

I desire you'll be secret and give your advice:

Though cunt be not coy, reputation is nice.

Then the knight tells her to retire "to some cellar in Sodom."

Where porters with black-pots sit round a coal-fire;

There open your case, and Your Grace cannot fail

Of a dozen of pricks for a dozen of ale.

Charles laughed heartily as Rochester took a bow. "I will tell her your lines and she will knock you straight on your back."

"If she does, I will beg to be allowed to kiss the hand that felled me."

"John, if I must order you banished, it will certainly be a black day for me."

"And for England, Your Majesty."

As Charles grabbed both of Rochester's shoulders and shook him vigorously, he caught sight of Lord Brinton standing at the door. "Come join us, Henry."

"I fear I have unpleasant news, Your Majesty."

Rochester finished his wine in one swallow. "Then this is no place for the likes of me. I beg your leave, sire. I have a game of All Fours to prepare for."

After Rochester left the room, Brinton prefaced his news with a gratuitous "He will come to sorely disappoint you, my king."

"I have no doubt he will, but what tragedy do you wish to share with me this time, Henry?"

"I am saddened to tell you that we found this at the Countess Castlemaine's." Brinton signaled the elderly gentleman to come forward. "Nicholas, if you would give that to His Majesty."

"What is this?" A moment after he asked, Charles knew what it was.

"Nicholas here found the casket carefully hidden among the pieces of oak in Lady Castlemaine's front fireplace."

"The one she never uses."

"Yes. As she told me, Your Majesty."

Charles ran his finger along the depressed area where his father's knife had been placed—the knife found thrust in the body of Elizabeth Keller. After several moments of silence, the king asked, "What was her reaction when you discovered it, Henry?"

"She remained silent, as though . . . well, she was aloof and austere as always, Your Majesty." Brinton anticipated the king's next question.

"Perhaps someone placed it there to implicate her, Henry."

"And I have thought of that. And it is possible, I suppose. But with the evidence already given by Bridget Warren, I would serve you ill if I didn't advise that Lady Castlemaine be more carefully and intensely questioned. I have spoken to one of your most trusted legal advisers, the Earl of Gatesby, who has agreed to undertake the task. I don't recommend having her questioned by a committee or representative of Parliament, seeing that the body is no friend of yours."

"To hell with Parliament. Gatesby is preferable—just Gatesby alone and no committee."

"Of course, Your Majesty."

"And yet Gatesby has no love for Lady Castlemaine."

"Only because he has always desired to protect you and your reputation. You have often taken his advice. You trust him and know he has the wellness of the realm always forefront in his mind."

"When do you think she should be questioned?"

"Gatesby thinks it best that it be no later than tomorrow evening."

"Very well. I'll leave it up to you and Gatesby as to when and where. If Lady Castlemaine refuses to be questioned, inform her that it is my wish. No, rather it is my command that she agree to it."

"I will see it done, Your Majesty."

After Brinton reached his carriage, he turned to his elderly companion. "Nicholas, I am off to speak with Lord Gatesby. I only hope I can find him with his breeches pulled up and his cock settled in for the night."

The old man readjusted his periwig. "I'm confused, Lord Brinton. I've been with you every minute since we left Lady Castlemaine's apartments. When did you first speak to Lord Gatesby?"

"I didn't. He knows nothing about any of this. Have a good evening, Nicholas."

All the actors left the King's Theatre following the afternoon performance and the short rehearsal of tomorrow's play that followed it. Devlin arrived to witness only the final minutes of the rehearsal. Now he was alone with Joan Pegge, who was gnawing at the skin of an orange she had not sold during the performance.

"You've been of considerable assistance to me, Joan. Here is what I promised you." Devlin handed her a small purse, which she shook in order to hear the coins jangle inside.

"I trust I may have my position another year, Mr. Devlin."

"You may have it for as long as I am here."

"Good." She spit to the floor one of the orange peels she had raked off with her sharp but rotting bottom teeth.

"Now I want you to remember what I tell you now."

"My mind isn't so far gone with drink as not to remember what you tell me, sir."

"Tomorrow immediately after the performance, I am going down across the Thames to Lambeth, where I'm to see two young Spanish women, who have a desire to perform on the stage. I will remain there for the night and return here late the following morning. Remember that I have told you this."

"I will not forget, Mr. Devlin."

"Good. Now you may go home."

Ten minutes after they parted, Devlin stepped behind one of the stage doors and waited for his actor Francis Gottlieb, who had been dispatched to bring Richard Hansall to the theatre. The two men joined him at the exact time Devlin requested.

"Damn it, man. Are you having second thoughts?" Hansall was irritated by having been summoned to the theatre.

"You misjudge me. I have asked you here to make clear before we act tomorrow night that I expect directly to take part in the king's demise. I will not be relegated to standing watch for you or holding our horses while you act. My hand will be in it."

Hansall smiled. "I apologize for my suspicions, Michael. I assumed the worst of you. You will indeed assist me in the murder of the king. We will both wield whatever weapon we chose to dispatch him. Mr. Gottlieb here has assured me that he will take care of Willet's wife.

Devlin turned to his actor, who nodded approval of Hansall's plan. "I assume then that we will leave the house on foot."

"No we will have horses ready to take us further north from London for half a mile or so, before we turn back and reenter the city from the east. A cry will go out after we ride off, and His Majesty's guards will be told the assassins headed south and west."

"And who will point them in that direction? And who will see to our horses?"

"I have someone who will do both."

"Can this person be trusted?"

Oddly, Hansall laughed. "Yes. One of the true-believers. Trust can be assured."

Devlin glanced at Gottlieb to see if he knew the identity of the man who would perform such an important service, but the actor gave no indication that he did.

The three men shook hands and agreed to meet at a place near the Willet home—each arriving separately from different directions. Devlin felt relieved and satisfied by how matters would proceed, but he didn't like the inclusion of a fourth player. Who was the man? Could he indeed be trusted? Could Hansall?

CHAPTER 21

In the fading light, Abigail Fayette once more noticed Lord Durell heading for the high-hedged labyrinth behind Dove-Raven House. Lady Durell was in another part of the house speaking with her dressmaker about her new dress with the short sleeves over chemise sleeves. It seemed Charlotte wasn't at all pleased with the size of the four puffs on the sleeves. She asked Abby to wait in another part of the house. "I shouldn't wish you to see my angry side when I am disappointed with my dresses." Abby vividly recalled the time when a younger Charlotte attacked her hat-maker for the thickness of the plume he placed on her head dress, chasing and pummeling the poor fellow with the hat until he pleaded for mercy. As humorous as she found her friend's irritation at poorly fitted or constructed dresses and hats, Abby's mood was pensive as she observed Lord Durell waiting at the entrance to the labyrinth. What exactly was Charlotte's husband plotting?

While in Virginia, Abby heard many complaints about the king's character and policies, and once she overheard two visitors from London express their belief that Charles would be murdered before the year was out for "crimes against his people," which included the immoral company he kept—women and men both—and his "disgraceful and perjured" acts against the Irish and Scots, which led to betrayals of various kinds. Abby's father privately called the new king an indolent and dissipated man by nature— "more an indecent foreigner than a true Englishman, who devoted himself to ease and profligacy than to the betterment of the realm." He went on to predict that Charles "had best have a watchful guard with him wherever he goes, as well as throughout and near Whitehall." Was this why his daughter now believed Lord Durell might be involved in a plot against the king's life? Just as the darkness made impossible her seeing Lord Durell's figure plainly, she saw someone else come to him and then both disappear into the labyrinth. Who it was she couldn't be sure.

"What are you staring at, Abby? Can you even see anything out there at this time of day?" Charlotte seemed delighted, and Abby assumed she concluded business with her dressmaker on a satisfactory note. "Drag your face to a mirror and make what adjustments you must. We have a surprise guest." Abby hoped that Nell Gwynn decided to return to Dove-Raven house, but Charlotte's flutter suggested it was someone she felt more important.

"You don't mean the Queen, do you Charlotte?"

"In a manner of speaking. Countess Castlemaine has sent word ahead that she wishes another visit—one so soon after her last."

Abby wondered why Barbara decided to return. Charlotte had no idea, but guessed that something salacious had happened at court Lady Castlemaine simply had to share immediately. Still perplexed by what she overheard regarding Lord Durell's apparently secretive plans, Abby debated whether she should talk openly about her concerns to Charlotte, who had left the room to speak to Phoebe. One further glanced toward the labyrinth revealed nothing owing to the increasing darkness.

"Abby, I do so wish our friend Barbara had fewer enemies than she has at present." Charlotte returned to the room with a piece of fruit in her hand, which she cut and shared with her friend. "She has affected too much in this country merely because she has for so long been the king's favorite."

"But not exclusively so, as you have been at pains to remind me."

"Yes, but Barbara is the only one of the king's mistresses ever to determine public and foreign policy. Nellie doesn't care, as she says, a 'shit about it' and neither have any of the others who have been with the king. Barbara has been our real queen, Abby. Catherine is nothing, and the only way she might have been is for her to have conceived an heir. And she has been unable to do that. I am not as superstitious as many in this country, but I would not swear against Barbara's having done something to curse the queen's womb."

"Oh, Charlotte, you exaggerate wildly. Besides, you have implied that she has now lost much of her power and that Nellie and France's Louise are the present competitors for her now abandoned throne."

Charlotte began to pace—clearly agitated. "They may replace Barbara in Charles's bed, but neither—and no one to come—will ever claim her throne. It may be that the king is only now claiming his own throne, after ten years of allowing Lady Castlemaine to sit in it."

"Please excuse my interruption." Phoebe entered with a note, which she handed to Charlotte. Abby smiled at the servant, who raised her eyebrows in reply.

"It is from Louise de Kéroualle, Abby. She regrets she cannot come in the morning as promised. She says that the king—and she underlines "king" four times—demands her presence. She will, however, be happy to come later in the week, if I so wish it."

"And do you?"

"Of course." Charlotte ceased her pacing and cut another piece of fruit. Abby could only laugh.

"You wish to bring Louise into the lion's den you are apparently hollowing out."

"And I trust her fate will be worse than Daniel's." Charlotte suddenly began dancing a sprightly French *Rigaudon*. "But we shall have a clash of lions before that, Abby. Would you like another slice of fruit?"

"Can you tell me where she is, Mr. Lockwood? Please, I must know."

Lockwood stood at the door and looked down into the broad face of Bridget Warren, seeing her eyes and cheeks matted with tears. He couldn't imagine she had come with a message from the king; she was never employed for such services. Had she discovered something relating to the murder of Betty Keller? He knew she had discovered the body initially.

"Why must you know where she is, Bridget?"

"I must speak with her, sir. It is very important that I do so."

"She wishes such requests to come through me first—and you have given me no good reason why I should tell you where she is."

"I see you don't trust me, Thomas."

He bristled at her familiarity. His services to the Countess Castlemaine were far more intimate than those Bridget Warren performed for the king. "It is my duty to be suspicious, woman."

"It has to do with her safety—her life."

Lockwood had not expected such a response. He raised his fist and barely restrained himself from delivering a blow to the side of her head. Instead, he grabbed her by her hair and yanked forcefully. "Tell me what it is or I will pull every hair from your miserable head."

Bridget begged for his patience and promised she would tell him before she spoke to Lady Castlemaine. "Take me to her, sir. She will want to hear it from directly from me."

Offering an apology for his outburst, Lockwood released his grip, and the both of them went outside to secure a coach.

"You make Phoebe unable to say "Madam" without shaking, Barbara."

"As I said before, she fears me." Barbara attempted to readjust several wisps of her hair, which had come undone during the journey to Dove-Raven House. Abby was concerned Lady Castlemaine had experienced danger on the road from London, given that Barbara's face displayed signs of tension and fear.

Charlotte handed Barbara a glass of French *Bourgogne*. "Abby is interested in knowing more about your relationship with your husband. Would you mind speaking more of it?" Charlotte avoided looking at her friend; therefore she didn't detect Abby's anger at being used so.

Barbara seemed confused by the request, but acceded to it nevertheless. "It is not a subject I speak of with any pleasure, but I can understand why you find it interesting, Abby. My husband attempted to mold and then subdue me. He was doomed to fail from the moment he made his initial attempt. He could not understand that I had been in love before him, with Lord Chesterfield, who was both loving and cruel—and that, if anything, is what molded me."

Abby dismissed her momentary pique at Charlotte. "May I ask how long your husband was unaware of your relationship with the king?"

"Publicly, he acted as if it took months—months of suspicions unsatisfied, of gossip unsubstantiated. But in my heart, I know he realized immediately—even before I had been in His Majesty's bed. It was on my face and in the sound of my voice. A woman who loves can never disguise such things. And, then, he himself had an advantage of it, for when I was not able to be with Charles, I shared my violent passions with my husband, but with eyes tightly shut, acting out my deep and committed lust for the soon-to-be new and rightful King of England." She paused, realizing that the inflections of her voice had revealed too much. She attempted to regain her equanimity by quickly changing the subject. "But enough of that miserable topic. I'm sure you both would enjoy hearing what is happening at court.

The women spoke about the men and women at Whitehall with Barbara jocularly mentioning the poet Dryden's description of the age as a "laughing, quaffing, and unthinking time." Still, Abby couldn't fail to notice Barbara's evident concern over something she hadn't yet shared. Charlotte winked at Abby and mentioned Barbara's beauty in contrast with the plainness of Charles's queen.

"No, Charlotte, she has never been as ugly as many have portrayed her. Still, when I first saw her my heart leaped. A woman who shares intimate secrets with a man knows what he finds desirable. I immediately realized she could never satisfy him. Catherine of Braganza was the Portuguese Infanta, unknowing of any English when she arrived. Yes, I knew he would have to marry—he told me he needed an heir and the people a queen and that any well-placed virgin would do, except a German princess. But for the first two years of his being mine, I foolishly held to some hope that I would have my marriage annulled or that my husband would die. And then I would marry the king, have my daughter legitimized and then bear him a male heir to the throne, the very boy named Charles that I delivered soon after his marriage. When she came to England, he was with me, and she was forced to wait. And then when he left me to go to her, I rewarded him by striking his face as hard as I could."

Abby's face expanded. "Did the king strike you back?"

"Charles is too kind-hearted to ever hurt me in that way. He has on occasion drawn back his hand, but he would never hit his darling 'baby-face.' For that is what he once loved to call me—his 'darling and loving baby-face.'" Barbara's eyes dropped, and she brought the wine glass to her lips to hide her reaction to the memory.

Charlotte once again winked at Abby, who was displeased that her friend was once more attempting to elicit and manipulate Barbara's emotions. "But Catherine has not produced an heir—and that should please you, Barbara."

"Yes, she had several miscarriages. I cannot lie and say I regretted any of them. His other children, whether from the whore Moll Davis or his first from Lucy Walter, that charming young Monmouth, have caused me pain and concern for my own litter. But any children given him by Catherine would eventually have power over mine and would likely avenge the injury I had done to their mother and force mine into penury or exile. I have had to do everything I could to prevent such a thing from ever happening. The king refuses to own my last, though he loves the others and has provided for all of them. In each instance I had ways to force him to give my children what I wanted for them. But now I cannot move him."

Abby wished to soothe Barbara's noticeable pain. "The king is generous. He will always provide for them."

"He would go weeks without dining with his queen. He would stay with me through the night, go off early, and return to wake me before noon. I was so comfortable then, knowing each day what I was to expect."

"Barbara, tell Abby about the Duke of York's interest in you as well."

"There, Charlotte, you make me smile. James did at first, before he realized the intensity of Charles and my love. He always wanted what his brother had. All brothers do. But poor James's mistresses were often so plain and uninteresting that Charles would say they must have been 'imposed on him by his confessors as a kind of penance.' But in one important way James has passed his brother. He now has two legitimate children, daughters, who will come to the throne if Catherine produces no heir, which she will not. I will at least have that consolation."

"And there were others who also wished to bed you." This time, Charlotte caught the disapproving look of her friend Abby.

"I have taken what men have given, enjoyed their compliments, and dismissed all obligations to serve their interests. Others who have looked at me do so because I fascinate them, even now in my publicized decline. For a woman to know a man wants her in bed is flattering but often tedious. But when a woman knows the man would be completely enraptured if only he could hear her voice or touch her fingers or simply admire what she wears—that is the truest and most lasting pleasure a woman can know."

"But His Majesty always enjoyed your humor, Barbara."

"Yes, Charlotte, although we rarely laughed loudly when we shared our wit. I amused him only to the point of making him smile. Only once did I say something, a vulgar play on words I believe it was, that made him laugh uproariously. No, it was more quiet laughter, mainly smiles, the merriment restrained by his romantic preoccupations. I think a man who constantly desires a woman cannot forget his passions, no matter how amusing the moment."

"Did the king love your flattery of him?"

"No, Abby. He never liked me to flatter him, even though I would insist on doing so. You see, as a king he is always flattered, sincerely or not. A man constantly aware of his power to inspire servitude enjoys—in fact, needs—to serve another himself. He needs to be the one providing the compliments. And I only increased his ardor whenever I pretended not to hear them or if I received them with seeming indifference." Barbara sighed and looked away, visibly troubled. Charlotte brought the wine to refill Barbara's glass.

"Barbara, something has happened, hasn't it? You are not yourself. Tell me what it is."

Barbara rose and walked to the window, out from which she could only see darkness. "I came here to confide in you, Charlotte."

"Oh, I am deeply sorry. I will leave the two of you alone."

"No, no, Abby. You have not made me hesitate. I thought at first I would find relief in just talking about the latest gossip, but I have unforgivably revealed too many of my feelings. I have been a bore, I know."

"You have been no such thing. What relief are you seeking? What has happened to you?" Again, Abby believed Charlotte was too vigorous in her probing of Lady Castlemaine.

"You have no doubt heard of the murder at Whitehall—of Charles's recent plaything Elizabeth Keller."

"We have." Abby answered the question intended for Charlotte because she didn't wish her friend to give voice to her apparent interest and delight in the matter.

"Lord Brinton claims that I killed her—or had her killed."

"He cannot believe such a thing."

"But he does, Charlotte. I'm afraid of his influence over the king. I imagine myself being arrested in the middle of the night. I had to get away, so I came here. I may need you to provide me with a character—with some words that can convince the king I could never have done such a thing, in spite . . . in spite of what I may have said about the girl to others."

Abby imagined Barbara publicly threatened harm to Elizabeth Keller as well as to the king in private.

"You know I will do whatever I can to dissuade anyone from acting on Brinton's ridiculous assumption."

Barbara was about to kiss Charlotte goodbye when Phoebe entered the room.

"What is it, Phoebe?" This time Charlotte grinned at Abby.

Phoebe was evidently frightened to make the announcement. At that moment, Abby recalled Charlotte's remark about a forthcoming clash of lions and knew exactly who had just arrived.

CHAPTER 22

"Anne, you possess an intoxicating charm which will make you rise quickly among London's women players. You merely need further polish, and then you will outrank Betty Boutell, Moll Davis, Meg Hughes, Elizabeth Knepp, the Marshall sisters, and even our dear Nellie Gwynn herself." Devlin was unable articulate the name Elizabeth Keller.

"You make me blush, sir. I could never be as good as any of these women—and certainly never as good as Nellie."

Devlin couldn't tell if Anne truly felt her modesty or was merely playing coy. He didn't care. He only wanted to possess her person, which made him dismiss caution and patience over how long he would wait until he attempted to bed her. Thoughts of the act he would commit with Hansall and Gottlieb tomorrow night stimulated his aggression. Why wait any longer to indulge in such pleasure? The death of the king would upset her, and it might take him even longer to convince her to offer her body to him.

"I wish you to try on one of Nellie's costumes—to see if it needs altering before you assume the role." Anne's reaction was what he expected. She evinced a young girl's excitement at both donning the clothing of such a noted actress and at assuming she would soon be assaying Nell Gwynn's roles. Devlin handed her one of the outfits Nell wore in James Howard's *The Mad Couple* three years earlier. "Put it on, Anne."

She took the garment and waited for Devlin to leave the tiring-house where the actors made their costume changes, but he remained. "Sir, I will need to undress." After looking at her lovely and innocent face, Devlin finally agreed to turn his back while she removed her dress. "I would feel more comfortable behind this, then." She took Nellie's outfit and stepped behind the Chinese screen Devlin had recently purchased for the King's Theatre—to be used both on and off the stage. Anne attempted to converse with Devlin about this afternoon's performance but heard nothing from him. She ceased speaking as her dress fell to the floor and the screen folded open. "Mr. Devlin, I am not yet . . ." Her words conveyed more embarrassment than fear.

"As I long hoped to find you, dearest one." Devlin extended the palm of his hand and placed it on her exposed neck before sliding it down between her breasts. Anne was too stunned to pull his hand away. Instead, her head moved from side to side as her mouth shaped the word "no"—a word she was unable to fully articulate.

"You need not fear me. I wish now only to kiss you and feel your softness with my hands." His left hand joined his right massaging the top of her breasts. "Later, we will enjoy each other more fully." After a moment, Devlin lifted his hands and stopped Anne from moving her head. Her lips had just shaped another "no" when he brought his mouth to hers and kissed her ardently. As he expected, her breath tasted of the mint leaves she liked to chew. He broke his kiss and lowered his head to feel her neck and breasts with his lips. Now she was finally able to speak her "no." She quickly lowered her torso to pick up her dress and her chin slammed down on Devlin's nose. She made her escape from the dressing room while his eyes filled with tears from the pain. Once the discomfort subsided, Devlin's anger at her actions turned to confidence that she now understood what it would take for her to succeed as an actress with the King's Company. Devlin gave no thought to the possibility that his head might be hanging from Tower Bridge the next time Anne stepped on stage.

"Charlotte, what a liar you have become. You deliberately invited Lady Castlemaine here so the two of us might entertain you for an hour or so with our mutual antagonisms. I'm surprised you haven't arranged for Squinting Louise to make a threesome of it." Nell looked about for Barbara, while Charlotte continued to insist that Lady Castlemaine took it upon herself to come without invitation. "So I assume your friend Abigail is presently keeping the lioness at bay."

"When Barbara heard your voice in the hallway, she dragged poor Abby out to the garden, demanding I send you back to London."

Nell threw back her head and laughed. "Let the beast in. As I have told

JOHN VANCE

you, I fear her no longer. As for the French slut Louise, make wager how long I can be civil to my new rival before she forces my normally virginal tongue to spread its legs and begin its violent humping."

"You have quite a promiscuous sense of imagery, Nellie. Happily, you are not a poet."

"You are correct, dearest Charlotte. I have advanced myself far better by writhing between the sheets than by writing on the top of them."

"Indeed." Charlotte poured her guest wine and glanced out the window, but it was now too dark to see anyone moving about.

"But I return to the subject of Squintabella. You should ask the king about her endearing sense of time, Charlotte. The bitch only fascinates him more because she seems to have no conception of the clock."

Nor of the week, Charlotte concluded, because she had just received a note from Louise looking forward to her visit "next week." How wonderful it would have been to have all three of these women locked in a circle hurling recriminations. Abby surely would be impressed by her dear friend's ability to arrange that event. Charlotte handed Nell the glass of wine.

"Thank you, my dear Lady Durell." As Nellie took her initial sip, she grinned conspiratorially. "We'll be more easily manipulated on your board and more likely to shed blood if Lady Castlemaine and I are drunk—is that it? I assume you've also plied her with this delicious wine?"

"Something to that effect. Oh Nellie, I am horrible, aren't I?"

"Yes, but that is why I love you so dearly." She saw a half-drunk glass of wine resting on a table. "Is this the Countess Castlemaine's leavings?"

"I believe so, yes."

Then let me do what they say I do best. Devour her Ladyship's remnants." Nell tossed off the rest of her own glass and consumed in one draught the remaining wine in Barbara's. "Now, I am fully prepared for battle. Bring her on."

"She will emerge in a moment, I am sure. So tell me. Were you with His Majesty last night?"

"Don't you know that it is unseemly to ask a lady about something like that?"

"But as you have so proudly told me, you are no lady."

167

"Nor am I ever like to be. No, I slept alone last night. The king was without me, mourning the loss of his recent treat Betty Keller."

Charlotte poured Nell another glass. "What do you know of her death, Nellie? I sincerely hope you had nothing to do with it—or any knowledge of it before she was killed."

Nell's face dropped. "Hardly the subject for a social visit, Charlotte. The king spent the night with his queen, who was ill once again. It has long been her way of getting her husband's presence in her bedchamber. He sits and holds her hands and lets his dogs kiss them. There he sits, with his sick queen, her six frights—those dreadful Portuguese maids of hers—and His Majesty's four spaniels barking and licking his and Catherine's olive hands. I have told Charles that two more dogs would make six and therefore fit husbands for the frights. Well, I see that I have amused you with my assessment. I think it best I leave if Lady Castlemaine refuses to come inside and face me. After all, I am the intruder."

"You seem uncomfortable, Nellie. Are you that afraid of her?"

"Hardy that, Charlotte. Hardly that."

"Don't frighten the poor girl, Charlotte." Barbara stood at the other end of the room with a nervous Abby. "Perhaps she may have something of value to share with us." Abby thought the two women eyed each other as two mastiffs might a moment before they attacked each other's throat.

Charlotte's smile could not be suppressed, much to Abby's chagrin. "I believe we all are acquainted with each other."

Barbara lofted her chin in her best aloof manner. "Our circles do not overlap, Charlotte, even though you have attempted to make them do so. I was brought up a Villiers, one of the best family names in the realm—while poor Ellen here had her education under whatever man decided to part with his shillings for the night."

Nell remained where she was but hesitated not a bit with her response. "I prefer to receive all my schooling at court, Lady Castlemaine, at the instruction of His Majesty. In fact, he tells me he much prefers being allowed to instruct, rather than being instructed by a demanding mistress."

Barbara's eyes flashed, but Abby believed not with hatred. She seemed to enter the lists with Nellie with confidence and enthusiasm. "I am sure the king has been exposed to much he never dared consider before. Things common, to be sure, but so unlike what he has been used to receiving."

Abby never felt comfortable among combatants, whether men arguing politics or women questioning each other's morality. She used Nellie's laughter at Barbara's sharp retort as an opening to change the subject. "And have you dogs, Lady Castlemaine?" The three other women stared at her in moderate disbelief. "Forgive me. I have no idea why I would ask that."

Charlotte stepped forward with the wine. "Have some more of this wine, Abby. It will clear the fog you seem to be lost in at present."

Nellie tossed her head and trained her eyes on poor Abby's. "Did you really say—as has been rumored, Lady Castlemaine, who in the middle of a late-night fuck with his Majesty and noting the canine population at the foot of the bed—did you really say, "God bless Your Majesty, but God damn your dogs"?

Barbara also turned to Abby, as if she has become a filter for the words of both adversaries. "You are as perfectly vulgar as your reputation warrants, Nellie. No, I did not say that—nor have I had one of the king's hounds named for me, as you have."

Charlotte was particularly delighted by this bit of news. "What's this, Nellie?"

"The people are now calling our French tart Louise 'Snappy' and me 'Tutty.' For your benefit, Abby, these are the king's two favorite pampered pets. Amusing, isn't it, that he hasn't named one of his dearly loved dogs 'Babba'? But that would be purely unnecessary, wouldn't it?"

Barbara lifted her chin higher. "I wouldn't permit it. Besides, the king holds me in too high esteem to ever humiliate me in such a manner."

Nell grinned wickedly. "The irony, Charlotte and Abby, is that it is I who always carries the spaniel 'Snappy' in my arms—the little bitch. The king, though, wishes to carry sweet little 'Tutty' whenever he can. Sadly, his old hound 'Babba' has been relegated to her dog kennel where she will feel pampered as she withers slowly away."

"I held nothing but Charles in my arms, Nellie. I have been neither a Snappy nor a Tutty."

No, Barbara, only the realm's reigning bitch. Abby, you must understand that Lady Castlemaine doesn't like dogs. That is why she's not as popular among the English as I am."

Abby was amazed that so far neither woman had physically attacked the other. Instead they both held their ground, firing their cannon balls made of compacted insults. "We had very few dogs in Virginia, I am afraid. At least I can remember only a few when I was a girl." After this failed attempt to bring about a cease fire—neither adversary was willing to discuss the canine population in Virginia—Abby looked at Charlotte, who was still inordinately pleased by the battle being staged before her. "Well, I wonder then if Louise de Kéroualle grew up surrounded by pets."

Abby's mention of Louise's name seemed to do the trick. Both Barbara and Nell sighed with derision at the sound of their French rival's name, while Charlotte cast a sharp look at Abby.

Nell finally broke from her martial posture and sat on one of the sofas. "It has long been my belief that she is a French spy. That's one thing they cannot accuse me of, Abby. I could only spy for tavern keepers and orange wenches—and the king has no worries about their loyalty." Abby's thoughts returned to Lord Durell and the other men she had seen and heard speaking with him.

Not to be outdone by Nellie's movement to the sofa, Barbara took her seat on the matching chair directly opposite. Charlotte took a place in a chair near Barbara, while Abby remained standing. Barbara gestured to Abby for more wine. "And while I have some power left, I should see to it that Louise is hanged for treason to her friends, at the very least."

"Then I ask your ladyship to appoint me as head executioner. I look simply incomparable in a black hood." Abby was stunned by the amity in Nellie's reply. Both combatants smiled at each other across the distance between them. Barbara shook her lovely head no.

"You might have to relinquish that black hood to your superior, Nell."

"Oh, heaven's no, Lady Castlemaine. Your beautiful giant pearls would not look good around black hood."

"Perhaps they wouldn't." Barbara paused and then threw up her hands. "I might as well confess that I lied earlier. I too have had many of His Majesty's spaniels in my lap."

Nell saw the continued amazement on Abby's face—and the disappointment on Charlotte's. "Charlotte, you may ask Phoebe to send the carts back to London. There will be no casualties this day to be taken from the battlefield."

The next few moments were awkward as Nell and Barbara remained silent, while Charlotte fidgeted with her dress. Abby thought hard for a topic to push the conversation along. Finally she had something. "Barbara, Charlotte informs me that you influenced so much fashion at court as well as ice-skating and the playing of the guitar—an instrument I have not yet seen." Barbara smiled and looked at Nell, who nodded politely.

"There was always good food, good wine, and good conversation when I ruled the table. I loved to encourage that which was new. Charlotte here even tried to play the guitar."

"I was an utter failure at it." At least Charlotte made a contribution to the discussion.

Abby saw Barbara contemplating something troubling. "Charlotte also told me that Mr. Dryden wrote something highly flattering of you, Lady Castlemaine. What was it? Can you recall his words?"

Barbara offered the saddest smile Abby had ever seen. "He wrote, 'You, like the stars, not by reflection bright, / Are born to your own heaven and your own light.' But of course, Nellie no doubt wishes to quote other verses made about me."

"Yes, I could. But at the moment it seems neither witty nor appropriate to do so. I think I will instead drink. May I be served, Charlotte?"

Charlotte dutifully rose and poured Nellie another glass. She now regretted deciding against Phoebe's remaining in the room. Abby suppressed her amusement at poor Charlotte's defeated manner. Clearly, she hoped Nellie and Barbara would be by now rolling on the floor ripping out each other's hair in large clumps instead of calmly sitting on the sofa exchanging civilities. Charlotte refilled the glass of Lady Castlemaine, who directed her next words to Nell. "Perhaps it is true after all what Charlotte says of you, Nellie."

"Hmm. That I . . . ?"

"That you have more character than you demonstrate in public."

"To be so praised by the powerful and brilliant Countess Castlemaine— soon to be the Duchess of Cleveland—is an honor beyond the realm of believability."

Abby thought the moment simply delightful and now felt the power of one who controls political or social discourse, even though she understood she was assuming Lady Durell's place in doing so.

"Nellie, why do you think you and the other women actors have become so popular with those who attend theatre? Surely, you have been shouted at when you come out to perform your parts." Barbara lifted the wine to her mouth, blocking the expression of pain or disgust on her face—Abby couldn't tell which.

"Even the lewd comments shouted at me were of a different nature, in that there was always so much good will in them. The theatre is a place where everyone seems to realize that men and women can behave in the ways they truly desire to be. The Puritans refused to understand that—I think they were afraid to understand it—and are still afraid to do so. They would close the plays down again if they could—but this time, since women are so strong a part of the performances, I don't think the men will ever allow it to happen again. We must face facts. Today when a man goes into a theatre, he is in effect going joyfully into a woman's cunt."

It was all Barbara could do to keep the wine inside her mouth. She found her rival's vulgar remark highly amusing, even as Abby found it shocking. Only Charlotte failed to respond to it. Abby recovered and continued her questioning.

"But don't other women, good Church of England women, hold that acting in such a public place cheapens the sex? I heard in Virginia that one of your profession is no different, really, than a woman who sells her body for pleasure. Oh, not that I believe such a thing, of course."

Nell answered without a smile, which suggested her seriousness rather than her disapproval. "Women must realize, no matter what they say, that the theatre has given their sex the kind of fame only known before to queens and empresses. First, there are those who hawk the oranges. Do you know they are looked for and missed if they happen to be elsewhere and not doing their business in the theatre? Their names are known, and their spirits are warm and entertaining. Then the women's roles in the plays we perform are often so beloved of the audience. And they make everyone think of women and what a woman is and what she must endure—in a new way I cannot believe was felt in the times when men and boys assumed all the parts. The theatres have also allowed the public to see the women of the king and his brother—I mean their lovers, not simply their wives. They are looked at—as our dearest Lady Castlemaine has been for so long looked at—as they sit next or near to the king, everyone understanding the power they have, no matter what unflattering comments are whispered about them. And then there are the actresses themselves, doing what only a very few could ever do well or dare do at all. Every woman plays her many roles—even you Abby if you would think about it—but how many could ever do them so publicly, with such spirit. But the important point is that they talk about us. Men truly admire us as well and much as they want us. We women will never relinquish the stage. Never."

Abby looked at Barbara for her reaction to Nell's remark about her and the implication that the king took other lovers to the theatre. Barbara seemed withdrawn, as if she hadn't listened to anything Nell said. Charlotte asked Barbara if she was feeling ill.

"I must return to London. I have forgotten my time." Abby sensed Lady Castlemaine had something she wished to share with Charlotte, but that Nell gave no hint she was about to depart. With Nell expressing her regrets at Barbara's leaving, she remained seated while Charlotte walked her other guest to her coach, leaving Abby and Nell to their wine.

I think you may have bested her, Nellie. She has, as you might say, retired from the field."

"No, Abby. It wasn't me that forced her away. Something is troubling her mightily."

"The king?"

"No, she wouldn't let me see her in any forlorn state. It's something more political I would imagine. Perhaps one of her many dark secrets has been revealed at court."

CHAPTER 23

"And you are sure you haven't been found out?"

"No, sir. No one suspects anything. I am certain of it. I have been sent to London to bring back the portrait Sir Peter Lely finished of my lady—so I should be right where I am."

"Do you have the portrait with you?"

"Yes, it is in the coach. Do you wish to see it?"

"Yes, but we must not be seen together."

"The coach is in a darkened place. I informed the coachman that I would be gone half an hour, so he took himself to the Dog Tavern nearby. I promised to send someone in to fetch him when I was ready to return."

"You're a smart girl, Phoebe."

"Thank you, sir. Come."

She led her accomplice to the coach and unwrapped the painting of Lady Durell. It was done in the style of the "Windsor Beauties." "You see the grain placed in her hand? Lady Durell is portrayed as Ceres, the goddess of the harvest. She insisted she would be painted as one of the highest goddesses, especially so because Sir Peter painted Frances Stuart as Diana and Lady Castlemaine as Minerva. It's very well done, isn't it, sir?"

"Very, although I fail to see how Lady Durell could serve as a symbol of the mother. She has no Proserpina to mourn half a year—indeed, no children at all. But then like Ceres, she has the power to bless others with her favor and she can shift her moods suddenly from spring to winter, as you have often told me. I also recall that Ceres was the first to require bloody animal sacrifices to her so that she would renew life. And remember, Phoebe, that Ceres loathed the pig for what it did to crops newly planted."

"Well, sir. There your comparison fails. Lady Durell eats wholesomely of pork, however prepared."

After they shared a restrained laugh at Lady Durell's culinary habits,

Phoebe re-wrapped the portrait and took the several coins offered her."

"Thank you, sir."

"Phoebe, you deserve a bigger reward for your assistance. What you have told me of Lord Durell and his plans has likely saved my life. For that I am grateful beyond measure."

"I am happy to assist you, sir. We are the same in spirit, after all."

The man nodded and turned to go. Before he took three steps, Phoebe called to him. "Mr. Hansall, how does a good Puritan man such as you know so much about the heathen gods?"

A hundred yards from the gate of Dove-Raven House, Lady Castlemaine's coach met the one transporting Thomas Lockwood and Bridget Warren. After both vehicles stopped, Thomas Lockwood opened Barbara's door and informed his lady that Bridget had something important she should hear.

"Have her come forward." Bridget approached and curtsied when she saw Lady Castlemaine sitting regally in the coach. "What have you to tell me, Bridget?" Barbara had never liked the woman. She believed Bridget asserted herself too familiarly with her betters and had too much of the king's ear when it came to court gossip.

"Lady Castlemaine, I am sorry. I have come to ask your forgiveness for what I was forced to do."

Barbara stared incredulously at Lockwood. "My forgiveness for what exactly?"

Bridget was rendered mute by Lady Castlemaine's withering stare. Lockwood, who heard Bridget's story on the ride from London, stepped in front of the older woman. "My Lady Castlemaine, allow me to repeat what she confided in me." Barbara's demeanor lost its intemperance, as she invited Lockwood to enter the coach while Bridget stood on the road weathering the chilly December air.

Lockwood informed his lady of Lord Brinton's insistence that Bridget implicate Barbara in Betty Keller's murder and the promise of torture if Bridget did not comply.

"That explains why Brinton placed the knife box in my fireplace. I am not surprised by his cruelties to that woman and to me. He has despised me ever since I dispatched Lord Clarendon, even though Clarendon's absence encouraged His Majesty to rely more on Brinton for counsel."

"But there is more, Lady Castlemaine."

"Then proceed, Thomas."

Lockwood hesitated, his mind suddenly filled with appreciation of his lady's incomparable beauty and his fortune in being seated so close to her. At this moment, he couldn't find the strength to take his eyes off her majestic face.

Barbara met his gaze with her own appreciative glance. "Thomas, tell me what else she said."

He dropped his eyes so he could more easily reveal the rest of Bridget's revelation. "Bridget says she overheard Lord Brinton telling the king that you are also responsible for the killing of Sir Roger Earle, whose body has just been discovered—also stabbed to death."

The color drained from Barbara's features, as she slumped. Lockwood held out his hands to catch her if she fell forward, but she recovered enough to place her hands on his forearms and push herself back to a fully seated position. "You know that I have spoken publicly against Earle—and only recently insulted him to his face."

"But he was rude to you, my lady. You had every right." She had earlier informed Lockwood that at Whitehall, Lord Rochester spoke of writing a mock-epic satire on "The Heavenly Whores of Court," immediately after which Earle looked at her and whispered something in Rochester's ear, causing the courtier to laugh boisterously. Barbara told Lockwood she replied loud enough for everyone there to hear, "Then my good Lord, you must not fail to ask those whores why Sir Roger Earle never visits them without a device for their pleasure since he can, by himself, provide them none."

"I never told you this part, Thomas, but the king took his side and scolded me for my 'inappropriate and senseless remark.' I told His Majesty that Earle should be banished from court for insulting me in the manner he did. I revealed to the king that seven years earlier he had banished another because I had asked him to. His Majesty said to me, 'Seven years is a long time. Much has changed.'"

Lockwood was pained by the tears forming in his lady's eyes. "My lady, I will testify that you were nowhere near where Sir Roger was discovered slain—I will swear my life on it."

Barbara lifted her violet eyes, still matted with moisture. "But do you know where he was found, Thomas?"

"I do not, Lady Castlemaine."

"Then you would make a poor witness." She smiled and took his chin in her hand. "Thank you for all you have done for me, Thomas Lockwood." He was so stunned by the feel of her gloved fingers touching his face that he couldn't reply. "Here, give these coins to Bridget Warren and we will speak more on these matters tonight after you take her back to Whitehall." Thomas had barely stepped down from the coach before Barbara signaled her driver to move on. Lockwood took the shivering Bridget Warren back to their coach and soon they too headed to the city.

Some eighty yards back toward Dove-Raven House, a cloaked figure waited until Lockwood's coach was out of sight before mounting a horse and riding back to London.

"What is wrong with you, child?"

Mary Gibbons took young Anne's arm and led her into her small but attractive lodgings provided by Lord Brinton in payment for Mary's particular sexual services to him.

"Mr. Devlin has . . ." Anne dropped her head in apparent shame.

She had no need to say anything further; Mary knew the theatre manager had made some attempt at intimacy with his young actress. "How far did he take matters with you, Anne?"

Anne stepped back in great wonderment at the implications of Mary's question. "Do you think I would allow him such freedom?"

"Then why are you so upset? Mr. Devlin has felt his share of bosoms since I have been at the King's Theatre, and to my knowledge he has only wished to lick the cunt of pretty Betty Keller. He simply needs to feel that his increasing age has not left him impotent. "

"But why with me?"

"Don't be stupid, Anne. You are quite beautiful, as you must know."

"I am not. My nose is crooked and my eyes are too narrow."

"Your eyes are very alluring—dangerously so at your age."

"Stop it, Mary. Besides, what I look like has nothing to do with my fears."

Mary took in an involuntary breath. She walked to the table and poured Anne tea and unobtrusively added a small amount of rum to the concoction. Here, drink this. It will relax you and make you think clearly."

"Can you afford to serve tea to others, Mary?"

"I have a benefactor who provides me with all the tea I could ever wish to drink."

Anne's face darkened. "In exchange for your body?"

"No, dearest child. He has never but once brought his prick anywhere near my womanly place. Now drink and tell me what you fear."

Anne brought the tea to her lips. "This tastes horrible. What kind of tea is this?"

Mary laughed. "Not the kind our dear queen brought from Portugal. This particular tea is made more delicious by something brought in from the West Indies."

"It still tastes horrible." Despite her dour assessment, Anne took another sip and immediately sat. "My fear is that I will no longer be favored as an actress because I rejected Mr. Devlin."

Mary's face broadened in relief. "Oh, is that all? My dear Anne, I can assure you that Mr. Devlin is not that kind of a man. He will treat you as he has treated other actresses who have rejected his affections. You need only ask Nellie Gwynn and Betty Boutell. I cannot promise you he won't make a similar attempt in the days ahead, but he will not press you further on your rejection or punish you for saying no. He knows the king likes his actresses and won't risk offending His Majesty by dismissing you."

Anne ended her sniffling and brushed the last tear from her eye. "I am so grateful to you for scattering my fears, Mary. I am now happy again. You have made me happy. My affections for you are boundless."

"Finish your tea, Anne. I can see you really like it."

"I'm ashamed to say that suddenly I do. I really do."

With Charlotte having gone off to bed, Abby stepped into her friend's small library, which consisted of an economical eighty books unlike the six hundred volumes in Lord Durell's collection, "none of which he has ever bothered to open," according to his wife. Abby smiled upon discovering the five volumes of Rabelais's *The Life of Gargantua and of Pantagruel*. As girls in France, Abby and Charlotte had secretive readings of the hilarious and vulgar work of the sixteenth-century French author. Abby learned graphically about cuckoldry and was exposed to the various and shocking descriptions of the male and female genital and anal areas—the naughtiness of which Charlotte relished, teasing Abby about being too squeamish. Abby didn't need to re-read the same passages she had never been able to forget. How Charlotte giggled, and she blushed when they read the description of Panurge's interest in the lady of Paris—how he wished to "embrace her, to kiss her, and to rub his bacon with hers!"—even asserting, "Madam, know that I am so amorous of you that I can neither piss nor dung for love." Charlotte liked to tease whenever Abby needed to purge herself, "Oh, it seems, then, that Abby is in love. She is about to relieve herself of dung!"

Both girls claimed to be sickened by Rabelais's depiction of the old Sibyl of Panzoust: she was "ill appareled, worse nourished, toothless, blear-eyed, crook-shouldered, snotty, her nose still dropping, and herself still drooping, faint, and pithless." Other old women received the same heartless treatment: "The rest were old, weather-beaten, over-ridden, toothless, blear-eyed, tough, wrinkled, shriveled, tawny, moldy, phthisicky, decrepit hags, beldams, and walking carcasses." Heartless, to be sure, but also hilarious to the two young girls. Yet most telling, Abby recalled, was Charlotte's fascination with the Priestess Bacbuc at the very end of the fifth volume. This character kept to herself in the belly of the earth but would provide proper guidance to those who traveled to her lair. She had Panurge drink from her magic fountain and ordered him to dance in honor of the Roman God Bacchus—and then sing a verse, every line of which Charlotte had memorized. Abby couldn't help remembering several of them herself.

Bottle, whose Mysterious Deep

Do's ten thousand Secrets keep,
With attentive Ear I wait;
Ease my Mind, and speak my Fate.
Soul of Joy! Like Bacchus, we
More than India gain by thee.
Truths unborn thy Juice reveals,
Which Futurity conceals.

Charlotte adored the fact that after Panurge had sung, Bacbuc threw something into the fountain which made the water boil. Abby teased that she wanted to be a witch like Shakespeare's three in *Macbeth*, but Charlotte insisted that she preferred to be Ceres for the gifts she gave to mankind. Besides, Charlotte added, down below the ground, as Bacbuc was, she could be free from storms and fire. As Bacbuc told Panurge, "What you see in the sky, whatever the surface of the earth affords you, and the sea, and every river contain, is not to be compared with what is hid within the bowels of the earth." At the time, Abby laughed and predicted that Charlotte would marry a ferret and become herself a shrew. But now she understood her friend enjoyed the power she wielded from Dove-Raven House—as evidenced in her pitting important and powerful women against each other for her curiosity and amusement—which she far preferred to the activity at Court and in London. Now Abby saw even the high-hedged labyrinth was a kind of underground lair for Lady Durell.

Placing the volume back on the shelf, Abby looked about the small library and appreciated how meticulously decorated it was, each piece of furniture balancing perfectly with the shelves and color of the walls and curtains.

"Oh, excuse me, Abby. I didn't know you were in here."

"It is I who should apologize for wandering about the house. What do you have there, Phoebe?"

Phoebe hesitated before answering. "It's a portrait Lady Durell didn't want anyone to see it before she did, but I don't see why you couldn't. Just don't tell her that I let you."

"I won't Phoebe. You can trust me."

Phoebe un-wrapped the portrait. "It's Sir Peter Lely's new painting of

Lady Durell."

Abby was struck by the beauty of the presentation. The painter had caught her friend perfectly. A lovely face with a sight aura of reserve. "Is Lady Durell supposed to be Ceres, do you think?"

"I believe that was what she wanted, yes."

Abby grinned and looked back toward the Rabelais volumes. "Ceres—of course."

"Will you be going to bed soon?"

"I hope so, Phoebe. But I'm very wide awake at present I'm afraid."

"May I be excused then?"

"Oh, yes. I will need nothing for as long as I am up. You can extinguish the lights now. I'll carry this light with me so I can find my way back to my room. Good night."

Because she wasn't ready to sleep, Abby left the house and went out to the rear toward the labyrinth, believing the walk and the crisp air would help tire her. As she approached the labyrinth, she caught sight of two lanterns moving from the Raven side of the house, heading in her direction. She assumed that, like before, Lord Durell and one of his men or a visitor were going to speak about secretive matters. She feared revealing herself; therefore she groped her way to the entrance of the labyrinth and looked back to see if the two men would stop or deviate from the course they seemed to be taking. For a brief moment, she perversely imagined Lord Durell bringing a woman to the labyrinth for some kind of carnal activity. Phoebe, perhaps? But the lanterns were clearly heading in her direction. She moved forward into the labyrinth so that if the men merely stepped inside the entrance, she would not be seen. In a few moments she heard Lord Durell's voice.

"It doesn't matter who. That has nothing to do with our plans for tomorrow night."

"It gives me great pause, Lord Durell," the other man replied.

"It shouldn't. Sir Roger was not a vital player in our game. His death is insignificant."

"Many know he was an ally of yours and came out here often."

"Damn it, man. Don't you see that Earle's death—no matter who killed him—works to our benefit? He can never point his finger at us."

"Suppose he already has and was murdered *after* he confessed or implicated us."

"The king's guards would have by now brought us in for questioning if he had."

Abby tensed when neither of the men spoke further. Had they heard her moving or breathing? Were they about to walk further into the labyrinth and discover her?"

Finally the other man broke the silence. "How can I be sure you won't have me silenced for the same reason you killed Earle?"

"Me? Your fears have made you silly, Richard. I have killed no one."

"Nor will you tomorrow night, Lord Durell. But you will be just as guilty as I for the king's murder."

Abby was certain her gasp was loud enough to be heard. She waited for the men to find her, but neither came. She waited a full ten minutes to be certain Lord Durell and the man he called Richard had left the labyrinth and returned to the house before she attempted to move. With her first step, she fell forward. Her shaking legs failed to work properly.

Chapter 24

Richard Hansall had risen at six—as he habitually did throughout every season of the year. He took for his breakfast some coarse bread with a modest cut of salted meat and half a cup of beer. In this too he rarely deviated. Hansall ate his morning meal in silence, a habit of a decade's vintage, begun with the death of his wife in childbirth on the thirtieth of May 1660, the day after the new King's triumphal entry into London. Though illogical, this fact too fueled Hansall's hatred of Charles. Both his wife and child died with the arrival of the corrupt monarch. Yet, it was the death of his father shortly afterwards that made Hansall believe he had been chosen to perform the act. God had provided him with more than enough cause. That this day had taken so long in its preparation had never been expected, but Hansall had been patient awaiting the proper time— never doubting that his hour would come.

In a little more than twelve hours his responsibilities would be completed. He would kill the king on justifiable grounds other than what had happened to his family. Whether he would survive the regicide meant little to him now. Later tonight he would attempt to escape to the Netherlands with the assistance provided by Lord Durell, but he knew he stood a good chance of being slain by the king's guards. He was convinced God would not allow his avenger to be captured, tried, and executed in the manner of his father. If he did manage his escape, he would live knowing Lord Durell would be dead as well. Hansall had only yesterday arranged for Durell's murder. He had spent the past year cultivating his relationship with Durell and Sir Roger Earle, even though he despised both men and what they represented to him—Anglican royalist bastards born to privilege. Durell and Earle never imagined their Puritan accomplice realized they had planned to have him blamed and immediately slain—all of which he had learned from the unsuspected servant girl Phoebe.

Later this morning he would speak to both Michael Devlin and his actor

Gottlieb. If he sensed any hesitation on their part, Hansall was more than willing to make alone the attempt on Charles's life.

"There you see, Henry. Even my dogs bark at your ludicrous assertion." In fact, the spaniels had barked at a lively hare bounding past them in St. James's Park, but Charles used the barking to dismiss Lord Brinton's "incontrovertible proof" that Lady Castlemaine was responsible for the murder of Betty Keller.

"I remind Your Majesty that your father's knife box was found in her fireplace—the box that held the weapon that took the poor girl's life."

"I suppose you are to tell me that Lady Castlemaine crept into Whitehall and stabbed Betty herself."

"It is possible, Your Majesty. You cannot disagree that Lady Castlemaine is very familiar with Whitehall and still has the means to enter at any time of day or night."

Charles frowned. He knew Brinton was right. "But do you really believe she would do the act herself?"

"I only ask you to recall the many times she struck at you and the many times she hurled objects at you and at many others, myself included. And the many times she threatened bodily harm to you and many of us here."

"Pure bluster, Henry. She was the queen of threats to be sure, and she was quick to lash out. But murder is quite another thing. And please don't inform me that she had looks that could kill." The king laughed and commenced forward with his dogs. Brinton halted and let Charles take five steps before announcing. "You cannot deny she could easily convince someone else to kill for her."

Charles halted as his spaniels attempted to drag him forward. He did not turn back as he replied. "And whom would she have convinced, Henry?"

"I dare say many. I need not remind you of the many men who stated even publicly that they would do anything for her favors. This woman has for ten years sought the attention of everyone at court. How many times have Lely and others painted her? You are surely aware that her images were engraved and sold to many men. That she has been replaced by several of your favored women has likely brought her to the breaking point—and the murder of the Keller girl was proof she had gone beyond it. Her incessant vanity has for so very long been well noted, Your Majesty."

Charles smiled recalling her vow that she would become the most well-known woman in England. He had replied much to her satisfaction that, if not that, she would be known as "the most beautiful woman of the realm."

"And you know that Lady Castlemaine has never been modest about her political influence. She led the assault against Clarendon—a man who advised you well during your exile—and inspired many men to join her in those attacks. Because of her bewitching charm, you took her side and let Clarendon go. Your Majesty also knows she has taken a considerable amount of money for her influence. The French and Italian ambassadors have often noted her power over you and have made fools of themselves seeking her cooperation in political matters."

Recalling that he had once responded to those who despised her and her influence with a declaration that anyone who deemed Barbara an enemy would have the king as an enemy as well, Charles cast a hostile look at Brinton, who feared he had gone too far in his indictment against Lady Castlemaine. "So, Henry, you are arguing that her political history is also relevant to your belief that she killed or had killed Betty Keller?"

Brinton couldn't help himself; his hatred for Barbara Villiers would not be tempered. "This woman greedily took your generous and costly gifts and spent your money vainly and thoughtlessly. Your Majesty recalls the excessive displays of jewelry she would wear while accompanying you at the theatres. What did you once tell me? Thirty thousand pounds worth? And then she would think nothing of losing that amount at the gaming tables."

Brinton saw that now the king was deeper in thought. He felt confident that Charles was slowly accepting and agreeing with the case against Lady Castlemaine unveiled before him. Yet Brinton softened his voice and made his next damning point as would a sympathetic friend. "You have told me about the fiery arguments you both had and the threats she made against you. You do recall the time when she was big with child and vowed that if you refused to claim the infant as your own she would dash out its brains?"

Charles remembered well his serious doubts about the child's paternity and the humiliating act of his falling to his knees and asking her to pardon his suspicions. The battles between them had been fierce, yet the passion they shared in combat was always equaled if not surpassed by that they shared in the royal bed.

Brinton continued to press the argument. "I know you have pushed her away to the best of your ability, Your Majesty, but my love for you forces me to mention that she has had at least five other lovers since she became your favorite so long ago now."

In spite of his own promiscuity, Charles hated the thought of his Barbara with other men, even though he recently told her she could love whom she wished as long as she made "as little noise" about it as possible. Barbara had forced him to run counter to his better political judgments and expose himself to her artful yet at time cruel ways. He knew the response she received from others over the past decade was deeply felt—no one was indifferent to Lady Castlemaine. He recalled such wide-spread praise of her beauty being "beyond the power of art," as Peter Lely had said, but also that she was "enormously vicious and ravenous, foolish but imperious," according to Bishop Burnett. Many labeled her a "whore," and one writer vilified her further by claiming she was "a vulgar mannered, arrogant slut," who was "the curse of the nation."

"Henry, I will see her and find if there is truth in your claim."

"Then there is no need for Gatesby to formally question her?"

"None. I will see her tomorrow."

Brinton was most pleased by the king's decision, especially since Gatesby demonstrated a surprising lack of enthusiasm for interrogating Lady Castlemaine when they spoke earlier. But Brinton detected one potential problem with the king's decision.

"But I hope Your Majesty will allow me to have her brought to you at Whitehall. It would leave the worst impression if you visited her—that is, if you find she is indeed guilty of Betty Keller's death."

The King hesitated for a moment before responding. "Very well, Henry. Have her brought to me at noon. Now, I should like you to have the dogs brought back to Whitehall. I prefer to walk alone for a time."

Brinton called forward Burgess the dog handler and held back the rest of the king's entourage while Charles walked ahead some twenty yards. "What else did you see when you followed Lady Castlemaine out to Dove-Raven House last night, Burgess? Anything that could further implicate her? Think, man." Last night when he returned to Whitehall, Burgess informed Brinton of the meeting on the road between Lady Castlemaine and Thomas Lockwood, who had brought Bridget Warren with him—but he could think of nothing else of significance." Brinton nodded and then signaled Burgess to leave. As Brinton followed the king, keeping distance between them, he felt the newly cold December breeze as something that warmed him.

"Your character is dispatched before half the play is over, Francis. Let both Betty Boutell and Mr. Hart know you wish to leave for Richmond before it gets too dark. I will meet you at Southampton Market at the time Hansall advised.

Gottlieb asked Devlin if he had arranged a similar deception. "I have. I will have announced that I'll be leaving the theatre before the play is completed and that I'm to meet the two woman players Mr. Lowther has brought over from Spain. The truth is he will not return from Spain for several days, but no one will know that is so. Gottlieb nodded but with concern imbedded into his face. "Francis, have no fear. The plan will go smoothly. Our route of escape tonight is set. Tomorrow we'll 'awake' and react to the stunning news that Charles is dead. And you will have seven hundred pounds in your pocket thanks to our benefactor's generosity. That is six hundred and fifty more than you received for assailing that ingrate Talbot last spring." Gottlieb attacked one of the more troublesome actors of the King's Company for threatening Devlin's life following the manager's severe assessment of the man's lack of commitment to the theatre. The beating was serious enough to cause Talbot to flee to the north out of fear once he recovered from his injuries. In gratitude, Devlin made Gottlieb the recipient of fifty pounds, some of which was owed to Talbot for his performances. Because Gottlieb assaulted Talbot in darkness, his identity as the assailant was unknown to the others at the King's Theatre. Devlin promised Gottlieb to keep his attack secret, and the grateful actor vowed to serve the theatre manager in whatever way he could. Devlin had asked little of him until now.

With a reminder of his forthcoming payment, Gottlieb's dour concern transformed itself into expressive satisfaction before he parted from Devlin. Devlin too smiled with contentment at the thought of the fifteen-hundred pounds he was promised by Durell.

Devlin allowed himself several minutes to ponder his life under a new king. Assuming James the Duke of York would succeed, the new monarch would be as generous to the theatres as his brother was. James was a frequent attendee and always ogled pretty women, like those who appeared on the stage. If somehow a revolution occurred and Charles's bastard son the young Duke of Monmouth assumed the crown, the theatres would still be royally supported. After all, Devlin thought, Monmouth was his father's son and also would likely seek actresses for his royal bed.

These thoughts again brought his darling Anne Whitworth to mind. Devlin reaffirmed his belief that he would break her resistance and have her. She still maintained too many of the scruples her family poured into her head, but Devlin had seen the same thing happen before with women in the theatre. Soon enough, almost every one of them lost their inhibitions and spread their legs before fellow actors and king alike. Besides, in the wake of Charles's assassination, Devlin would take her in his arms and comfort her—which would be a prelude to caressing her breasts and completing his seduction to both of their satisfactions.

Bridget went about her late morning duties at Whitehall. Each room received its daily spot cleaning and the windows were checked for cracked or dirty glass. With difficulty, Bridget entered the bedroom where she discovered sweet Betty Keller with the knife once belonging to the martyred King Charles I plunged into her lower abdomen. The pressures thrust upon Bridget since that morning had affected the kindly woman beyond her power to rationalize. Why had she been forced by Lord Brinton to implicate Lady Castlemaine? Why had he chosen her to threaten and intimidate? Bridget stared at the spot where the bed was placed before it was dismantled and burned along with the bedding stained with Betty's blood. Now only the walls remained as a silent witness to who had actually stabbed the young woman. Yes, it may well have been Lady Castlemaine. She had the temperament for it. Many times over the years she had expressed her displeasure with Bridget in a number of ways—some of them including violent threats. But Bridget actually felt sympathy for the Countess when she was forced to move from her apartments in Whitehall when the lively Nell Gwynn began to hold sway over the king's passions. As Bridget surveyed the entire room, she wondered if Nell could have done Betty in. As His Majesty's recent favorite, she may well have felt that Betty Keller was assuming her rightful place in the king's heart. Yet something told Bridget that the murderer was a man. And Lord Brinton more likely than anyone else. Or at least that Brinton ordered the death of Betty and had someone else wield the knife. But who might that have been? One of his men? Something then struck Bridget's imagination that forced her to grab the doorway to prevent herself from falling. Who was Brinton most intimate with? A woman who, if the rumors begun by other servants held true, catered to his perverse sexual desires—a woman who Bridget knew possessed the strength, temperament, and daring to commit such a foul deed—the actress Mary Gibbons.

Yet, Bridget knew she could not act upon her suspicions. Lord Brinton would surely have her silenced if she accused either him or Mary. The king would never put any credence in her beliefs to do anything to save her. Overcome with a palpable feeling of helplessness, Bridget cried. She would be used as a witness to implicate Lady Castlemaine. She would carry her lie to her grave, and God would never forgive her.

CHAPTER 25

During her morning meal, Abby found it surprising she was able to keep to herself what she overheard last night and earlier from Lord Durell. She rationalized her silence in two ways. First, she didn't want to cause her dear friend to approach her husband and accuse him of a plot against the king. Lord Durell would deny such an accusation, of course, and then accuse Abby of slandering him. But the other reason was even more terrifying to ponder. What if Charlotte was part of the plot or cognizant of what it entailed? Lady Durell would then dismiss their long friendship and, like her husband, charge her friend with slander or something worse. Fearful for her own safety, Abby thought it wise to say nothing to Charlotte, but she was determined to warn the king of the potential plot against his life—whether she implicated Lord Durell or claimed she heard some unidentified men speak of it.

"Is there anything you need, Abby?"

"Oh, you started me, Phoebe."

"Please forgive me. I tried to enter heavily."

Abby laughed at Phoebe's novel expression. "No, no. I have been in thought and didn't hear your steps." Charlotte hadn't shown herself this morning, and the hour was approaching noon. "Does Lady Durell often sleep this late?"

"She wishes me to say she is not feeling well and will keep to her bed most of the day. She suggests you go to the city and attend another play at the King's Theatre."

Abby couldn't believe her good fortune. Charlotte's recommendation provided her an acceptable reason why she would return to London. When she arrived she would make her way to Whitehall and beg to see the king.

"Very well, then. I will take in a play."

Phoebe appeared delighted. "I have to go back to London myself for Lady Durell, so I could accompany you, if you think it proper. I'll be your lady's maid. I can help you dress your hair and hook your necklace. And if you need something sewed I am also your woman." Phoebe's cheerful demeanor brought another smile to Abby's face, even though she was concerned that Phoebe would remain with her and prevent her attempt to speak with the king.

"Tell me, Phoebe. Do you intend the view a play as well?"

"Alas, no. I must do special errands for Lady Durell. We will have to meet when the play is over and come right back."

Abby's spirits rose further. "Then you must help me prepare myself for an afternoon at the theatre. Shall I inform Lady Durell I will do what she suggested?"

"Oh, no. Lady Durell expressly ordered she be not disturbed—by anyone."

Abby was taken aback by Phoebe's insistence on the matter. "Very well. You can now perform your duties as my lady in waiting."

"The King has ordered you to Whitehall tomorrow morning at ten o'clock."

"You could have sent a messenger to deliver that bit of news, Lord Brinton." Barbara's contempt for the king's counselor was evident in her tone and on her face.

"I thought such important and, may I say dire, news should be given by one of my rank, Lady Castlemaine."

"*Dire* news?"

"I say that only because the crime of which you are being suspected is far greater than any of your others."

"So you have convinced His Majesty to accept your absurd belief regarding Betty Keller's death?"

"The evidence convinced him, my lady, not I." Brinton's face registered bemusement, a radical contrast to the fear now overtaking the contempt on Barbara's features.

"Evidence you had placed to implicate me."

"Evidence we were fortunate enough to discover here in your residence, Lady Castlemaine."

Brinton's mock politeness pushed her beyond the borders of decorum. "You vile lying bastard!" She lifted her hands to rake her nails down his face, but he quickly grabbed both her wrists, as if he was were prepared for such a violent outburst.

"You need to regain your civility, my lady. If it were up to me, the king would confront you now, but he is busy today and this evening and wishes not to lay his eyes on you until tomorrow." Brinton waited until Barbara's arms relaxed before he released her wrists. "We will come for you in the late morning."

The moment Brinton left her apartments Barbara called for Lockwood and informed him he was to turn away anyone else who might arrive at her door. She went to her wardrobe and selected the king's favorite dress of hers, which she would wear when she visited him at Whitehall. She would convince him Brinton had lied about her and that she never wished to harm Betty Keller. That would be a lie she could make him believe. It was no different than the others she had told him. Her charms would be as effective on his sensibilities as they always were. She would feel him once again inside her and afterward he would refuse to hear another word said against her—from Brinton or anyone else.

Upon arrival at the King's Theatre on Bridges Street, Abby and Phoebe stepped down from their carriage and were at once caught in the whirlpool of theatre patrons passing hurriedly near and loudly conversing outside the structure. In a moment Phoebe raised her hand as if to signal someone. Through the crowd came an elderly man in fine clothing befitting his apparent elevated status. But Abby noted he was dressed much younger than the man's apparent age. The pink feather in his hat was ostentatious and the purple ribbons on his shoes equally noteworthy if not appalling. The left side of his gold-brown periwig was inadvertently tucked under the shoulder section of his pink and purple jacket and his silver cravat was tied in a fashion Abby had never before seen.

"Abby, the man coming toward us is Sir Benjamin Jolly. He was a friend of Lord Durell's father and a former member of Commons. A messenger was sent ahead to arrange for his appearance here. He will be your company for this afternoon's performance."

Abby suppressed a laugh at the man's bizarre appearance. "My company?"

"Of course. You—a fine woman—cannot be expected to sit alone in the gallery. Have no fear. Sir Benjamin is beyond causing a woman any concern." Phoebe laughed at her own muted though bawdy joke.

Abby's smile dropped. Her plan to wait until Phoebe left to attend to her errands and then make her way to Whitehall to warn the king was now compromised. When Sir Benjamin doffed his hat and bowed, Abby feared he might be unable to straighten up again. After Phoebe made the introduction, she excused herself and was off. The old gentleman had just begun his obviously rehearsed praise of Abby's appearance when she heard a familiar voice.

"What are you doing here, Abby? Has Charlotte sent you here to spy on me?"

"Nellie?" Abby spoke the name with a mixture of pleasure and intense relief. Nell informed her she was attending today's performance of Mr. Joyner's *The Roman Empress* as a favor to her fellow player Betty Boutell, whose role was by Betty's own admission "very well acted." Nell had come with her former lover Charles Sackville, who was titled Lord Buckhurst.

"He's one of my three lovers named Charles I spoke to you about—remember? Charles Sackville, my fellow actor Charles Hart, and His Majesty."

Abby laughed openly. "Oh, Nellie. You are so very wicked. Does His Majesty know you are with one of your other Charleses?"

"He doesn't care. In fact, he's entertaining the little tart Squintabella while we speak."

"Louise de Kérouaille?"

"The very same. Abby, what is that look that has just come over your face?"

Abby pulled at Nell's arm to take her further from Sir Benjamin's hearing, as debilitated as it might have been.

"I would really like to meet the king this afternoon. It may be my only chance. Is there a way you could introduce him to me?"

Nell grinned. "And for that you would miss *The Roman Empress*? And worse, that you would wish me to miss it too?"

"If you would make the sacrifice along with me, I would be so grateful."

"Oh, poor Lord Buckhurst will be heart-broken. It is true we have stopped crawling into the same bed, but he still believes he can rekindle our recent carnal past. Even though he was rewarded handsomely for delivering me to His Majesty, I do so like him just as much as ever. He is charming, cultured and dissolute—a wonderful mix of virtue and vice. He is one of the merry gang of wits you have heard about. So, who have you come with, Abby?"

With considerable embarrassment, Abby whispered. "Do you see that old gentleman with the pink feather in his hat?"

"Oh, dear God. You have come with Sir Benjamin Jolly."

"Shhh, Nellie. No, I haven't come with him. Charlotte must have decided to repay me for some childhood trick I played on her by having him sent here to meet me and be my companion during the play." Abby added that Charlotte was feeling ill and had remained at Dove-Raven House for the day.

"Wait here, Abby." Nell scampered to where Lord Buckhurst conversed with four other gentlemen. She whispered something into his ear, which he began to protest but quickly ceased when his company continued addressing questions to him.

"Is everything all right, Lady Abigail?" Sir Benjamin had come up behind her." "We should perhaps take our place in the gallery. I do not wish to miss hearing the music that precedes the play." Abby noticed that when he smiled he displayed two overly large front teeth—one of which was riddled with decay. Before she could respond that she wasn't a Lady anything, Nell returned.

"Lord Buckhurst has been informed I will not be attending the performance. Oh, there you are, Sir Benjamin."

"How do ye do, madam?"

"Remarkably well. I am sorry but Abigail here is going with me to Whitehall. Your services are no longer required." The old man was lost in confusion. "But I have an idea. Why don't you go in with Lord Buckhurst and take my seat in the gallery. I know he would be honored to sit and converse with you during the play."

"Oh, no, madam. That honor would be all mine."

Nell pushed Jolly toward the gathering of gentleman surrounding Lord Buckhurst. As soon as he felt confident he had his bearings, Sir Benjamin joined the group and made his salutations.

"Come on Abby, we'll ride to Whitehall in my carriage."

As Nell grabbed her hand, Abby caught sight of the orange woman Joan Pegge staring at her and Nell. It was obvious the unsightly woman had been watching them—but for how long Abby couldn't be sure.

"And you have done all I asked at Dove-Raven House?"

"Yes, sir. And Lady Durell's friend Abigail is presently attending the theatre play. I will meet her after it is concluded, and I will inform her, as you have instructed me, that our coach has been damaged due to a collision with another vehicle and that she must spend the night here in London. I have already made arrangements for her to stay with a family on Tothill Street near the Abbey." Phoebe laughed. "So Abby will be put up near the Abbey."

Richard Hansall was too consumed with his thoughts to catch the pun. "What?"

"Oh, nothing, sir. I just want to thank you again for allowing me to arrange for her safety. Abby is a good woman and has been very kind to me since she arrived. She doesn't deserve to perish along with the others at Dove-Raven House." Still, Hansall remained pensive. "How many men did you say would go out there tonight?"

"Three men of God, Phoebe. Men of the true word. Men who remember how Lord Durell and his royal kind arranged and cheered for the deaths of those who had rescued this country and placed it in God's hands. Men like Durell should have been punished years ago, but it has taken war, a plague, and a fire to remind us what we have failed to do. But now the time has come. There can be no further delays."

Phoebe remained silent while Hansall spoke. She believed in what he had done and would do, although her spirits were tempered by compassion and resignation. Tonight she would leave London for Cambridge to visit one of her sisters. She would stay there a few days before sailing for Amsterdam, where she would join Hansall. She supposed that he would either marry her then or introduce her to younger men of good non-conformist stock, from which she might choose one to be her husband. But he would know beforehand that she would come to the marriage bed already experienced in the ways of Venus, as Nell Gwynn would say.

"Come, Phoebe. We will go where we can be alone. If God wills my death tonight, I want to die having once more enjoyed the pleasures of your body. You comfort me and give me hope. What we have shared is no sin. It has been sanctioned by God."

Chapter 26

"You look especially nervous, Abby. Have you not seen the king in the flesh?"

"Not in the manner you have, Nellie." Both women smiled at Abby's witticism. The moment helped relax Abby, who feared the king would refuse to see her. She would then have to confess her suspicions about Lord Durell to someone else, and she could only imagine how her warning might be taken. She might in fact be interrogated as though she were part of the plot. But as she examined Nellie's wonderful face—with her full cheeks and dimples, upturned nose, and most kissable full lips—Abby was struck by the comforting thought that she could tell Nellie, who would then inform the king. "I have seen His Majesty only yesterday. He was walking in the park."

"With my rivals?"

"No, Nellie. I assure you. He had no women with him."

"I mean my real rivals. His dogs."

Abby couldn't believe the irresistible force sitting across from her. This was a young woman—only twenty as Charlotte said—and yet she seemed so worldly wise and confident. Abby believed she could confide matters to Nellie she would never dare reveal to Charlotte.

"What will the king say if he knows you have arrived at Whitehall while he is in the company of Louise?"

"Abby you ask that as if they are presently fucking. No, I doubt Squintabella would allow herself to be taken so early in the day."

"Your name for her makes me laugh."

"As it should. I also call her 'The Weeping Willow' because of her habit of breaking into sobs whenever she can't have her way or doesn't receive the praise she feels is due her. Yet Charles still finds her attractive for all that. She has such a child's-face that he feels he would conquer an innocent virgin—which of course is every man's wish. But I know the whore dwells inside her, scratching to get out. Barbara believes Louise's appeal to the king is all political—all part of some agreement with the French over some treaty I could never understand but apparently Lady Castlemaine does. But I know better."

"Yet you don't seem to hate Louise."

"I don't. There is much I like about her. We have gotten together for tea and have played cards with one another as well. We have not pulled out each other's hair. Nor have we slapped each other's face. She told me that as a young woman of her social bearing, she would never stoop to violence. But I know she fears I'd beat her senseless. No lady in waiting has a chance against a girl of good tavern stock such as I am. She was formed at Versailles as a reserved young lady of the aristocracy who loved mirrors and manners, while I came of age in the theatres as a playful orange wench who adored bawdy jokes and rough talk."

As the carriage approached the New Exchange, Abby experienced a flush of panic at the prospect of telling the king that Lord Durell might well be plotting an assassination. Again, should His Majesty refuse to believe her, she risked serious punishment for making such a claim. Her friendship with Charlotte would be finished regardless, and if she were allowed to leave London she would travel over two hundred miles southwest to her uncle's home near Plymouth and never return to London for the rest of her life.

"Dearest Abby, what is the matter?" Nell immediately put up her hand. "No, no. You need not tell me. You are nervous about meeting the king. Either that or you are afraid he'll try to make a mistress out of you. You are handsome enough to be sure. Should that happen, you should heed my advice. First, do not bore him with serious conversation. Only Barbara has been able to get away with that. Charles will want you to pamper him."

"Nellie, stop! You are making me blush. Such a prospect is embarrassing."

Nell merely shrugged. "Remember that His Majesty adores the company of women and making love to them most vigorously, so I hope you've had plenty of practice and know how to push back."

Abby's head dropped toward her lap and she spread her fingers so that the sole of each hand rested over her ears.

"He wants pleasure but also understanding and flattery. There is no compliment you could pay him that he would find excessive. Oh, and be sure to ask him about racing horses, swimming, and Pelle Melle."

Abby leaped at the opportunity to change the subject. "What is Pelle Melle?" Nell explained that it was a game imported from France in which players take mallets and hit wooden balls through hoops. "You will also need to love clocks."

"Clocks?"

"His Majesty had seven of them in his bedroom—and none of them are in harmony with another—so that the chiming drives his attendants to the brink of madness. Oh, do you speak Dutch, Abby?"

"Only a few words here and there."

"Then be warned that Charles will want to teach you words and sentences in Dutch that have the most vulgar translations. He has done that with his Portuguese queen, teaching her lewd English words and having her repeat them in front of Lord Brinton and others."

They had now reached Charing Cross, and as the carriage turned down King Street, Abby fought her returning anxiety by asking Nell about her fame in the theatre. "How did you progress from selling oranges to acting on the stage?"

Nell informed her that one of her friends, Mary Meggs—"who once sold her body for profit"—received a license to offer for purchase oranges, lemons, and sweetmeats inside the theatre. "She then was known as 'Orange Moll,' and she asked me and my older sister Rose to work in the theatre with her. We wore our dresses low to show the men other sweetmeats and sold for sixpence our small china oranges." As the carriage approached Whitehall, Nell added she would deliver messages from the men to the actresses behind the stage or in the tiring-house and receive extra money for that work. "But before a full year was done as an orange girl, I was being trained by Mr. Devlin and Charles Hart. Mr. Lacy taught me dancing, and when I was fifteen and as Mr. Hart's lover I took on a role in one of Mr. Dryden's plays." The carriage stopped in front of the palace when Nell finished her account. "Three years later I made my first performance in the king's bed. It became a role I came to do very well."

Abby was too frightened to blush at Nell's witticism. She could barely step down from the carriage owing to her distress. What would the king say about her warning? Or more significantly, what would he believe?

"She is a friend of Lady Durell, you say?"

"Yes, Mr. Devlin. She and Lady Durell have been friends since childhood. Abigail Fayette has returned from Virginia and has been staying at Dove-Raven House."

"And your man overheard her asking Nellie to take her to Whitehall?" Devlin had grown reliant on the information his orange wench Joan Pegge had provided him. Her impressive cadre of spies included both men and women, from stagehands to seamstresses—from street vendors to prostitutes.

"He did. For what reason Abigail wishes to go there I cannot guess—except to meet the king." Joan cocked her heard in that attitude of one who probes for a tell-tale sign or clue to some mystery.

"Thank you, Joan. Here, take these coins with my thanks and continue to bring me news."

She was pleased by his generosity, but she was also aware that the information she had imparted had special significance for Devlin. "I'll head back to my duties inside now, sir."

"Yes, yes. Do so. Do so." Devlin walked away from the theatre to seek a quieter environment in which to think. Could it be that Abigail Fayette had learned something about Lord Durell's plot against the king? Had she in fact overheard Durell speaking with Richard Hansall or Sir Roger Earle about it? If so, she might be at Whitehall warning the king. And if she had overheard much, might she know that the manager of the King's Theatre was involved? But if she only knew of Lord Durell's involvement or had heard Durell speaking with Hansall or Earle, she likely would have no idea that Michael Devlin was part of the plot. In that case, he would very likely escape arrest. If Durell implicated him, he would deny any association, reminding the king that he had never been to Dove-Raven House. Yet, Devlin desired to speak to Hansall as soon as possible. Fortunately he knew where the Puritan would be the entire afternoon.

Anne Whitworth left the King's Theatre midway through the play and made her way to the rear of the theatre. She didn't wish to watch any more of *The Roman Empress* but not because of the acting or the writing. It was because the august name of the title character brought to mind in a painful way the one who had such influence on her life, especially in the past several weeks. She had come to London never expecting to be so influenced by others or by her own desires. She had simply deferred to those stronger than she and wished only to please. Still, she had become enamored of the attention she received and the prospects of becoming the leading actress of the King's Company. But as it now stood, she assumed she would never achieve her desire to be the darling of the London theatre world—or the future favorite of the king, once he tired of Nell Gwynn.

"Here you are. I've been searching the galleries for you. You are not going to view the rest of the play?"

The presence of Mary Gibbons upset her. She wanted to be alone so she could think, and now Mary was going to order her to go somewhere or do something. Summoning up her strength, Anne let the words escape, although she couldn't look her fellow actress in the eye.

"Mary, I wish to be alone now."

"Why in heaven's name? What has happened? Has Mr. Devlin attempted something lewd?" Mary's grin belied the seriousness of such a possibility.

"I don't wish to talk about anything. I simply want to think."

"And to fear or to regret?"

"I don't understand you."

"There you lie. You most certainly do." Mary paused before approaching Anne. "Give me your hand." Anne did as Mary ordered. "Be careful in your thinking, my sweet Anne. You could much damage your future if you react poorly and without balanced thought. Cry if you must, but don't say or do anything you will regret. I want to see you prosper here with the King's Company. I want to stand with you on stage when you become the favorite of the town—which you most certainly will if you continue to play the part off the stage you still believe you are not equipped to perform. Go home now, and I will come to you at eight."

Anne watched Mary disappear toward the front of the theatre. She looked at the darkening sky and fell forward, her hands now in cold mud, her dress now soiled. She brought her head up and clutched her dirty hands together in an attitude of sincere prayer. She took one more look skyward and closed her eyes.

CHAPTER 27

The King had just left the Banqueting House at Whitehall and was speaking with Henry Bennet, Earl of Arlington in the Privy Garden when Nell and Abby arrived with their palace escort. Nell whispered to Abby that Arlington was one of the "dull" advisers at court. "No one has ever caught him with any woman other than his wife." Arlington parted from the king as one of Charles's spaniels ran to Nell and began leaping upon her.

"You best pray you have no mud on your paws!" Nell shouted with mock seriousness. "Abby, this is Prince Nip, my favorite. I love the black and white spaniels especially—with that brownish rust color mixed in around his adorable face." Nell calmed the spaniel down and knelt to pet it, and in a moment Abby did likewise. Abby was not at all surprised that the animal took so to Nell Gwynn. She wondered how anyone could dislike this incredibly vivacious young woman. By the time Abby looked up, His Majesty was standing a foot away. He called for one of his men to take the dogs to Mr. Burgess as he hovered over his two female guests, a look of bemusement in his rugged and handsome face.

"Oh, Your Majesty, please forgive me." Abby had lost her balance just enough to make her rise most unladylike. She wanted to fall prostrate on her stomach, she was so embarrassed. Suddenly, Charles grabbed her hand and assisted her to her feet. Abby immediately bowed, this time with at least a modicum of grace.

Nell cleared her throat loudly. "Am I to receive no help in rising?"

Without thinking, Abby reached down for Nell's hand, while the king roared with approval. Nell stared at her new friend with playful disdain.

After Nell made the proper introduction and the king asked several questions about Abby's opinion of Virginia and her recent ocean voyage back to England, Nell asked with a matter-of-fact tone, "Am I to suppose that Squintabella has returned to her French handlers?" Smiling, Charles shook his head at Nell's temerity and raised his eyebrows as he looked at

Abby.

"Here, Abigail, let me—"

"Oh, call her Abby, Your Majesty. She doesn't stand on formality."

Through her discomfort, Abby managed to squeak out a "You may call me what you like, Your Majesty."

Nell nudged the king. "There, you see. You have her permission to call her Abby." Abby audibly groaned at the implications of Nell's translation. She tried to explain that she never meant to sound as though she was giving the king permission, but he graciously dismissed her attempt with "Nellie is like a fisherman. She casts her net wide for any opportunity to shock and embarrass those in her company. Much to everyone's discomfort, she always catches what she casts for."

Nell ignored the playful jab while giving credence to it. "Abby, do you know that the most exciting thing His Majesty and his queen have done together is fish. I enjoy all the king's games—his tennis, his swimming, his riding, and his horse racing. But fishing, never. Somehow it all seems so appropriate. The king and his wife dropping a line in the water waiting for that to happen which means nothing anyway. A tug on the line, and a loud "Houza!" when Catherine Queen pulls up a silly little limp fish, not enough to feed a street urchin.

"You should be whipped and exiled for slandering the queen," Charles replied in mock ferocity.

"Me—never. You love me too much and will not have me sent away—at least not yet. My day will come, Abby, I am sure, but I have made His Majesty promise that if he dies before I do, his last words will be 'Be sure Nellie remains fed'—or something to that effect."

Abby waited until the king laughed before she even allowed herself a smile, but after this moment of merry bantering, she knew it was time to explain why she wanted to see him. Since she hadn't told Nell, she accepted she would have to tell them both at the same time. Once more her stomach tightened as she searched for the right words to broach the subject, but Charles went on to tell her about Whitehall Palace—the largest in Europe, he boasted. He spoke about its "well over a thousand" rooms, its Tennis Courts, and Banquet Hall, where he had come after his triumphal return to England ten years earlier. Charles added a short history of Whitehall, going back to the time of Henry VIII. "I shall show you the Banquet House, Abby, but then I must prepare myself for short journey to fight a number of serious of battles." Abby was confused by the military reference. Nell made the allusion clear.

"His Majesty is going to gamble tonight at Sir Joseph Willet's in the northern part of the city."

Abby hesitated before responding. "Is that something you do often, Your Majesty?"

"Not often enough to win as much as I would like. It seems I need more of Nellie's luck, I'm afraid."

"I have gambled and won all my life, Abby."

Abby couldn't let her elaborate. She had to find herself an opening to share with the king what she had heard. "Is Sir Joseph's where you frequently play, Your Majesty?"

"Why do you ask? Do you want a place at the table?" Abby appreciated the king's playfulness toward her. Perhaps, then, he might be more inclined to believe her and heed her warning.

"Do many know you go there for your gambling, Your Majesty, or is that a secret known to few?"

Charles seemed puzzled by the specificity of Abby's question, but he indulged her curiosity. "It is no secret that I go there to gamble. His slight emphasis on "gamble" grabbed Nell's attention. Abby felt this was the moment she needed to reveal what she knew, but the king took her by the arm and led her toward an object Abby judged as close to ten feet tall. "Let me show my sun dial." Abby now felt queasy from the suppression of the information she held within her, but she couldn't interrupt the king as she spoke of his prized and elaborate sun dial, constructed with brass, wood, stone, ironwork, and painted glass panels. The works inside the structure reminded Abby of a fountain of glass. "Do you see, Abby? It reveals not only the hours of the day but it also provides information about the stars."

"His Majesty is a star gazer, Abby." Nell again thought to tease the king. "Do you see over there—right off the Stone Gallery?" The Privy Garden was hemmed in by some of the buildings and walls of Whitehall. "Those are the royal apartments, and there is a screen set in one of the windows so that anyone walking here will not see His Royal Majesty's nakedness while he bathes in his tub large enough to serve as a boat." Abby looked at the king for any signs on anger, but he remained charmed by Nellie's brazenness. "Oh, and some *former* residents here used to place their undergarments to air in sight of those who walked here in the Privy Garden. In fact, you have met one of those residents—Lady Castlemaine, whose intimate garments were often commented on by those who saw them fluttering in the breeze." This time, Charles looked disapprovingly at Nell, who twitched her lips and sighed. "I need to use the Royal Chamber Pot. I hope the Royal Gong Farmer has emptied it, Your Majesty. If not I will flood the floor with piss." It was clear to Abby that Nell was upset at Charles's sour reaction to her mention of Lady Castlemaine's undergarments.

As Nell walked briskly toward the palace, the king looked at Abby and shrugged his shoulders. Now was the moment. Abby pushed forward the words she had been waiting to speak since she arrived at Whitehall. "Your Majesty, I have news I must share with you. It has to do with a plot against you—or so I cannot help believing." Although she spoke rapidly, none of her words were lost on the king. She shared with him what she overheard and saw at Dove-Raven House. She added she was nearly certain an attempt on his life would be made this evening. "Please remain here tonight. Do not go to Sir Joseph Willet's."

Initially the King uttered only a name. "Lord Durell." Abby pleaded again for the king to remain at Whitehall. "No, I will go to Sir Joseph's tonight. You see, Lord Durell is not the kind of man who would take an active role in such treasonous activity. There will be others to do his work for him. I must catch them in the attempt. Did you see Sir Roger Earle at Dove-Raven House, Abby?"

"I was not introduced to him, but I was told he was there."

"Recently?"

"Yes. I know there was a man who talked to Lord Durell in the darkness last night, and I heard them speak. But I don't know if it was Sir Roger Earle."

"It was not he."

Knowing nothing of his recent murder, Abby assumed Earle was at Whitehall or that the king was having him watched.

"I wish you to be near Sir Joseph's house tonight, Abby."

"Me, Your Majesty?" She was startled by the suggestion.

"Yes. I will see to it that you are safe, never fear. My men will watch over you. You will wait nearby and then come forward to identify by face or voice any who are involved."

"Yes, Your Majesty." She knew it would be fruitless to protest.

"Such plots we always fear. Do not go or send any message back to Dove-Raven House."

Nell returned to the Privy Garden. The king asked her to show Abby the Banquet House and Tennis Courts. "The two of you will then sup together at Whitehall." Because the king brushed her lovely face before he walked back to into the palace, Nell's mood brightened. Yet Abby's sense of accomplishment had transformed to one of deep concern. What if there was no attempt made tonight at Sir Joseph's? What would the king's reaction be to what she had warned him of? Did the king consider the possibility that she was being used by the plotters or was even a willing participant in an assassination attempt? Abby couldn't believe she was now praying for the plotters actually to make their attempt on the king.

"It's time to go, Francis. I assume you have told no one where you are going."

Gottlieb assured the theatre manager he did not, but he was bothered by one matter. "And are you sure we will receive our payment sometime tomorrow?"

Devlin tried unsuccessfully to contain his frustration. "As I have told you several times already—yes. Likely before daybreak, as a matter of fact." Richard Hansall already handed Devlin one hundred pounds—money he said he had received from Lord Durell. Hansall also assured Devlin that neither he nor Gottlieb's identity were known to Durell. Devlin reminded Gottlieb once again of the promise he would be handsomely rewarded. That calmed the tightly-strung actor. "Francis let's go over our actions once or twice more so that we are sure to make no mistakes."

Gottlieb nodded somewhat wearily, suggesting he felt the exercise completely unnecessary. The men would take slightly different routes to the meeting place off Holborn and not far from the home of Sir Joseph Willet. Devlin knew the odds of seeing the morning sun as a wealthy man were not as much in his favor as he would prefer. On the other hand, he knew that Francis Gottlieb's chances were utterly nil.

Thomas Lockwood picked up one of his Lady's handkerchiefs, which she had inadvertently dropped in a moment of violent agitation at the prospects of Lord Brinton bringing her to ruin. Lockwood felt the moisture on the fabric and knew it came from the tears his lady shed after her anger was expelled. Lockwood had been thinking of nothing but saving the woman he adored from such a fate—from such a humiliation. The king trusted Brinton explicitly—and the man was a clever and persuasive prosecutor. Lockwood accepted he would never be fortunate enough to lie in bed with his lady or enjoy her physical affections, but he drew upon the tales of three centuries earlier, in which knights would sacrifice all—even their lives—to serve the women they loved. Perhaps he could kill Brinton and escape detection; after all, he had done other deeds in service to Lady Castlemaine that remained unknown to everyone other than her—and at times even unknown to her. Placing the moist handkerchief to his nose, he absorbed the fragrance that lingered on it as if it were an elixir that filled him with both purpose and courage. He would die if need be, but he would protect his lady.

"Do not ask me any further questions, Samuel. You know only what you need to know and what you need to do."

"Very well, Lord Durell. I understand fully."

Durell stared into Greenham's eyes for assurance that his man both knew what was expected of him and was committed to doing it. Satisfied, Durell smiled. "Samuel, you have long served me as well as your father served mine. Do you recall the first major task you performed for me?"

Greenham answered Durell's smile with one of his own. "Yes, my Lord.

We were in Paris, and you wished me to intrude on a gathering of woman-what the French now call Salons—and then cull you out two or three of the youngest and prettiest ones to keep you company."

"And do you remember the names of the two you brought to me?"

"Ninon and Henriette, my Lord, and you were particularly taken with Henriette."

"Yes, she was a twenty-year old exquisite beauty—beyond compare. Do you remember what she said when she first beheld me?"

"I do indeed. She said, '*Il est seulement un petit garçon!*'"

"'He is only a little boy!' But I was not that little for my age—for a nine-year-old boy."

"But at least Ninon remained and humored you."

"She most assuredly did. With her tales of sea monsters and cave-dwelling beasts while I stared at her two lovely mounds half exposed from her dress."

Greenham felt there was something of a valedictory nature in Lord Durell's reminiscences, but it was good to see Durell smile again. He had been quite serious and morose for a good two months or more.

"Go now, Samuel. Do as I have bid you."

"Shall I go to the other side of the house and greet Lady Durell before I go."

"That won't be necessary, Samuel. I'm sure she is engaged in social plotting of some nature."

"Excuse the question, my Lord, but have you spent more time together in recent weeks, or . . ."

"About the same as always. She has her desires and schemes and I have mine—and they are not compatible."

"I have had it all day and have not opened it."

"You haven't opened it? But it is from the king!" Mary Gibbons was dumbfounded by young Anne Whitworth's naiveté. "Child, you cannot ignore a message from Whitehall. You could be . . . here give it to me." Mary took the note, broke the seal, and read the contents.

To the lovely Anne,

I have seen you twice on the stage of the King's Theatre and should like you to take a morning walk with me the day after tomorrow in St. James's Park and have some tea or chocolate afterwards. I would wish of course to discuss your performances. When you arrive at Whitehall, ask for Bridget Warren, and she will bring you to me.

Anne looked frightened. "It's what I feared. The king has been disappointed in my acting and wishes me to leave the stage."

Mary rolled her eyes skyward. "You stupid girl. His Majesty is interested in you for other talents he believes you possess. He will not ask you to leave the stage—at least not at present."

"Why are you laughing at me?" Anne was nearly in tears.

"Oh, my dearest angel. I laugh not at you but at your misunderstanding of the king's intentions. He loves all actresses, but seems to have taken a special liking of you. We must choose a fine dress for you to wear."

"Then I'm to meet him?"

"Yes, you lovely but brainless girl. And I will give you some topics about which to speak to His Majesty to keep his interest in you alive throughout your walk and tea."

Chapter 28

At the home of Sir Joseph Willet, Abby sat conversing with Sir Joseph's wife Amanda and Elinor Middleton, the wife of one of the men playing cards with the king in an adjoining room. Trying her best to answer Elinor's questions about her years in Virginia, Abby was both anxious and confused by the king's apparently carefree behavior as he played *Jeu Royal de la Guerre*, a French card game Charles had become most fond of. How could he seem so relaxed when he knew there was an imminent attempt on his life? What did he know that permitted him such freedom from fear?

Abby was most disappointed when the His Majesty informed Nell she wouldn't be accompanying them to Willet's home off Holborn. As he informed Abby after a frustrated Nell left Whitehall, he wished to prevent his mistress from worrying about his safety. "Besides," he added, "she'll want to play at the table, and I cannot afford to lose to such a clever gambler. I believe you were wise in keeping what you knew from her."

Having been told that the king preferred her in the Willet house and not in another residence nearby, Abby tried her best to listen as the men spoke during their "royal game of war," wondering if Charles would say anything to the others about Lord Durell's plot. She learned from overhearing that they played a trick-taking game with a war theme, with four suit-less cards designated as *Death, Force, Army General*, and *Prisoner of War*. The four aces in the deck were labeled *cannoneer, a soldier with a drawn rapier, a battalion,* and *a squadron of horsemen,* and the men played for liberal amounts of money, much of which the king won, either by chance or by the cooperation of his fellow card players seeking to humor their monarch. Although Abby didn't fully understand the rules of the game, she was quick to learn that one loses immediately if he holds the *Death* card. The relevance of the game to the reason she was here with the king was pronounced and terrifying.

After several hours of the men's card play and the women's

conversation and cups of tea, Amanda Willet excused herself and promised to return before Abby went to bed. This was Abby's first indication she would be spending the night at the Willet's. "Where is Amanda going, I wonder?" Abby asked Elinor Middleton.

"Oh, my dear girl, don't you know? She is going to meet the king nearby."

"For what purpose?" Abby immediately felt foolish for having asked such an ignorant question. For a moment she felt sad for Nell, but quickly remembered the king was hardly a loyal lover to his favorite women. After a few minutes, she heard Charles in the other room excuse himself for a time and promise that he too would return to finish the game. Abby feared the king would put himself in grave danger by meeting privately with Amanda Willet. Would his men be close enough by to protect him if an attempt was made on his life? Abby's next thoughts were once more about Charlotte. What would happen to her if the king arrested Lord Durell for treason?

"Willet's wife has entered the house across the way." Gottlieb informed Devlin that only one of the household servants—an elderly women—accompanied Amanda Willet.

"Tell Hansall." Gottlieb headed to where the Puritan was awaiting word—behind another house in the immediate area. Devlin took up the position that gave him an unimpeded view of the distance between the Willet house and the one used for the king's periodic assignations with Willet's wife. Having watched the area for almost an hour, Devlin and Gottlieb had seen none of Charles's men come to the empty house. By the time Gottlieb returned with Hansall, all three men caught sight of the king making his way to the house which Amanda Willet and her woman recently entered. By the time Charles made it to the front of the residence, one room on the lower level had been lit by candles—one of the bedrooms, Devlin assumed. Hansall took his position next to Devlin, and they observed Charles gesture to the three men accompanying him—apparently instructing them to guard the front door. After the king entered, his three men remained where they were. The plotters watched for an additional five minutes to see if one of these men would take up watch near the rear entrance of the house, but none of them moved from their places. Rather, two of the guards lit clay pipes and smoked tobacco.

Hansall whispered to Devlin, "The king's lust has always dominated his better sense—as I suspected it would tonight. Come." The three men placed over their heads black hoods with cut-outs for their eyes and made their way walking ten yards apart to the rear of the house in which the king and Willet's wife were surely beginning their lovemaking. When the men made it to the rear door undetected, Hansall easily and quietly opened it with the straighter of the two knives he had on his person. The men waited another minute before moving toward the one lighted room forty feet away. They took out their blades the moment they heard the sound of Amanda Willet in evident sexual arousal. Hansall smiled thinking of the justice to be served by executing the king in the middle of his perverse and sinful act with another man's wife, whom the men had already agreed to leave unharmed provided she obeyed their command to be silent. Gottlieb had the responsibility of placing his hand or bed clothing over her mouth and instructing her not to scream while Devlin and Hansall dispatched the king. As Hansall earlier instructed them, Gottlieb would tie a gag around her mouth and bind her hands to the bedpost, giving them more than enough time to escape out the door they had entered through and then go separate ways until their arranged meeting before daybreak. Only Devlin knew Gottlieb would not live to collect the money promised him by Lord Durell. He would dispatch his actor not simply for reasons of greed—but rather of prudence. He believed Gottlieb had too much of a conscience to be depended on to remain silent for any length of time.

The men were grateful that Amanda Willet was a demonstrative lover, because her passionate cries covered any sound they made slowly walking across the wooden floor. When the men reached the slightly ajar door to the bedroom, Hansall replaced his straight knife with the one with a curved handle and wider blade. Devlin reacted viscerally to the sight of Hansall's weapon and knew the Puritan could both stab and carve into the flesh of the king. At that moment, they heard both male and female moans indicate that the sex act had reached its culmination. Hansall bolted into the room followed by Devlin and Gottlieb. They were stunned by what they saw.

The bed was empty.

Standing against the far wall was one of the king's men and a female none of them recognized. The confused men stepped further into the room and began to look behind them, but their shoulders had barely turned when each man was set upon by five more of the king's men, who had been waiting on the inside of the room, on both sides of the door. Two of the guards disarmed each of the plotters and removed their black hoods. Holding swords to the throat of each would-be assassin, the king's men also bound the plotters' hands behind them. Hansall, Devlin, and Gottlieb were led out of the room and shoved forward until they reached the house's withdrawing room.

The king sat regally in one of the chairs, with Amanda Willet placed next to him. Four more of Charles's guards stood to either side of the chairs. The population of the room had now swollen with the three plotters, ten of the king's men, Amanda and her elderly attendant, and the young woman who had provided the mock sounds of passion in the bedroom. The king addressed the three prisoners.

"Did you really believe I had no idea of what was plotted in my own city?" Devlin and Gottlieb had their heads down; Hansall kept his hateful eyes trained on the king's. "My men have been waiting in this house for three hours, fully aware you would enter through the back door. In fact, I made that rather simple for you. You should have realized you were only permitted to enter a trap. I give you credit for knowing that I have had my occasional moments alone with the Willet's lovely wife Amanda here." Amanda also had her head down—in embarrassment over the apparent fact that others knew of her liaisons with the king." Charles called forth the young woman who had been in the bedroom. "This is a woman who in her trade has had frequent experience expressing passion when she felt none. Meriall, I believe your name is."

"Yes, Your Majesty."

"I wanted everything to sound enticing to the three of you, you see. Thank you, my dear." Charles signaled one of his men to pay Meriall for her special services, which she took gratefully and left the room. As she did, she passed Abigail Fayette coming into the house.

On her heels was Lord Brinton. "Please excuse my delay in arriving, Your Majesty."

"No, Henry, you have arrived exactly at the right moment. Now Abby, do you recognize any of these men?" Charles ordered that Devlin and Gottlieb lift their heads. Tears were evident on Gottlieb's face.

Abby's stomach tightened. How she wished she were anywhere else than in this room. "Yes, Your Majesty. I recognize Mr. Devlin from the theatre. I don't know the other man."

"And?" Charles pointed toward Hansall.

"I am certain he was the man I saw meet with Lord Durell by the labyrinth."

"Would you care to hear him speak to be certain? Go on, man, greet the lady." Hansall's eyes narrowed and his jaw tightened, indicating to the king that he would say nothing. "Well, it is unnecessary, Abby. You have identified him. So, I assume that Lord Durell has paid for the three of you to murder your king."

"You are not my king." None in the room expected Hansall to speak only seconds after he indicated he wouldn't.

Charles raised his eyebrows. "I shan't be *your* king for long—we can at least agree on that."

Abby marveled at how serene the king was in the aftermath of an attempt on his life. He almost seemed pleased.

Hansall spoke with fury and bitterness. "You, Charles Stuart, are the murderer. We are heaven's agents to punish your sins against us men and against Almighty God."

"Heaven had chosen the wrong men, then. Take him from my presence." Three of the king's guards dragged Hansall out of the house. "Now, Mr. Devlin, I will not spend much time castigating you for your ingratitude. After all, I permitted you to run my theatre and saw to it that you had fine actors to perform the plays. But you thought to stage your own drama—which you believed would be a comedy, but has turned out to be a most bitter tragedy for you."

Panic swept over Devlin's countenance. "It was Lord Durell, Your Majesty. I will testify to the fact. Hansall assured me he would pay me handsomely." Devlin ceased speaking; he realized he had done himself no favors with his admission.

"My only confusion is how did Richard Hansall—a Puritan who despised the theatre as did all his stock, come to depend on someone like you who represented all he loathed. But that is no matter now. Perhaps we will learn the answer in the days ahead. Take him." Two guards led Devlin away. Francis Gottlieb began to sob, which affected Abby's sympathies. "And you, Gottlieb. I never thought you were much of an actor—but that might be your saving grace. Tell me why you took part in this matter. Gottlieb struggled to get the words out, but he managed to admit that Devlin had power over him and his livelihood and that he too had been promised seven hundred pounds from Lord Durell, although he had never met the man.

"I wasn't to stab you, Your Majesty. I was only to keep the lady there silent." He pointed to Amanda Willet. "And then bind her to the bedposts so we could all escape. I am no murderer, Your Majesty. Please, please know that I am not. I will speak against Mr. Devlin and Mr. Hansall in the court. I swear it." Abby began to step toward the king so she could plead for the poor man's life when Charles issued his sentence. "Upon your being found guilty, you will be sent to prison, but you will have your life." Abby articulated a soft sound to suggest that she wished the sentence to be more lenient. Charles could barely suppress his smile. "Upon a second thought, you will be spared the misery of Newgate, Gottlieb, but you will spend the next ten years without your freedom. Charles cast a glance at Abby, whose face suggested that the sentence was still too strict. "As I said, you will spend the next six years without your freedom." Gottlieb fell to his knees and thanked the king through a torrent of tears. The sight of this large man reduced to a childlike display affected Abby to the point that she touched him after the king ordered he be taken away.

"Well, Abby, I owe you many thanks for sharing what you overheard. We will discuss tomorrow how I may repay you."

Abby thought better of protesting any reward because she feared it might be an insult to the king. An unwelcomed thought slipped into her mind. What if the king wished to share his bed with her as her proper reward? She immediately chastised herself and her vanity for imagining such a possibility, but how could she help it given what he learned about the king and his sexual conquests in just the few days she had been in London.

"Henry?"

Brinton stepped forward from behind the king. "Yes, Your Majesty?"

Charles cast a sly glance at Abby. "It's been an eventful evening and I'm too tired to deal with Lord Durell tonight. Have him brought to the palace tomorrow morning right before the noon hour."

"Should I arrest him tonight?"

"Let's give the traitor one last night of 'pleasant' sleep. I have already sent men to watch Dove-Raven House to prevent his riding off should he hear the news that his plot has failed. He will keep until morning."

Abby asked to be heard. "Your Majesty, is there any way I can go there tonight and be with Lady Durell? She is my dear friend, and the news of her husband's horrid act of betrayal will devastate her."

"You would then spoil Lord Durell's morning surprise. But I will see that she is brought to Whitehall with her husband and you may comfort her then. And surely there will be much for which she will need comforting. She is soon to be a widow. Henry, be sure you bring her to the palace with that despicable and traitorous husband of hers."

"I will, Your Majesty. But let me remind you that you are to see Lady Castlemaine tomorrow at noon as well."

"Yes, Barbara." Abby thought the king appeared greatly saddened by the prospect.

"Pardon me, Your Majesty, but am I to sleep here tonight?"

"No, Abby. I have changed my mind. You will sleep at Whitehall. I promise that you will enjoy the accommodations there. Besides, you will need to be present when Lord Durell is brought before me. You are an important witness, you know. Both you and I will sleep until late morning, and then I will see to it that you have a hearty early dinner before we set to our business." Abby heard nothing past the king's "you and I will sleep until late morning"; her entire body felt as though it were going numb. Charles read the concern on her face easily enough. "Never fear, Abby. You will sleep alone—unless, that is, you should like company. I will then send two of my spaniels to your room to warm your sheets." The king paused for the laugh that came immediately from the men in the room—even from Lord Brinton. The only one who frowned at the witticism was Amanda Willet. Her plans for a pleasurable evening with the monarch had been dashed.

Chapter 29

Phoebe had no idea where Abby went after the play. She waited half an hour after the patrons dispersed before she headed to the Willet house to the north of the city. Her instructions were to inform the king's men that the assailants had gone to the south and west after the king's murder. But something went terribly wrong and the plot failed. Phoebe waited until she saw the bound Richard Hansall taken from the house near the Willet's before she joined the elderly non-conformist husband and wife Hansall had hired to take her to her sister's home in Cambridge following the murder of the king. They began their sixty-mile trip almost immediately. Wondering if Abby left the play early with someone she knew, Phoebe feared Abby would return to Dove-Raven House and be there when the three men also hired by Hansall arrived to murder Lord Durell and perhaps others in Durell's employ. "Please be safe, Abby," Phoebe whispered to herself as she began her journey to Cambridge.

Hansall's crew arrived near the grounds of Dove-Raven House at four in the morning. One of the men went ahead to investigate the premises for signs of anyone up and about. When the man didn't return within twenty minutes, the other two decided to ride around the grounds to the east and come upon the house from the rear. They hadn't ridden one hundred yards before they were halted by members of the king's guard.

"You have awakened me this early for a mere tweak of conscience?"

Mary Gibbons opened her door to a highly agitated Anne Whitworth, who had evidently been crying for some time. "I cannot help it, Mary. I dreamt of him. He was looking up at me, with blood coming from his body, asking me why I had done it."

Mary pulled Anne almost violently into a chair. "That was a dream. It didn't . . . It has nothing to do with reality."

"Oh, but it does. I'm afraid I will never sleep again without seeing him. What can I do? Oh, Mary. What can I do?"

Her elder friend's annoyance and frustration quickly turned to deep concern. "You can stop these foolish thoughts is what you can do. I have a little rum left. Would you like some to calm you?"

"No. I must . . . No, but perhaps a small sip of red wine." Anne's eyes danced about the room as Mary found the bottle and poured her a healthy amount.

"Here, drink this." Anne took but a small sip and handed the cup back to Mary. "Are you settled a bit now?"

"Yes, thank you." A smile came to Anne's lips as though she had solved a difficulty of some kind. "Forgive me, Mary. I am all right now. I'm sorry I woke you."

Mary was hardly convinced. "Why don't you stay? You can lie with me and sleep another hour or so."

"No, I am awake. I will go about my business now. I am to be at a rehearsal for tomorrow's play at noon."

"I know that, silly girl. I'm in the same play—remember?"

"Oh, yes. I forgot. Goodbye—I mean good morning, Mary." Anne blithely turned and headed out the door. Mary remained troubled. She thought Anne impressionable, yet still dependable. Now she wasn't sure.

Abby presented herself to the king a few minutes before noon. She barely slept during the night and the early morning hours. She couldn't numb herself to the impending dread of what would happen to Lord Durell, because she knew how affected Charlotte would be by the events of the preceding night. Abby prayed that her dear childhood friend would not be forsaken or falsely accused by the king or by Lord Brinton.

"I have played tennis, walked in St. James's Park with my spaniels, and looked in on my racing horses while you slumbered, Abby."

"I fear I did little slumbering, Your Majesty. My eyes should inform you of that."

Charles laughed as though nothing serious had happened the previous night or would take place on this day. "I even had time this morning to . . . communicate with a very pretty actress."

To her surprise, Abby found the king's admission of his early sexual activities both amusing and charming. "Should I be told of such things, Your Majesty?" She couldn't help smiling at her monarch. They had clearly developed a harmony between them in the mere eighteen hours they had known each other.

"Oh, I do believe you misconstrue, Abby. I am shocked you would imagine such a bawdy thing. Fortunately, Lord Rochester isn't here. I know he would immortalize you in one of his verses as a bad woman."

Abby was completely confused. "Then I must beg Your Majesty's forgiveness."

"I easily grant it. Although I am afraid it will be the last forgiveness I will grant today." Charles's smile dropped as he signaled to one of his men. In a moment Lord Brinton came to his side. "Let us begin with our surprise business, Henry. Have her brought in."

"A surprise indeed, Your Majesty." Brinton had no idea what this matter was about. Abby saw that upon his signal a lovely young woman took her place before the king. Her eyes were opened wide but her demeanor was settled. Was this the actress Charles had "communicated" with earlier?

"I have spoken with this woman already and she has a most interesting tale to share. Tell Lord Brinton what you have done, my dear." Anne Whitworth turned to Brinton and spoke without hesitation.

"I helped kill Sir Roger Earle, my Lord."

"You?" Brinton laughed.

"Listen to what she has to say, before you dismiss her claim."

"Yes, Your Majesty."

Charles instructed Anne to repeat what she told him earlier. Anne revealed considerable relief as she commenced.

"I led Sir Roger to his death at the hands of another."

Abby believed the young actress only meant she was with Earle when he was set upon, but Anne soon disabused her of that assumption. Anne spoke of posing as a prostitute by the name of Lucy and luring Sir Roger into a nearby house. "I said to him what I was instructed to say, and soon he gave in to his lust, completely unaware of another's presence in the room. When he was stabbed, I immediately ran out of the house and returned to my lodging as I was also told to do.

Brinton shook his head as if he had only that moment awakened, "Who killed him, then?"

Abby felt sympathy for the young woman, as Anne's face twisted in pain and tears formed in her lovely eyes.

"I have told His Majesty. I cannot mention the name again. Please forgive me. I didn't realize what would happen to Sir Roger. I only thought that a witness would be brought in to see what he was attempting to do to me. I didn't want him dead. I didn't." She broke down and sank to her knees. Abby rushed over to assist her, and Charles called for a chair.

Brinton looked at the king. "You know who it was who killed him, Your Majesty?"

"I do." Once more he nodded to one of his men.

Brinton was horrified when Mary Gibbons was brought into the room. She stared at him intently, with a look that seemed to command him to assist her, not merely to ask him for assistance. Mary shifted her eyes to the tortured Anne Whitworth, who fully expected the vile language Mary assaulted her with.

"You ungrateful slut of a bitch. How could you betray me like this, you pathetic whore."

Abby glared at the women with disgust, but she wasn't free to say anything. Instead, Anne raised her head and responded in a voice that was both pleading and terrified. "Forgive me, Mary. I didn't wish to, but I knew it was necessary for my soul to speak truth. I cannot add to my . . ."

"Your what, you pathetic slut?" Mary once more glared at Brinton, whose head shook slightly side to side.

Suddenly, Anne seemed hopeful. She rose to her feet and took a step toward Mary, who was restrained by two of the king's guards. "Just tell them that you had good reason to slay him, Mary. Your Majesty, will you hear what she had endured from Sir Roger?" The king looked bemused as he gestured his permission with his right hand.

Mary spat at her former friend and accomplice. "You fool. You silly little foolish bitch."

Anne's hopeful expression was not at all affected by Mary's epithets. "His Majesty will understand, Mary. He will."

Charles sighed in exasperation. "Just tell me of your relationship with the man." He cast a glance at Abby, who let him know she sympathized with his impatience. But still Mary said nothing.

"Oh, I will reveal it then." Anne informed the king that she and Mary had overheard Sir Roger Earle speaking with a Puritan man named Hansall about an event they were planning for the king. "Sir Roger said that Mary had agreed to do whatever she could to make sure the event went as they had planned, but that—"

"Liar!" Mary struggled further against her captors. "She lies!"

"Take her out of the room." Charles's leaned forward in his chair, his expression having lost all its bemusement as his men dragged Mary Gibbons away. "Continue your tale, Anne."

"Mary later overheard Sir Roger tell Mr. Hansall she would serve them better by being blamed if matters went wrong, and that since she was keeping lewd company with someone named Henry, the two of them could be held responsible if the event was a failure."

Charles turned toward Lord Brinton, whose face registered grave concern and humiliation.

"Your Majesty, I . . . "

Charles leaned forward, his anger evident. "Do you know this Gibbons woman, Lord Brinton?"

Anne's eyes broadened, as fear overcame her. Abby once more came to her side to steady her.

"I do know her. I have been . . . But I assure you that I knew nothing of what this young woman speaks. I swear that to you, Your Majesty."

Charles curled his bottom lip inside his mouth as he took measure of what he had just heard and learned, "No, Henry. I don't believe you did. Logic suggests to me that Sir Roger was one of the plotters and you were to be used if I escaped my death."

"Your death?" Anne's words were barely articulated as she began to tremble.

"I'm sure you didn't know what they were planning to do, young woman. Now tell me. Mary Gibbons killed Earle because . . ."

"Because she hated him for betraying her and abusing her body, as she told me, when they . . ." Suddenly, Anne realized Mary was part of the plot to assassinate the king. "Then she wished you dead, Your Majesty?"

"Apparently so." The king regained his bemused demeanor. He looked at Brinton. "Relax, Henry. You are guilty of bad judgment regarding your choice of lovers but nothing more it seems to me."

"Exactly, Your Majesty." Brinton still feared that Mary Gibbons, who expected him to come to her aid, would reveal the sordid nature of their sexual encounters. Now that he knew she had been willing to assist in the death of the king, he was overcome by the fact that he had chosen her to satisfy his need for sexual stimulation through physical punishment. But his humiliation was tempered by the announcement that Lady Castlemaine had arrived at Whitehall. There was still the matter of the actress Betty Keller's death. Brinton felt justified in planting evidence in Lady Castlemaine's fireplace, because he was not only certain she was responsible for the murder but also highly desirous that she be blamed. But now there was the distinct possibility that the Countess Castlemaine had hired Mary Gibbons to kill Betty Keller in her sleep. Lady Castlemaine could easily have gained the woman entrance to Whitehall. Would the king discover his chief adviser's unusual sexual proclivities when he learned that Mary had murdered both Sir Roger Earle and Betty Keller? And now Brinton came to another realization—that Mary had in one sense cuckolded him with Earle. She had assured Brinton she would have no sexual experiences with other men as long as Brinton required her services.

Abby noticed Brinton's agitation, with a tinge of fear evident on his face. Her attention then shifted to the entrance of a man she did not recognize. Charles threw up his hands.

"And who gave you permission to enter my presence, Thomas?"

Before Lockwood could reply, one of the king's men begged Charles's indulgence. "Your Majesty, this man insists he has information for you that could not wait. He said it was necessary you hear him out."

Once more the king glanced at Abby, with an expression that seemed to beg for her sympathy. "Is Lady Castlemaine here, Thomas?"

"She is, but it is important I precede her."

"Does she know you have done so?"

"No, Your Majesty. She has no idea."

Charles stared at Lockwood for several moments, before venting his frustration. "Then in God's name speak, man."

Lockwood bowed and expressed his gratitude for being permitted to address the king."

"Damn it, Thomas, if you don't get to the point immediately, I'll have you locked away for trying my patience."

"Your Majesty, I know Lord Brinton believes my Lady Castlemaine is responsible for killing the young actress here at Whitehall. But . . . I swear she is innocent of any such crime or even knowing of it beforehand."

Brinton stepped toward Lockwood as though he would strike him. "And just how do you know this? Are you privy to all she has done or plans to do? You serve her. You are not her lover." Brinton paused. "Or are you?"

"Henry." Charles responded with only slightly muted anger at Brinton's implication. "Then I assume you know who killed Betty Keller, Thomas?"

"Yes, Your Majesty." Brinton braced for the name Mary Gibbons to come from Lockwood's mouth. "I did. I killed her."

"You, Thomas?" The king oddly smiled at the confession. Brinton was relieved that Mary wasn't named, but he would not allow Lady Castlemaine to escape responsibility.

"And who put you up to it, Lockwood?"

"No one, Lord Brinton. I swear it."

"The Countess Castlemaine ordered you to do it, didn't she?"

"No, My Lord, she did not. Nor does she know even now that I was responsible."

Brinton's voice reflected his intense agitation. "You lie, man. You are only covering for that woman. You cannot deny it. The king knows you are speaking falsely. He knows." Brinton looked at Charles for corroboration. The king immediately gave it.

"That's exactly what I believe too, Henry." Brinton was too flushed with self-satisfaction to notice the wry smile on Charles's face.

"No, no, Your Majesty. It is not so. I speak true." Lockwood attempted further to refute Brinton's conclusion, but the king cut him off.

"Thomas you *are* doing your best to protect your lady, but you are doing it out of simple devotion." Lockwood attempted to speak again, but Charles held up his hand. "It has long been obvious to me that you love Lady Castlemaine and wish daily to prove that love. I know as well that you have aided her in some of her more insensitive schemes—but you would not kill for her, even if she begged you to. You're too good a man for that."

Brinton stepped toward the king. "Your Majesty, you must realize—"

"Keep silent, Henry. I don't wish to dismiss you from my presence, but I will if you interrupt again."

Brinton had no choice but to accede to the king's demand. "Forgive me, Your Majesty."

Charles smiled at Lockwood as he would a child who had lied for an unselfish reason. "Tell me the truth this time, Thomas, and I will forgive your earlier lie."

Thomas knelt. He couldn't look at the king. "I so feared she would be blamed that I felt I must take the responsibility for the horrible act—just to protect her. She is my lady, Your Majesty."

Charles stood and lifted Lockwood to his feet. "Would that you were not born the son of a merchant, Thomas. I would be pleased to have you close to me. I would treasure your loyalty."

One of the king's guards approached. "Lord Durell is here now, Your Majesty."

"I would have preferred to see Lady Castlemaine first and have that business concluded, but I will not wait a second longer to view this traitor to his king and country. Bring him in."

Abby wondered where Charlotte was at present. She assumed Lady Durell would be brought with her husband. Had anyone told her what Lord Durell had done? Charlotte was either in such a state of shock for having learned the truth or soon would be. Abby wanted to comfort Charlotte in whatever way she could, but her contemplations were halted by the king's voice.

"Abby, you will excuse us for the time being." One of Charles's guards took her out of the room. Everyone else remained. When Abby left, Charles nodded. In a moment, two of his men brought forward Lord Durell. Durell was young enough to resist vigorously, as the blood seeping from one of the guard's lips revealed. A third man joined the other two and pushed Durell to his knees in front of the king, who stared down at him with eyes more sad than hateful.

"Look at me." Durell slowly lifted his eyes. "If you deny organizing the attempt on my life, I will bring a witness who has overheard you and Richard Hansall together in close conversation. I have always known you felt insulted not being named to my group of advisers, but I assumed that my gift of what you now call Dove-Raven House was enough to temper your jealousy and resentment. Apparently, I was incorrect in my judgment. So, Lord Durell, do you deny being behind the plot on my life?"

Durell's bitter expression never gave way to fear or contrition. "I do not deny it. I should be pleased if you put me to death today—as soon as possible."

The king shook his head in pity. "I will determine the manner and day of your death when it pleases *me*." Another of Charles's men translated his silent nod. They took Durell from the room and began the journey to the Tower and ultimately to Tower Hill for his execution after his trial.

CHAPTER 30

Abby sat alone in one of the lavishly furnished rooms at Whitehall when she heard footsteps approaching her open door. She stood up, anticipating the visitors, but the two men and the woman did not stop. Rather, they walked past the door at modest pace. Abby caught sight of the woman. It was Barbara, Countess of Castlemaine. Abby raced to the door after the others had passed and looked down the hall at the regal bearing of the beautiful and notorious royal mistress. Perhaps sensing someone was staring at her, Lady Castlemaine turned her head and saw her recently-made acquaintance. Without halting stride, Barbara smiled at Abby and then continued on with the king's men.

Abby knew Barbara was accused of having Betty Keller murdered. Dismissing the possibility that Barbara herself killed the young actress, Abby wondered who could have committed the crime. Thomas Lockwood's "confession" was from its beginning too eager to be plausible—the king immediately making the same judgment. It was someone else Barbara had hired or convinced to do the deed—perhaps even Mary Gibbons, who had killed Sir Roger Earle. Could the king believe Lady Castlemaine was behind the murder and still forgive or spare her for having Betty Keller killed? This day was already a most unfortunate one. Would it be even more dreadful in the moments ahead?

Abby just returned to the sofa when a palace attendant stepped into the room. He nodded to Abby and stepped back into the hallway. When he returned to the room he was holding up Lady Durell, who was barely able to walk. Upon seeing Abby, she uttered a pathetic moan.

"Charlotte." Abby put her arm around her friend's waist and signaled for the attendant to leave the room. "Oh, Charlotte. I am so very sorry."

It took Charlotte several moments to speak through her sobbing. "They have blamed my husband for a plot against the king's life."

Abby was utterly miserable. It was her coming to the king and

228

informing him of what she had seen and heard at Dove-Raven House that brought Charlotte to this devastating emotional state. Even though she really had no choice in the matter, Abby knew her conscience would be forever tormented. What kind of future would—could—Charlotte have? Abby had not lived in London to know what happened to the wives of noblemen who were found guilty of such horrendous crimes. Would Charlotte be accused and punished? If so, how severely? Would she be banished from London or entirely from England? Abby sat Charlotte on the sofa and quickly formulated how she might assist her childhood friend.

"Charlotte, please know you may come and live with me if you are left with no other place to go."

"Your Majesty, may I know why I am brought before you in the company of others?" Lady Castlemaine saw several of the king's men, her nemesis Lord Brinton, the deeply grieved Thomas Lockwood, the evidently frightened Bridget Warren, and a winsome young woman she did not recognize. She stared almost malevolently at Anne Whitworth, assuming the girl was yet another of the king's bed partners. For her part, Anne had yet to learn her fate for aiding Mary Gibbons in the murder of Sir Roger Earle. Anne wished the woman called Abby would return and assure her all would be well.

Barbara understood she was being accused of either killing or having killed Betty Keller in one of the bedrooms at Whitehall, and she was certain that Brinton had poisoned the king's mind against her. She looked at Lockwood and smiled, assuming he had given his assurance to the king that his Lady could not have been guilty of so heinous an act. That Thomas was in the room suggested to her that perhaps he had lessened the king's belief in Lord Brinton's accusations. She would insist to the king that an accomplice of Brinton's had placed in her fireplace the knife box belonging to the martyred King Charles I and that she had never touched it or the knife used in the murder. "I ask again, Your Majesty. Why am I standing in such a public place as this room? Do you wish to humiliate me? Is that part of an undeserved punishment I am to receive?"

Charles stared at his lover of some ten years with a mixture of concern, disappointment, and affection. When she asked if she could speak to the king in private, Brinton said she could not but then quickly apologized for speaking before the king. Charles shook his head, but remained silent. Barbara realized he would not trust himself to be alone with her and that she had to address him in front of the others. She seemed to tremble for a moment before she began her defense.

"Since I came with you to London, I have been accused of betraying you with other men and betraying England with my supposed plots with those who wished you ill. Many have written verses decrying me as a 'whore' and 'villain' unworthy of your attention and deserving of exile or worse. Do you remember the couplet 'Full forty men a day provided for this whore, / Yet like a *bitch* she wags her tail for more'?—which you though more witty than insulting?"

Charles lowered his eyes for a moment in gesture of regret for over the years having waved off the hurt she suffered from insults like these.

"It has been said by many that I set the palace on fire and tore my children to pieces. Oh yes, I am the goddess of war Bellona—not Minerva, as Mr. Lely painted me—mocking those who would dare challenge my power. I have supposedly demanded a man be castrated for having falsely claimed to have lain with me. I have been confronted with sordid libels against me and no one doubts it was I referred to in "the Poor Whore's Petition" that amused so many. Your wife the queen and her ladies in waiting believe I am a sorceress, and I had to bear in silence the humiliation of seeing your wife cross herself when I entered her company. It is said about you, in case you have forgotten: 'Give the king the Countess of Castlemaine and he cares not what the nation suffers.'"

Barbara fought to maintain her composure and dignity as she looked at the others in the room—all of whom were silent—and only Lord Brinton wore disgust on his face.

"That I care for both my king and country cannot be fairly denied. Have I not warned His Majesty that the Court and the common people believe your pretty Louise is at best a French spy for King Louis and at worst a French slut, who has had King Louis between her legs. I cannot tell Your Majesty how many times I have heard a loud cry in the streets of 'Hang the French bitch!' I have tried to warn you she has been chosen by *others* to be your favorite mistress."

Charles dropped his eyes only momentarily before looking again at Barbara's incredible face revealing a vulnerability he had never before discovered on it.

"Those who depict me in the most horrible of ways have never seen how playful, kind, and fair-minded I can be. They see me frown and never realize—as you have my king—how much I love to smile. How we have smiled at so much for these many years in spite of our disagreements. Have you not praised me for my dinners, for my dancing and my society? Did you not call me your 'baby-face'? Were you not proud that many have called me 'The Great Lady' and said I deserved such an attribution? Did you not see yourself reflected in me, so much that you once told me that if God had made you a woman, you would wish to be no other than your Barbara? Did you not admire my opinions? Have I not always believed in you—no matter the times I attempted to influence your course?"

Charles closed his eyes and debated whether he should excuse the others and hear Barbara privately, but he didn't wish to endure Brinton's inevitable protest.

"I always sought to gain your admiration in places other than in your bed. Yes, I fought very hard to have my way, and I insisted you live up to every single promise you made to me. I fought ferociously only because I felt if I lost any battle with you, no matter how trivial, I might then lose you entirely. I could not let that happen. I did hate men like Clarendon, not simply because he despised me so, but because he threatened my existence with you. He threatened my place."

For the first time, she turned her head and looked at Brinton—but only for a brief moment. When she returned her gaze to Charles, he had re-opened his eyes.

"I remember that you would leave me in the gray dawn and then after your walk return for morning chocolate, while I sat with my head propped up in the bed talking with you regarding the affairs of state. I have always believed it was my incorrigible wickedness—perhaps my potential for cruelty that you could not understand, not possessing that quality yourself, but wished so much to embrace. You once said that for a man to love a woman she must of course capture his heart. But you added that I took more than your heart—I also conquered your imagination. I have always known that, deep inside, you felt imprisoned by the intensity of your passion for me and fought hard against it. But then all I had to do was talk with you intimately, to whisper so very quietly, and you were mine again. When, I wonder, was I banished from your imagination?" Tears began to drop from her violet eyes, so often marked upon as cold, austere, fiery, and frightening. "I fear it does me little good at this moment to claim I will always be the greatest love of your life. That I was once the king's favorite— the greatest love of your life—for I am not your favorite now.

Barbara kept her body erect and her head elevated as she openly cried—while Charles placed his face between his hands. For several seconds nothing was heard except Lady Castlemaine's muted sobbing. But the relative silence was shattered by Lord Brinton.

"Your Majesty, she is playing a part—can't you see that? Do not be moved by these manufactured tears. She has admitted she has conspired against others to maintain her power over you. She will do anything to escape punishment for having the sweet girl Elizabeth Keller murdered right here in Whitehall. She had it done, if she didn't do it herself, because she could take no more rivals for her place and the power she believes she can still wield. She is guilty, my king. You must see that."

The cry startled all in the room. It was no less agonizing for having come from that particular female voice.

"You are both to come with me."

Abby looked at Bridget Warren who punctuated her words with a forceful nod. Abby lifted Charlotte's head from her shoulder and let her know they needed to leave the room. Charlotte was dazed, still overcome with the grief of learning about her husband's treasonous activities. Abby hoped the king's business was completed and he would offer them a meal and speak of where Lady Durell was to reside in the days to come. Surely he would not punish her for her husband's treachery. If so, Abby knew she would plead with the king to reconsider such a decision, against which she would testify.

As they approached the room from which Abby earlier left, she heard painful feminine sobs. She couldn't believe Lady Castlemaine had been brought that low to cry in such a manner. Had the king truly been convinced she was culpable of murdering the young actress in one of the bedrooms at Whitehall? But when they entered the room, Abby saw a relatively composed Countess of Castlemaine, yet with streaks of tears still visible on her face. The sobbing came from young Anne Whitworth.

The king stood. "Abby, this young woman has confessed to murdering Betty Keller, and I have no doubt she has done so." Abby saw Lord Brinton retreating several steps, a look of utter confusion on his face. In spite of what she heard, Abby could not believe Anne had committed the crime on her own. Surely someone else had encouraged her to do it. The name was out of Abby's lips before she could question the wisdom of uttering it.

"Mary Gibbons made her do it, Your Majesty."

"I am afraid you are mistaken, Abby. Isn't that so, Anne?"

The young woman swallowed her sobs and looked at the others in the room—the king's men, Lady Castlemaine, Bridget Warren, Lord Brinton, and the king. She turned to address Abby. "Please don't think horribly of me, Abby. I'm not so much of a sinner as you must think. I only wanted to keep acting on the stage. It meant so much to me. And I thought that if I—" She abruptly stopped and ran the bottom of her hands across her tear-streaked cheeks. "You tell them what I mean to say, Lady Durell. You must tell them."

Charlotte had been staring at the floor from the moment she stepped into the room. She closed her eyes as though she could somehow escape the moment. Charles called Abby to him.

"As we have learned from Anne, she was brought to Dove-Raven House to meet Lady Durell, who told her she had admired her performance on the stage in the smaller parts she played. On two other occasions she was similarly summoned and made to promise that the topic of their conversation would remain between them."

Anne took a deep breath. "Lady Durell told me Mr. Devlin was going to release me because Betty Keller was going to play the parts I wanted to play for at least five more years. Lady Durell convinced me that something Mr. Devlin did was known by Betty and that she promised to reveal what it was if he didn't let her play the main parts—the ones Nellie Gwynn would have played if she hadn't become the king's . . ." Anne's face flushed as she glanced at the king, who continued the account.

"Lady Durell made her believe she would do both herself and Michael Devlin a good deed by killing Betty Keller. Having been to Whitehall on a number of occasions, Lady Durell instructed Anne how to find the bedroom, after Mary Gibbons informed Lady Durell where Betty would be sleeping. Lady Durell had seen where I kept my father's knife and case—as I have always been proud to show it to my guests. Apparently, Lady Durell did not trust Mary Gibbons with the murder, but paid her handsomely to keep the truth to herself. I will see to it that Mary Gibbons confesses to her part of this horrible event. Anne did as she was instructed and remained silent because, as she says, she feared losing her position at the King's Theatre and believed she did a worthy service by aiding Lady Durell and Mr. Devlin as well as herself. The only question yet to be answered is why Lady Durell wished Betty Keller dead."

Charlotte kept her back to the king and the others as she began to speak. "Why? It is very simple, Your Majesty. Abby here can tell you how much I spoke of you when we were girls. I believe I made the bold prediction that you would make me your queen."

Abby would never forget the brazenness of her close friend, who even at the age of thirteen made clear that Charles would have no better lover than Charlotte Hollier, daughter of Sir John Hollier, Charles's friend and former Ambassador to France. Throughout the years she and Abby were separated by an ocean, Charlotte wrote lovingly of the king and predicted, even after Charles wed Catherine of Braganza, that she would become his favorite mistress in spite of the hold Lady Castlemaine had on his affections. Abby dismissed the sentiment then, but during the time of the great London fire of 1666 Charlotte wrote to say that her heart was broken owing to the king's indifference to her and highly insulted when Charles suggested the match with Lord Durell. Abby believed it was merely temporary petulance—the effect of having one's girlhood dreams ruined.

"I could have born your rejection of me, Your Majesty, had you kept only Lady Castlemaine and Nell Gwynn as your favorites, but when I learned another mere actress was climbing in your esteem, I couldn't bear another insult and proof of your indifference to me. I had Mary Gibbons leave a note I had written in an altered hand threatening that girl if she continued loving the king, but then I knew Betty wouldn't stop, and so . . . Your Majesty, did I not speak to you in terms of love, even after I married Lord Durell? Had I not written you of my desire for your attentions? And yet you never replied. I was filled with hurt and rage—that only lessened when I learned Anne had done what I had asked of her. The death of Elizabeth Keller elevated my hopes once again. Once more I had only Lady Castlemaine and Nell Gwynn ahead of me." Charlotte turned to the king, her eyes broadened as she re-shaped her mouth more provocatively. "What of your latest find, the French Louise, you may wonder? She would have been poisoned. I would have soon convinced Anne to do it, I have no doubt." She took several steps toward the king, her arms now free from the grasp of the stunned guards. "I am still young, Your Majesty, and as you can see, younger than Lady Castlemaine. I possess a beauty still. Mr. Lely has painted me. My lying with my husband has ceased. I was preparing myself for you. I am ready—ready if you will have me."

CHAPTER 31

"And I missed all of it—which I will make the king most assuredly regret. I have special ways to exact my revenge on him."

Abby smiled at Nell Gwynn's "threat," but the events of the morning left her too exhausted to laugh. She had just informed Nellie of what transpired the previous evening near Sir Joseph Willet's house and the following day in the room at Whitehall. Nell was particularly anxious to know how Lady Castlemaine responded after the truth about Berry Keller's murder was revealed.

"I wasn't in the room to note her initial reaction when Anne Whitworth admitted to killing Betty, but after Charlotte entered the room, her features slowly changed into those of great sorrow—as did mine—when the full weight of Charlotte's guilt pressed upon us. The king refused to allow me to accompany Charlotte when they took her away; therefore, I was able to witness Barbara looking at the king, not with anger or disgust but rather with special pleading—as if she wanted him to apologize for suspecting her of having Betty murdered. His Majesty only glanced at her briefly with a look I could only characterize as great relief. I know she saw his expression and seemed both grateful and resigned to the fact that he would say nothing to her at the moment. When she turned to leave, she stopped in front of Lord Brinton. I could only see his face, so I don't know what expression she gave him, but he lowered his eyes and nodded to her as she left."

Abby and Nell talked further about Lady Durell's reasons for all she did, and both women expressed regret for being insensitive to the possibility that Charlotte had been deeply affected by the king's lack of interest in her. Nell took Abby's hand. "So now she faces a punishment I cannot even imagine."

"The king told those of us left in the room that he would be as merciful as he could allow himself to be, although some would pay with their lives. I am sure Lord Durell, Richard Hansall and Mr. Devlin will be executed, and Lord Brinton spoke of having Mary Gibbons declared a 'demon witch' and then executing her. Poor Bridget Warren pleaded with the king to forgive her lying about Lady Castlemaine because Lord Brinton had threatened her. Lord Brinton's apology to Bridget seemed to satisfy the king, who assured Bridget she would not be punished. His Majesty only shook his head in pity as they took young Anne from the room—a gesture I hope suggests he will be merciful. He has given me permission to visit him tomorrow to plead for Anne."

"And that leaves our friend Charlotte. What could you make of the king's inclinations regarding her?"

"I couldn't tell. His face spoke disgust but not hatred. Perhaps he will be moved by the arguments I will make for her when I see him tomorrow."

"Severe punishments are nothing His Majesty enjoys inflicting on his sinful or criminal subjects—so I think you will help both young Anne and Charlotte with your pleadings. I know I will want you to plead for me when I infuriate His Majesty to the point that he threatens to have me burned like a witch."

Abby was finally able to laugh. "Oh, that will never happen. You are going to be his favorite for many years."

"That is my intention, even if I have to share the title with that weeping French crust Louise."

The two women continued their stroll in St. James's Park. "Abby, what do you plan to do after you see His Majesty tomorrow?"

"I suppose I will go to visit relations as I had planned to do after my stay at Dove-Raven House ended."

"Stay with me for another week, Abby. There is much in this city you have not seen and much I wish to show you. After that we can decide what you might do to remain in London."

"Here? And just what would I do?"

"While you are waiting on a man to make you his wife, you could be on the stage. I could train you."

Abby gave full throat to her laughter. "I have no ability—or the inclination, I'm afraid."

"There will be a new manager of the King's Theatre, and whoever he is, he will listen to me. I will teach you what you need to do and then you can become admired by the town and cursed by the Puritans. The king will then come to his theatre, see you in all your loveliness, and then take you back to Whitehall for a good fucking."

"Nellie—that is enough!" Abby looked around to be sure no one heard this scandalous prediction.

"Who knows? You might then replace me, Lady Castlemaine, and Squintabella as the king's favorite."

—THE END—

Appendix
List of Historical Characters

In the Novel:

King Charles II
Barbara Villiers, Lady Castlemaine
Nell Gwynn
Frances Stuart, Duchess of Richmond
John Wilmot, Lord Rochester
Sir Charles Sedley
Earl of Mulgrave
Charles Sackville, Lord Buckhurst
Henry Bennet, Earl of Arlington

Alluded to:

Anne Marshall
Arabella Churchill
Bishop Burnett
Catherine Pegge
Charles Hart
Charles Stuart, Duke of Richmond
Count de Gramont
Earl of Chesterfield
Earl of Lauderdale
Elizabeth Boutell
Elizabeth Knepp
Elizabeth Mallet
George Villiers, Duke of Buckingham
Henrietta, *Duchesse d'Orleans* (Minette)
Henry Hyde, Lord Clarendon
James Howard
James, Duke of Monmouth
James, Duke of York

Jane Needham
John Dryden
John Lacy
King Charles I
Louis XIV of France
Louise de Kérouaille
Lucy Waller
Margaret Hughes
Mary Meggs
Michael Mohun
Moll Davis
Nicholas Burt
Oliver Cromwell
Praise-God Barebone (and son)
Prince Rupert
Queen Catherine of Braganza
Rebecca Marshall
Richard Cromwell
Roger Palmer
Simon Verelst
Sir Edward Fairfax
Sir John Coventry
Sir Peter Lely
Thomas Betterton
William Joyner

View other Black Rose Writing titles at www.blackrosewriting.com/books and use promo code **PRINT** to receive a **20% discount** when purchasing.

BLACK ROSE
writing™